BURN

ALBERT WHITMAN & COMPANY
CHICAGO, ILLINOIS

FOR MOM

Library of Congress Cataloging-in-Publication
data is on file with the publisher.

Text copyright © 2015 by Mandy Mikulencak
Hardcover edition published in 2015 by Albert Whitman & Company
Paperback edition published in 2016 by Albert Whitman & Company
ISBN 978-0-8075-0942-5

Printed in the United States of America
10 9 8 7 6 5 4 3 2 1 LB 20 19 18 17 16

Design by Jordan Kost
Cover image © Shutterstock.com

For more information about Albert Whitman & Company,
visit our web site at www.albertwhitman.com.

CHAPTER 1
TWO WEEKS AGO—FOUND AND LOST

I'm positive Mom wanted me to find her body. I'd been taking care of us both for so many years that she trusted I'd know how to handle things. She'd say, "Arlie, if something ever happens to me, don't let the police or ambulance boys find me in a compromising position." Translation: flush any remaining drugs down the toilet, make sure she had on clean panties, and tidy up the motel room. By the time I had to carry out her wishes, I knew exactly what to do.

What she hadn't prepared me for was life without her. I wasn't afraid to be alone. Mom had a way of making me feel lonely even when she was right by my side. The scariest thing was that I was no longer invisible. Her death cast a spotlight on us both, and hiding wasn't an option.

I was numb when I dialed 911.

"I'd like to report a death," I said. "My mother's."

Two police cars arrived within minutes. The Animas View Motel could have been on their speed dial. Assaults and drug busts were frequent, deaths not so much.

Sticky, sleety rain cloaked the cruiser where they told me to sit and wait. Its heater, turned on high, was as suffocating as their questions.

"Are you all right?"

"Do you have any idea what happened to your mom?"

"Is there anyone we can call?"

No, no, and no, I could've answered, but I stayed mostly silent while two officers poked around the room and Mom's body. They'd left the motel-room door open, but I couldn't make out their movements from the squad car.

The cop babysitting me was chatty without asking too much. I was a minor. We both knew an adult had to be present.

"I could get you some cocoa or juice from the motel lobby if you like." She turned sideways in the driver's seat.

"It's not that kind of motel and you know it." I pressed my cheek against the ice-cold window, fogging it with my breath.

"My name is Reagan," she said.

I didn't need to know her name. She wasn't my friend. I wasn't hers. I closed my eyes and wished for sleep—the feverish, flu-like kind where the world drifts away.

"What time did you say you found your mom's body?" Her good-cop tone was chipper, like she'd just asked what flavor ice cream I preferred.

I'd already lied and told them I'd stayed at my best friend Mo's house last night and only found Mom early this morning. The truth was that I'd spent the entire night in a chair in the corner of the motel room, too exhausted to run and too afraid to ask for help, even from Mo. Her parents would have just judged me more than they already did.

But when I woke at dawn, a strange and unsettling thought

picked at my brain: what if I just let someone else make the decisions now?

"There will be a counselor available when we get to the station," the officer said. "I can imagine this is all very hard on you."

This. Is. All. Very. Hard. I picked apart each word as if she were speaking a foreign language. She had no clue.

The two investigating officers were now outside on the balcony. One laughed at something the other had said.

"What are they laughing about?" I shouted at the female officer. "And why are they done? They've been in there less than fifteen minutes."

"They're not finished, Arlie," she said. "An investigative team will be here soon. And I'm sure they're not laughing about your mom. I'm sorry they're being insensitive."

She opened her door and shouted to the other officers that she was taking me to the police station.

"We can't go yet." I slapped my hand against the passenger-side window. I had just realized that when I flushed the drugs, I'd probably destroyed the very evidence that could prove whether she'd left me on purpose. "What about the coroner? Will there be an autopsy?"

"The funeral home will pick up the body," Reagan said. "In the case of suicide or overdose, the coroner doesn't usually come to the scene."

Suicide. Overdose.

"Social services will find you somewhere safe to stay tonight," she continued.

Somewhere safe.

Whatever they'd gleaned in a few minutes led them to believe I hadn't been safe before.

"So I'm going to a foster home?" It'd been six years since the last time I was in foster care, but I wasn't surprised that's where I'd end up tonight. It's not like they'd let a sixteen-year-old stay in a motel room—especially one where someone had died—just because it was paid up until the end of the week. And staying with Dora, our friend who lived a few doors down, wasn't an option either. Social services would say the motel wasn't suitable for children.

"Yes, a foster family will be identified. You're sure there's no one else we can call?" the officer asked for a third time.

I looked up at the room—a tiny, sad place I'd tried to make a home for us, but failed.

"No," I said. "I'm ready to go."

CHAPTER 2

My sessions with a court-appointed therapist played out the same way each time I saw her. I stared at the clock while Jane asked questions that didn't have right or wrong answers. She'd often bring the conversation back around to my mom's instructions and ask if I believed her suicide was selfish. I wasn't ready to believe Mom killed herself, but who was going to believe me when the police officers had scanned the room for a whole five minutes before making up their minds?

I'd despised how disconnected they'd seemed. As if Mom hadn't been a real person and we hadn't been a real family. They couldn't wait to seal up the room and make me someone else's problem. Yet I was just as angry at myself. By carrying out her wishes—flushing her drugs, erasing all traces of her life—I'd ensured the truth would never be found.

"Arlie, you're not paying attention."

I appreciated that Jane didn't use a soothing, singsong therapist tone with me, the type designed to make a person feel cared about or special in some backhanded way. I wasn't special, and I didn't need to be cared for. I was here because some caseworker who didn't know me had decided I couldn't possibly be okay if my mother was dead.

"I'm listening," I said.

"I asked if you're adjusting."

"To high school? It's only been a couple of weeks."

I sat cross-legged on the overstuffed love seat, the one spot in Jane's office where I could stare out the window at Perins Peak, the highest ridgeline visible from downtown Durango. When we first met, I avoided looking directly at her. She probably thought I was embarrassed by what had happened to my face. The truth is that I just didn't want to look at her. Her stare suggested she knew something about me that even I didn't know.

"Do you like your classes?" She paused for an answer. "Have you made any other friends?"

"Yes to the classes, no to the friends. Don't need them."

"Why do you say that?"

"Some people aren't worth knowing."

Ever since the accident that left my face disfigured seven years ago, I had refused to attend school. Mom had felt so much guilt that I could've done anything I wanted. I may not have been in the school system, but I'd still run into students at the library and Boys and Girls Club, even on the hiking trails around town.

Most had made up their minds about me a long time ago, and I about them. Just this week, someone had written "fire freak" on my locker with lipstick. It had to have been Brittany, a junior who'd taken it personally that I dared to grace the steps of her beloved Durango High School.

"Maybe you should give it some time," Jane said.

"Yeah, maybe."

She looked over the top of her glasses, delicate things that were probably Danish or German. Everything about her seemed European, or what I imagined a European to look like: tailored knits in black or dark gray, brightly colored silk scarves, ballet flats.

I wondered what I'd look like in such sophisticated clothing. Most of my wardrobe came from the thrift store, but I also gravitated to black and gray, straight lines, nothing too flashy. The dark, muted clothing and my black hair made me feel like a moving shadow, capable of disappearing at any moment. Except, of course, from Jane's office.

"Did you bring your notebook?" she asked.

I rummaged through my backpack to find the hardcover sketchbook that doubled as my journal. "Aren't journals supposed to be private?"

"They are. And you get to decide what you want to share, or if you want to share at all. I just think it puts you more directly in touch with your feelings if you read something you felt strongly enough to capture on paper."

I ignored the obvious therapist angle and turned toward her, my feet squarely on the floor. A bookmark held the place where I'd started a new list yesterday. Lists were easier than writing pages and pages of feelings, although Jane would've been thrilled if I had.

"Names I'm Called by Insensitive Shitheads," I began.

"Interesting title."

I resisted the urge to throw the thing at her. I had to keep it together in front of Jane to prove I didn't need to be there.

"It's my list," I said.

"I wasn't judging. Go on." She removed her glasses and settled into the back cushion of her chair.

"Ash-hole, Fire Freak, Arlie Krueger..."

"Krueger?"

"You know, Freddy Krueger. The dude in *A Nightmare on Elm Street* with the burned face and long knives for fingers."

"How do those names make you feel?" Jane leaned forward as if I might have something profound to share.

I closed my journal and leaned forward to mimic her stance. "I've looked like this almost half my life," I said. "The names aren't even original. Well, the Krueger bit is."

"If you say so." Jane didn't acknowledge my half-assed attempt at a joke. "Must be a reason you wrote about the name-calling this week."

"Had to write about something," I said. "Doesn't mean it bothers me."

Sometimes, I figured there had to be right answers to Jane's questions—answers that could possibly bring these forced appointments to an end. I'd learned over the years what adults wanted to hear and had gotten good at it.

"Little girl, are you living in that car with your mother?"

"Oh no, officer. We're moving to Florida and just pulled over to rest. Been a long drive."

At least Jane didn't hand me a bunch of bullshit, and she wouldn't stand for mine. I trusted her because of that.

"Sleeping better?" she asked.

"I'm sleeping some, but if you're asking about the nightmares, I still have them."

"About your stepfather?"

"Who else?"

Lloyd. The real-life boogeyman I couldn't hide from no matter how many miles and years separated us. Mom and I left

Albuquerque six years ago, and she was fanatical about making sure he didn't find us.

"He'd hurt us if he found us," she'd say. Only later, when I was older, did I realize that both she and Lloyd were wanted for manslaughter. The meth lab he'd constructed in our apartment kitchen had exploded, killing Rosa, our elderly neighbor who took care of me almost every day. Throw in child endangerment and manufacturing of a controlled substance, and both Mom and Lloyd had plenty of reasons to stay hidden.

Of course I blamed Lloyd for the accident that burned my face and took away the only person who cared if I was fed or got to school on time, but placing blame was a tricky business. After all, Mom chose Lloyd and the drugs over me.

"He makes me crazy angry," I told Jane. "Not just because of what he's done, but because I still have to think about him. That I have to talk about him now."

"Why do you think your mother believed he'd hurt you?" Jane asked.

"She never said exactly, but he wasn't a nice guy. Especially to her."

"Do you want to see him again?"

The question caught me off guard. He and Mom disappeared after the accident so the police wouldn't find them. I spent the next year in the hospital and burn rehab, and then in a foster home before Mom finally resurfaced, saying she was sorry and promising she'd stay clean. She wanted us to move to Durango. We stole away in the middle of the night so my foster family wouldn't know. She didn't mention then that she was still wanted by the law and that we would be mother-daughter fugitives.

"No," I finally said.

"He's your stepdad."

"And that's supposed to mean something?"

"He's the only family you have left," she said.

I bit back my anger. "He's not my real dad. I've told you that before."

Jane let the moment hang heavily between us. She did this when she wanted me to keep talking. If she pressed any harder, I might start screaming and never stop.

"Do you think he'll seek you out one day?"

"What would he want of me?" I asked. "And why do we even have to talk about him?"

"Because he still causes you pain."

I used to think Mom was paranoid for thinking Lloyd lived and breathed with the sole purpose of hunting us down. When she'd have nightmares about him, I'd be the one to console her, to convince her he'd probably gone to Mexico or California to start a new life. But the night she died, the universe seemed to transfer her nightmares to my subconscious—and the paranoia followed soon after.

I stared at the clock on the far wall and wondered if I'd have the guts to kill my stepfather if he ever found me. I shuddered at my own thoughts. He definitely deserved to die, but I wouldn't be the one to make it happen. If he still ran with the same drug crowds, he'd end up in the ground before he became an old man anyway.

"He made her a drug addict," I said. He was the reason for everything bad that had happened in my life. Mom's death was no different.

"Addiction is complicated…"

Jane's words receded into muted gibberish. I watched the

sunlight change the color of Perins Peak and wondered how cold it was outside where Mo waited for me.

"What are you thinking about, Arlie?"

"What to wear to Mom's funeral."

Jane looked confused. "The county set a date? When?"

"Monday," I said. "My foster mom is taking me. And I think the social-services lady will be there."

"Why'd you wait until the end of our session to share that news?" she asked.

Jane already knew the answer. It was the same reason I didn't tell her that social services had discovered I had an uncle living in Texas. And that he'd be in Durango in time to help bury his sister. Secrets were the only thing truly my own.

* * *

"Did you cry?" Mo struggled to keep up with my long strides. Her short legs required two steps for each one of mine so I slowed down.

"Why would I do that?" I asked.

"She probably wants you to show some emotion…you know, to prove you're in touch with your feelings, that you're dealing with everything."

"Everything?"

"Well, your mom's death for one."

"And?"

"You know…your face. The accident."

"Technically, I think her job is to make sure I'm not permanently messed up. She can take her pick of the reasons why."

"I wish you'd take this seriously. I'm sorry you're being forced into therapy, but I think it's a good thing." Mo and I were both sixteen, but you wouldn't know it by the way she mothered me.

"I appreciate your analysis, Dr. Mo." I elbowed her in hopes of knocking the seriousness from her expression.

"You haven't cried much. At least not around me." She squinted against the sun in her eyes, which gave the impression that she was smiling, not grimacing.

"Is that how you gauge that I'm 'processing'?" I put air quotes around the word. "I'm not a crier. You know that."

"Sometimes that worries me," she said.

As an emotion, worry was overrated. Just an attempt to feel useful and in control, when we can't control anything except the moment we're in—and sometimes not even that.

"Okay, you didn't cry. Then what did you talk about today?"

"She wanted to know if I was making friends. I said I didn't need friends, and she wanted to know why."

Mo grabbed my elbow so forcefully that I almost stumbled off the sidewalk curb.

"What do you mean, you don't need friends?" she asked. "What the hell am I?"

Fury showed up as ruddy splotches on Mo's otherwise pale cheeks, but today something flashed in her eyes—an unnamed emotion that made me want to hug her and say I was sorry.

I hip-bumped her instead, then grabbed her hand. "Maureen Elizabeth Mooney. I only need one friend and that's you."

"Arlene Marie Betts. Then don't you ever forget it." She returned the bump.

"Fine. As long as you quit calling me Arlene."

"You called me Maureen first." She pressed her forefinger into my chest, and I batted it away.

We walked down Main Avenue for a few blocks. The pavement and sidewalks were dry—unusual for late January in

Colorado—and the temperature was warm enough that I only needed a hoodie. Smiling tourists were everywhere, searching for recreation or food, or both, since the snow was a no-show at the resort this season. Even the man-made stuff was melting.

Mo, however, wasn't smiling. Whenever a group of tourists passed us, she stopped at a boutique window and pointed something out to me, shielding me from their stares.

"Stop it, Mo. Really. They can't help it." I flipped back my long bangs to better see our reflections in the window. Cords of pink scar tissue pulled at the edges of the slick, taut skin on my left cheek. The grafted skin wrapped from my eyebrow to my jawline and down my neck. The area lacked natural pigment and looked even paler next to my dark hair.

"It's rude," she said loudly enough for a couple to hear as they walked past. Her disapproving stare quickened their steps.

"Well, if it doesn't bother me, then it shouldn't bother you." I pulled my hair back down over my face.

"You don't get to decide what bothers another person."

We walked in silence for another block before I took her hand.

"The freckles on your nose get darker when you're mad," I said.

Mo rubbed her nose. "Don't joke."

I had to joke. Things had been too serious between me and Mo since Mom died. Mo's mothering had kicked into overdrive. I owed her so much, but it was getting harder and harder to be around her. She stared at me, like all the time, trying to gauge my mood. It was worse than the assholes who gawked at my scar.

"Did you tell Jane about your uncle?" she asked.

"Not yet."

Mo shook her head. "This isn't some game. She could help

you. Things are going to change when that guy shows up. He'll be your guardian."

She didn't have to state the obvious. When Mom died, rules emerged where rules had never been. A foster family. High school. Therapy. Now, an uncle. I had no idea what to expect from Frank, but I could always make it on my own if things didn't work out.

"Tammy is driving me to Mom's funeral," I said. "She asked for a day off from work. Said it was her responsibility as my foster mother. Plus, we have an appointment at social services later in the day."

"You don't want me to go?" Mo's defensiveness couldn't hide the hurt behind the question.

"That's not what I meant. I just know how you feel about funerals. I'd understand if it's too hard."

Mo's sister, Celine, had died from leukemia when she was five years old and Mo was eight. Just a couple of years ago, Mo couldn't even bring herself to attend her grandmother's funeral.

"CeeCee died a long time ago. I'll be fine."

I knew Mo was lying but didn't call her on it. Everything in my life was changing, even the way she and I were around each other.

We made our way down the street, hand in hand but not talking. I assumed we were headed to the Book Nook. Mo insisted on buying me a book for each therapy session I attended—sort of like the lollipop a doctor gives kids after a shot. I didn't need babying. I resisted the initial offer, since the court required me to see Jane twice a week for the foreseeable future because of my "unusual family circumstances."

We'd finally agreed on one book a week and I'd accepted,

especially since her parents probably wouldn't mind book purchases showing up on their credit card. And Mo usually ended up borrowing the books she'd purchased for me in the first place.

When we reached the bookstore's entrance, Mo kept walking.

"No Book Nook?" I asked.

"Not today," she said. "Your mom will need something nice to be buried in. I'll help you pick something out. My mom gave me money. She didn't want you to worry."

Embarrassment flooded my cheeks. I hadn't thought about a dress for Mom. Of course Mo's mother would know what had to be done. I experienced an odd panic that there were other important decisions and I'd never even know they had to be made.

I found it strange that with all the instructions Mom had left me, she never mentioned how to handle her funeral. Maybe she hadn't planned on leaving me after all.

* * *

Mo parked in front of JCPenney and suggested we walk the length of the mall until we found a dress. She opened the car door. After a moment she shut it again when she noticed I wasn't getting out of the car.

"You want to go somewhere else?"

"No... I don't know." I leaned back against the headrest. A ferocious headache had been brewing since my therapy session ended.

"Arl?" Mo placed a hand on my thigh.

"I never asked for anything from her. All she had to do was stay alive. And she couldn't even do that for me."

Mo turned the key partway in the ignition so that the heater would work. She held both hands in front of the stream of warm air. "You know it's never been about you, right?"

"Well, it should have been," I said. "She took the easy way out."

"You're right," Mo said. "You deserved better."

I stared out the passenger window, which had begun to fog over. I wrote my name in the condensation, then wiped it off with my sleeve.

"I never begged her to be anyone other than who she was, even though I wanted to almost every day. Maybe things could have been different if only she'd tried."

Mo shook her head. "Did you really think she'd ever turn things around?"

"You didn't know her."

"Maybe not, but I've known you for five years. Nothing changed in all that time except that she relied on you more and more. Do you know how hard it was for me to see you play the tough girl when she disappointed you over and over again?"

"Mo, stop."

"I'm not trying to hurt you. I have no idea what it's like to lose a mother," she said. "But I did lose a sister. I know what it's like to beat yourself up with what-ifs."

Did Mo expect me to give them up so easily? What-ifs had been the mainstay of my daydreams since I was small. *What if Lloyd got in a car accident and died? What if the explosion hadn't happened and my face hadn't been burned? What if Mom got a job and we could afford a nice apartment? What if my real dad returned one day and forced Mom into rehab?*

I reached over and turned the key a half turn more so that the engine came back to life. "Would you mind if we went to Goodwill instead?" I asked.

* * *

The dress I finally chose was too lightweight for winter, but Mom would be in a closed casket, not wearing it outside on a snowy day. The fabric was lipstick red with just the slightest sheen, probably someone's discarded holiday dress. She would have liked the color but would've said it wasn't short enough. She didn't have a say in the matter. Besides, the dress met my main criterion: it had long sleeves to cover the track marks on her arms.

While I browsed through the crowded racks, Mo found a pair of black patent pumps in a size six and a wide, black leather belt she insisted would look great with the dress. Mom had never worn anything remotely like the items we selected. It felt like picking out a Halloween costume. At the checkout counter, Mo looked through the glass case full of costume jewelry. Before she could even ask, I touched her arm and whispered, "No."

The cashier stuffed the items in a plastic grocery-store bag. Mo handed over eleven dollars and change while I rushed out of the stuffy store into the brisk air.

* * *

Mo suggested seeing a movie or going for milk shakes, but I refused. "It's okay. Just take me back to Tammy's."

My foster mom left me alone for the most part and didn't pry about Mom's death. She did insist that all her fosters have breakfast and dinner together because she said it created a sense of family even if we weren't related by blood. I could tell these meals meant something to the younger kids so I did it more for them than for Tammy.

"Is she expecting you at a certain time?" Mo asked. "I don't want to leave you when you're upset like this."

"I'm fine. I'm just tired."

We didn't talk as Mo drove up North Main. The afternoon clouds hung low and pale gray. I'd never known what people meant by "snow clouds," but I hoped these weren't that kind. I wanted Mom to be buried on a sunny day. It was hard enough to think about her casket in the rock-hard winter ground.

When we neared the City Market, I asked Mo to pull over. "Just drop me off here. I want to buy some hose to go with Mom's dress. I can walk the rest of the way home."

"Arlie, don't do it."

"Do what?" I asked, even though I knew exactly what she meant.

"Don't go back there." She looked across the street toward the Animas View Motel where Mom and I had lived off and on the last few years.

"I haven't told Dora about the funeral. She'd want to be there."

Dora was a long-term resident of the motel and probably the closest thing to a friend my mother ever had, although they never did anything socially and Dora was almost sixty years old. In truth, Dora had hung around mostly to check up on me, to see that I was safe and fed. Like Rosa had done years before in the apartment complex in Albuquerque, Dora stepped in when Mom disappeared into a meth binge and forgot she had a daughter.

"You can call her," Mo said.

"I owe Dora more than that. Please understand."

There was no reasoning with Mo where Dora was concerned. I'd stopped mentioning her after Mo blew up when I gave Dora the Subaru. Mo thought I should keep it and get my driver's license, but I didn't want it. The car reeked of cigarettes and memories I'd rather forget. It was the car we'd used to escape from our life with Lloyd, and I wanted nothing to tie me to him. Plus, Dora would never be able to afford a car. It made me feel good to thank her for what she'd done for me and Mom.

Mo reached across and opened my door. Cold air rushed into the car. "I can't stop you."

"Don't be mad."

"Here, take my coat," she said. "You'll freeze in just your hoodie."

Mo had been mad at me plenty of times. She just rarely allowed herself to express it for fear it might upset the balance in my precarious world. I shoved my arms into her down coat and kissed her quickly before running across the street toward the motel's entrance.

* * *

Dora wasn't in her room so I sat on the cement walkway, my back against her door, until she arrived from her shift at the Manna Soup Kitchen. By the time she found me, it was growing dark. I'd lost feeling in my hands and feet.

"Arlene! My sweet girl!" Dora helped me up and I leaned into her bear hug. She brought a hand up to my unscarred cheek. "Saints in heaven! You're ice cold. Come in right this minute."

I made a beeline to the heating unit beneath the window. I turned it on high and sat on the vent, grateful for its instant warmth through my jeans.

"I'm sorry I haven't called," I said. "Things got crazy after…"

"I know, girl. I know. I figured you needed time to adjust to your foster family."

"Won't be with them much longer," I said. "Turns out I have an uncle in Texas. He's coming to Durango."

Dora retrieved a Tupperware container from her large tote bag and poured the contents into a small pot. She set the pot on a hot plate and turned back to me. "You're staying for supper. Tell me about this uncle."

She sat on the edge of the bed closest to the heater. Her graying hair was wound in two braids twisted into a single bun at the nape of her neck. She'd look grandmotherly except that her skin was satiny with only a few lines around her eyes.

Although Dora must have been exhausted after her shift, she gave me her complete attention, as she always had when we talked. It didn't matter if I was eleven or sixteen. She made me feel that everything coming out of my mouth had to be important.

"Nothing to tell. Haven't met him yet," I said. "I'm here because I wanted to tell you about Mom's funeral. It's Monday."

"I figured she was buried by now." Dora leaned toward me and pushed my hair behind my ears. "There, I can see your beautiful face."

I blushed even though Dora had always encouraged me to wear my hair off my face. "Why hide your scar? It says you're a survivor," she'd said. And in her presence, I could allow myself to feel that.

Her room always made me feel safe, like I didn't have to be on guard. Dora didn't use the motel for temporary housing as Mom and I had. She'd been in the same room for years. The manager allowed her to hang pictures and use her own bedding. Her sewing machine occupied the table.

At first, she'd chosen the motel because it made economic sense. There was no way she'd have enough money for first and last months' rent at an apartment, or for utility deposits. She ended up staying, solidifying her role as fairy godmother to the children whose parents were absent, either physically or emotionally.

When she heard the soup bubbling, Dora got up and spooned

some into two paper cups. She handed me one and I slurped it dutifully even though I wasn't hungry. The liquid scalded the roof of my mouth.

"I always wondered why you called the police after you found your mom," she said. "You had to have known things would change. We could have figured something out together."

"I wasn't really thinking. I just wanted the world to stop."

"And did it?"

I laughed weakly. "Just the opposite."

"You could have taken the car and gone anywhere," she said.

"Where would I have gone? At least here I have you and Mo. And you need the car more than I do." I couldn't admit to her that a vehicle would make it easier for authorities to track me, should I decide to leave Durango one day. If I could make it to a large city, being on foot would allow me to slip into the shadows, untraceable.

While Dora ate, I showed her the dress and shoes that Mo and I had chosen for Mom. She approved. I laughed when she confirmed that Mom would have liked something shorter.

It was getting dark outside and the temperature would dip below freezing soon. Not wanting Tammy to worry, I called and said I'd stayed over at Mo's for dinner. I couldn't leave just yet. Dora and I snuggled beneath the bedspread and turned on the TV.

It took some time to work up the courage to ask what I'd come to ask. "Did you see anything unusual the night Mom died?"

"What do you mean?"

"Did anyone stop by? Someone you didn't recognize?" My heart pounded in anticipation of her answer.

"What's this about?" She cupped an arm around my shoulder and pulled me to her. I buried my face in her neck. I hadn't cried in front of Jane or Mo or Tammy since Mom's death, but Dora was part of a world they'd never understand. She'd lived with addiction—her own and that of her former partner. She'd been homeless for more years than I'd been alive. Even so, the tears wouldn't fall.

"What if Mom didn't kill herself?"

Dora kissed the top of my head. "Ah, sweet child. It was an accident. Don't read more into it. You'll make yourself sick."

"But what if someone else was involved?"

Dora stiffened at my question. "You think someone killed your mother?"

I explained that when I found Mom, so much about the room looked wrong. Too much meth had been left behind, as well as paraphernalia I didn't recognize. She wouldn't have had the money to buy it.

And if she'd been with her junkie friends, they'd never have left behind such a stash. But everything I said made me sound more and more pathetic, as if I couldn't face the truth…that I wasn't a good enough reason to fight to stay alive.

I got up from the bed and swung my arms back and forth, trying to shake off the emotion overtaking me because I hadn't gotten the answers I wanted. Dora stood and grabbed both my hands.

"Listen to me. Bad things happen. There doesn't have to be a reason. She died, but you're alive. You have all the chances she never got. And more smarts to boot."

I smiled when she grabbed my chin for emphasis.

A loud rap startled us both. Dora moved toward the door.

"Leave the chain on," I said.

"Of course." She shook her head at my obvious caution.

The door opened just three inches, but enough to see a sliver of Mo's face.

"What are you doing here?" I asked.

"Thought you could use a ride to Tammy's," she said. "It's getting colder."

I kissed Dora good-bye and followed Mo back to her warm car. We'd met on a day much colder than this one, when I'd let my guard down and begun to think having a friend was possible. She'd become much more.

CHAPTER 3
FIVE YEARS AGO—MEETING MO

The November wind cut through my jeans. I was too cold to walk to the library so I dropped to the ground and leaned against the dumpster behind the Animas View Motel.

Mom shouldn't have invited those people into our room. She promised she wouldn't, but that was yesterday. She changed her mind a lot and yet I still wanted to believe her.

"Doesn't it stink down there?" The girl's voice carried above the wind. She sat on top of the cinder-block wall at the back edge of the motel parking lot. In hot-pink sweatpants and a purple down jacket, she looked like a Barbie doll on a ski trip.

"Nah," I called out. I hadn't been able to smell anything since the accident, but I didn't need to tell a stranger that.

Although the wall was at least six feet high, the short girl jumped down like the distance meant nothing, her blond ponytails flying behind her. I stood and brushed the gravel off my jeans.

"You live in the motel?" she asked.

"What's it to you?"

She shrugged. On tiptoes, she peered into the open dumpster. "You lied. It does stink."

"I'm not a liar."

"Didn't mean it like that," she said. "Don't be mad."

I wondered what she wanted.

"We see you out here a lot," she said. "But you don't go to school."

"Who's 'we'?" I stuck my hands in my jacket and stepped from side to side to stay warm. She must be freezing in those girlie sweatpants.

"Me and my neighbor, Brittany. She says you're white trash and I'm stupid for talking to you."

"Then why are you?"

"She can't tell me who to be friends with."

Friends? The girl acted like she already knew me.

"You always have a book, but not today," she said. "I love reading too."

"It's too cold to hold a book. You spy on everybody?"

I jumped back when she laughed. She sounded like a donkey, and I couldn't believe such a big noise came out of such a small girl.

"I haven't been spying. I live on the other side of the wall and a few blocks over. I just notice things."

"Like?"

"Like your face."

I pulled my hair down over the scar. For those few minutes I'd forgotten about it.

"You don't have to hide it. Were you in an accident?"

I nodded. "Three years ago. In Albuquerque."

I wasn't supposed to tell anyone where we'd come from, and

now I'd told this weird girl who'd been spying on us.

"That's too bad," she said. "By the way, my name is Mo."

I was shocked she didn't ask any more questions about the accident.

"Mo's a boy's name," I said.

"Short for Maureen. It's an old lady name, but my mom said I should like it because it's my grandmother's name. What's yours?"

"Arlie," I said, giving away a second secret I shouldn't have.

"That's a nickname. What's your real name?"

"Arlene."

"That's an old lady name too. What are the chances?" She gave another donkey laugh.

"You know, I could bring you the homework assignments I get at school," Mo said. "Then if you ever go back, you won't be behind. How old are you?"

"I'm eleven," I said. "Today."

I'd tried to wake up Mom this morning, to remind her she promised we'd go to the movies to celebrate. She rolled over and said I was wrong, that my birthday was next month.

"Oh, happy birthday!" Mo squealed this time instead of making the donkey noise. "Then we're both in the sixth grade."

I took her word for it.

"What are you doing to celebrate?" she asked. "Did you open your present yet?"

"I'm saving my present to open tonight after we go out for pizza," I lied. There'd be no movie or pizza or presents. I just wanted someone to know it really was my birthday.

She looked over my shoulder. "You can go back inside now. They're gone."

I turned to look. Three men got into a dark blue van and left.

If Mo had been watching us for a while, she knew more than Mom would like her to know.

When I turned back to her, she was already skipping toward the wall. The wind drowned out her words, but it sounded like she was singing "Happy Birthday."

Later, I plopped onto the bed to read. Mom was lying on her side, talking to herself like she normally did when her visitors left. I couldn't make out her words, but I rarely could. Her legs and arms jerked, but I'd stopped worrying about that a long time ago. I folded the bedspread over her like a burrito, partly to keep her warm and partly because I didn't want to look at her.

It was after 8 p.m. when I heard a knock on the door. Even though Mom told me never to answer the door, I asked her if I could. She didn't respond so I took a chance.

I left the chain on and opened the door slowly. No one was there. My eyes moved to the doormat. On it sat a cardboard bakery box from the City Market grocery store directly across the street. I could see through the clear plastic lid to the pink rose decorations on a round cake. The writing on top said: *Happy Birthday, Arlene.*

I ate nearly half of the chocolate cake even though I couldn't enjoy it. A funny metal taste filled my mouth, and I only felt the cake crumbs and the greasy frosting. I couldn't remember what chocolate even tasted like.

Mo was right to call me a liar. Whenever Mom asked me if I could smell anything, I still said no when I really could. I smelled and tasted our old apartment. I smelled and tasted the explosion.

CHAPTER 4

For the last two weeks, I dreamed every night of a never-ending wall of stainless-steel doors, the top row accessible only with a rolling ladder like those found in libraries and bookstores. Behind each door, the dead waited their turn to be drained of blood, washed and clothed by a stranger, laid in a satin-lined casket, and grieved over by tearful loved ones.

In the dream, the room always glowed with a bluish light whose source wasn't apparent. My bare feet ached from the cold of the cement floor, and my white breath fogged my vision. I'd hear Mom screaming for me to let her out, but I didn't know which door to open. When I opened the wrong door, Lloyd's decaying corpse reached for me with bony arms draped in bits of muscle and skin. Sometimes his icy hand wrapped around my throat.

Those few times that I cried out in my sleep, my foster mom would wake and come into my room. She'd say, "Your mama isn't in the mortuary. She's in heaven with God and the angels."

I didn't tell Tammy about Lloyd's recurring role in my

nightmares. But I truly appreciated the comfort she tried to give me on those black nights. The despair I felt came from the fact that Tammy couldn't provide proof of her version of the afterlife. How could she be so certain Mom was in a better place? No matter what Tammy said, Mom was indeed at the mortuary. She'd been waiting behind her steel door for twenty-one days, locked in an ice-cold holding pattern until next of kin could be found. Next of kin with the means to pay for the burial, that is.

The day after Mom died, I'd met with a social worker. She'd explained that after all avenues were exhausted, Mom would be buried in the indigent portion of the cemetery in a numbered grave paid for by the county. She whispered the word "indigent" as if it meant something profane instead of just poor. Now that they'd found my uncle, he'd foot the bill. I hoped he had enough money to pay for a nice headstone too, instead of the numbered metal plate the social worker had described.

* * *

"Mama Tammy said it's vulgar you picked out a red dress for your mom to be buried in."

My foster sister, Jess, sat at the end of my twin bed even though hers was just two feet away. At seven, she was just a myna bird, repeating everything anyone else said.

"She said your friend Maureen is a bad influence." Jess picked her nose and wiped her finger on my bedspread without bothering to inspect it first. I made a mental note to throw the spread in the washing machine later.

"Mo didn't choose the dress. I did."

"Mama Tammy still doesn't like it."

"Shut up, okay?" I was dangerously close to knocking her off the bed or throwing her out into the hallway.

"You can't tell me to shut up. You're not my mother." Her whine grated like fingers on a chalkboard.

"You don't have a mother. That's why you live with Tammy."

Jess was still in that honeymoon phase of foster care, where kids think their foster parents will adopt them and they'd all live happily ever after. She'd soon find out that no one really wants strays after they're no longer cute and cuddly toddlers.

Jess's eyes narrowed. "You're not a nice person."

I should've apologized—and would have if she'd started crying—but I couldn't be bothered. I needed to dress. Not knowing how cold it'd be at the cemetery or how long a graveside service would last, I chose a slouchy sweater and scarf, and black jeans tucked into boots.

"That's not very dressy," she said.

I ignored her and pulled my duffel bag from the closet. I hadn't bothered to unpack it when I got placed in Tammy's temporary care. Mom had taught me to keep few possessions and to always be prepared for a fast getaway. Besides, the foster home wasn't home. Having two drawers in a dresser to call my own didn't make it so, nor did sitting around a dinner table, holding hands and saying grace with other parentless children.

"So, you're going to live with your uncle?"

"Appears so."

"Hope he's as nice as Mama Tammy."

I really didn't care. As long as he was nicer than Lloyd and as long as he could get me out of here.

* * *

Greenmount Cemetery occupied a small mesa overlooking downtown Durango. The winding road, typically slick with ice and snow this time of year, was clear. The afternoon sun shone through the trees, casting long shadows. The one cemetery I'd seen in Albuquerque was a wide-open lawn with a grid of headstones and an occasional urn of fake flowers. Greenmount's residents had thick-trunked cedars and pines to shield their graves. I liked the idea of Mom having these evergreen sentinels watching over her since I couldn't anymore.

Tammy and I weren't the first to arrive. A man I assumed was the preacher stood by the grave site, a prayer book in his hands. A cemetery worker stood farther back, huddled against a tree. Carol, my case manager from social services, hadn't arrived yet. And neither had my uncle, even though he'd assured Carol he'd be here.

Mom's casket and a large square of green artificial turf concealed the hole in the ground where she'd be placed. I don't know why I'd expected a perfectly rectangular dirt pit like those on TV shows where the bad guys made some dude dig his own grave.

"You must be Arlie. I'm Reverend Knox from First Presbyterian. I'm sorry for your loss." The lanky minister held out his gloved hand, so I shook it to be polite. His nose and ears were redder than Mom's dress. No one told me how he'd been chosen to perform the service, but then again, I'd never asked. It didn't matter. Mom hadn't been religious. I remembered she mentioned going to Sunday school as a kid, but she never specified a denomination. Funny that she'd mention something like Sunday school but not that she had an older brother.

While my foster mother introduced herself to the minister, Mo huddled close to me. "You okay?" she asked.

"I'll be okay. How about you?"

Mo had said she lost her best friend when she lost her sister.

Attending Mom's funeral had to dredge up painful memories for her. I didn't even know where CeeCee was buried in the cemetery. Mo and I had never visited the grave.

"We'll get through this together," she said.

I craned my neck to look down the road toward town. The service was about to start and still no sign of my uncle. He probably didn't make it up from Texas as quickly as he'd hoped. Or maybe he'd decided to skip the funeral altogether and would meet me at the social services office.

"You looking for someone?" Mo asked.

"Nah. Doesn't matter anyway."

"Follow me." Mo grabbed my hand and led me toward the stocky, disheveled guy standing on the other side of the grave site. His unruly red hair stood up in the back. His beard concealed his cheeks and most of his thick neck. He seemed unfazed by the cold.

"Hi, I'm Mo and this is Arlie."

I couldn't understand why my best friend insisted I meet the cemetery worker who would later cover my mom with a ton of black dirt.

"Pleased to meet you both. Especially you, Arlie." The man kept his hands tucked in the pockets of his faded peacoat. "I'm Frank."

"Thought so," Mo mumbled.

My mouth and brain wouldn't engage so I just stared at him.

"Your uncle," he clarified.

"Yes…yes…I understand. I just didn't expect…I mean, you don't look like my mom."

A sad grin emerged from behind his ragged beard. He looked only at my eyes, as if trying hard not to stare at my scar. "You look a lot like her. Or at least the way she looked when we were in high school. Luckily she took after our mom instead of our dad."

My grandparents. "Are they still alive?"

"No, I'm afraid not," Frank said. "But we can talk about that later. We have a lot of catching up to do."

Once my case manager finally arrived, the minister motioned for us to join him closer to the grave site. I dipped my shoulder away from Tammy, who was trying to put an arm around me. Instead, I looped my arm through Mo's and listened to the preacher say kind words about a woman he'd never met.

* * *

When Reverend Knox was finished, he asked Frank and me if we'd like to say a few words. Frank shook his head no, so I spoke up.

"I'd like to sing something instead, if that'd be okay."

Mo rubbed my back and then stepped away as if my lungs and grief needed plenty of space.

Before I could start, a familiar car pulled up near the hearse. Mo's mom. I didn't know she was coming. Mrs. Mooney was always late for everything, but I didn't care. She'd been really nice to me over the years, despite what Mo's dad thought of me. She hurriedly took her place near Mo and blew me a kiss. Perhaps she was here for Mo as much as for me.

The song I'd chosen was "Angel," which I'd sung to Mom dozens of times over the years. When the voices made it hard for her to sleep, I'd stroke her hair and sing Sarah McLachlan's sad lyrics that seemed even more appropriate for her funeral.

In the arms of the angel, fly away from here,
From this dark, cold hotel room and the endlessness that you fear.

When I'd finished singing, Tammy and Carol dabbed at their

eyes, as if following some funeral playbook.

Mo wrapped an arm around my waist and laid her head on my shoulder, and her mom hugged us both. I didn't cry. I used to think my tears dried up sometime after the accident when the saltiness of tears stung the burns that were trying to heal. It embarrassed me to think people were waiting for me to show some emotion. Today, I just felt abandoned.

Frank's eyes were red and glassy, but he didn't cry outright either. Maybe he was only here because he felt he had to be.

While the minister expressed his condolences to us again, Frank approached the man who'd driven the hearse from the funeral home. He nodded and pointed in my direction. The two of them walked over.

"Miss, your uncle would like permission to open the casket to view his sister. Would that be all right?"

I blinked several times, letting the request sink in. My first reaction was "Hell no," but I had no good reason to object. Except that I was pissed Frank hadn't been a part of Mom's life when she was alive and I didn't think he deserved to ask anything of me, especially today.

"It's okay, Arlie. I shouldn't have asked. I'm sorry." He flipped up his coat collar against the chill and blew into his hands. That beard didn't protect him so much after all.

"I guess I don't mind," I finally answered.

Frank nodded and mouthed "thank you" before walking away.

"That was kind of you." Mo's mother stroked my hair. The move startled me and she dropped her hand quickly.

"Thank you for being here, Mrs. Mooney," I said. "It means a lot."

Mo leaned in to her mom. They remained in a silent embrace,

probably acknowledging memories of CeeCee's funeral. Mrs. Mooney whispered something in Mo's ear and then walked to her car.

I stood next to Mo and we watched her drive off. Mo swiped at tears that remained on her cheeks.

"I'm glad you're here," I said.

"It never crossed my mind not to be." She rubbed her mittened hands together.

"Since we're already here, would you like to visit CeeCee's grave?"

Mo stiffened. "No, I don't believe in visiting graves. That's not my sister in the ground anyway."

My friend was always asking me to talk about *my* feelings, even though it was hard to admit her own. Still, we both knew we didn't have to visit graves to remember the family we'd lost.

"It's getting colder. Let's go sit in Tammy's car," I suggested.

"Umm…not exactly fond of your foster mom," Mo said, but she followed me anyway.

The sun had heated the inside of Tammy's Corolla so I shucked off my coat. Tammy was already in the driver's seat and asked if I was ready to head to social services. They'd asked for a meeting with my uncle and me to talk about living arrangements. It was just another appointment on this strange day.

"Not just yet," I said. "Could we wait a bit?"

Mo stood by my door, hugging her arms across her chest. "I'm going back for last period. You sure you're okay?" she asked.

I nodded. "Go to school. *Really.*"

"Call me later?"

"Sure," I said.

Mo bent down and kissed my cheek before running to her car.

"Is that girl even old enough to drive?" Tammy asked. "Her parents must have some money to buy her a nice car."

"It's a used Honda," I muttered.

Tammy acted as if she hadn't heard me and continued to give her opinion on Mo's directness and overconfidence. She wondered aloud if she should tell Frank about her concerns.

I ignored my foster mother and instead watched as the funeral director opened the lid of the casket and stepped aside. Frank's back was to me so I couldn't tell if he was saying his good-byes or crying or just standing there. After a couple of minutes he leaned over and kissed my mother's forehead. I bit my lip to stop it from trembling.

I'd decided not to view her at the funeral home because I didn't want the last memory of my mother to be of a made-up, plastic version. I'd made a mistake. Now, my last memory would always be of her dead body on the motel-room bed, surrounded by the drugs she loved more than me.

Frank stepped back from the grave site and spoke to the funeral director again. The man pointed toward a large piece of equipment that looked as if it had been used to dig the grave. Frank shook his head. *What did he want now?*

After the funeral director nodded, Frank marched briskly toward Tammy's car so I opened my door again.

"Hey, I'll be just a few minutes late to our meeting. Don't start without me."

He jogged back to the grave and removed his peacoat, tossing it on the ground. A cemetery worker returned from his pickup with a shovel and handed it to Frank. My uncle looked over at me one last time and waved us on. He'd be the one to cover my mom with dirt after all. It helped to soften my horror of leaving her.

I almost asked Tammy if I could stay and help. Perhaps then the nightmares would stop once and for all.

CHAPTER 5

I stayed at Tammy's for the next month while Frank made arrangements to move to Durango. I'd assumed he would want me to move back to Texas with him, but he said I'd had enough upheaval in my life. He added that he'd always wanted to live in the mountains anyway. I couldn't tell if he was lying for my benefit, but I didn't press him. At least that meant Mo and Dora would remain in my life.

Frank bought me a smartphone and insisted we talk every few days. These check-ins were brief, neither of us feeling all that comfortable. During one call, he informed me he was bringing his thirty-one-foot Airstream trailer back to Durango for us to live in. I couldn't imagine being in such close quarters with someone I barely knew.

Tammy disapproved as soon as she saw the thing.

"You're going to live in a rundown trailer?" She ignored Frank, who waved to us from the wooden steps attached to the Airstream's entrance.

"It's no big deal," I said. "He's lived in it for years, and he probably wants to save a few bucks on rent."

"Look at him," she said. "He dresses like a homeless person. Does he even own a comb? You know you can call me if things don't work out, right?"

Tammy would be the last person I'd call, but I nodded anyway. I got out of the car and retrieved my few belongings from the backseat before she could hug me or offer any more snark about Frank.

As she drove off, I stood for a minute, taking in how large the trailer actually was. Frank had positioned it at the far side of a huge lot that was mostly dirt clods and weeds. I hadn't known lots this size were even available within the city limits. This one was situated at the north end of town behind a river-rafting company. Half a dozen brightly painted school buses that were used to haul rafters blocked the view of the residential area behind the lot. At least I'd be within a couple of blocks of the last stop on the town's trolley route and a short bike ride from Mo's house.

Frank motioned me over, so I joined him in the middle of the yard and set down my duffel. He'd already marked off a perfect square with wooden stakes and bright pink plastic tape.

"What's the project?" I asked.

"This is where the entrance will be. The downstairs will be one large great room with a staircase in the center." He waved his thick arms, pointing here and there at an image only he could see. "And there'll be two bedrooms, one upstairs and one downstairs."

"You're building yourself a house?"

"I'm building *us* a house. It'll be our new home."

Home. I'd lived in one-room apartments, motels, a beat-up

Subaru Outback, and an abandoned garage. I couldn't imagine living in a 1970s-style trailer with a stranger I'd just met a month ago. I didn't know if I could do this. Any of this. Returning to the foster home almost seemed like a good idea.

"You bought this lot?" I asked.

"Yep. The owner is letting me rent the lot for the trailer until the sale of the land closes early next month."

He'd made this decision on his own; not that I expected to have a vote. He'd moved awfully fast to establish us as a family, but still he didn't give me a say in the matter.

"You a millionaire or something?" I asked. "Land's not cheap here."

"Nothing to concern yourself with. Let me show you the tube."

He picked up my bag, but I grabbed it back. "I got it."

The interior felt more spacious than I'd thought it would, although it was definitely retro. The front door opened into a living area with a brown plaid sofa and an orange Formica table with a built-in bench on one side. Books stood in precarious piles under the table and near the sofa. Many more lined makeshift bookshelves along one wall and covered one of the few windows in the place. The inside of the trailer smelled old.

"Like books much?" I asked.

"I have hundreds more in a storage unit in Corpus Christi," he said proudly. "Climate-controlled, of course, since the humidity is damn thick down there."

I let out a low whistle. "Impressive."

"So…you get the bedroom." He pointed past the little galley kitchen to the plastic accordion door at the rear of the trailer.

"I don't want to put you out," I stammered.

"You're not putting me out," he said. "You need a door. Everyone needs a door."

"I don't understand."

"I'd go mad if I couldn't shut out the world at least a few minutes a day. From what I hear, you've never had a door to close. So this one's yours."

I swallowed hard against the growing lump in my throat. "I hadn't thought about it like that."

"I have," Frank said. "A kid should have a room…a messy room with clothes and junk everywhere…and a parent to yell at them to clean it up."

Parent? He wasn't my parent. I'd never had a room or someone who cared if it was messy or not. The thought was so completely overwhelming that I picked up my bag and retreated before Frank could say anything else. "Thanks. I'll be out in a minute."

I plopped down, burying my face in the bedspread. So, the guy was being nice. Isn't that what he had to do? I didn't ask him to move here. I didn't even know him.

I sat up and wiped my face. The room was basic and outdated. The double bed was covered in a simple floral bedspread—a relic from the 1970s. Mo would love it. She'd say retro was in. The walls were pale wood paneling without any photos or pictures, although you could tell by several darker spots on the wall where some had hung before. Frank had probably taken down his own stuff.

In the corner of the space was a wooden rod hanging from the ceiling by two chains, a makeshift open-air closet. That and the small chest of drawers would do, since I didn't have a lot of clothes.

My room. Mo would want to paint it right away and pick out curtains and probably a funky lamp. I could just see it now: orange and turquoise and hot pink, like Mo's personality. She'd want to pay for it all too, even though I had my own money. I'd always made sure I did because Mom hadn't.

We'd buried Mom just over a month ago and here I was, under the microscope of yet another person tasked with making sure I was okay. This one wanting to be my father.

* * *

When I emerged from my room, Frank was in the kitchenette chopping veggies. He could be described as a fireplug—thick across the chest, with massive arms that could pound anyone who dared to call him that. He wore an apron that read "You can kiss the cook, but keep your hands off my buns." Not exactly the picture of manliness.

"Stir-fry okay by you?" he asked.

I nodded. In our few brief visits with the social worker after Mom's funeral, I hadn't mentioned my inability to taste.

"Could I help with dinner?" I asked.

"Nope, just relax. I'll be done in a second." He waved me away with the knife.

"I'll just watch some TV then." I scanned the living area for the television.

"I don't have one. Rots your brain."

As much as I loved to read, I'd gotten used to having cable in our motel rooms. Almost every motel, no matter how shabby, had cable and at least one premium movie channel. One of the few perks of living in a moldy, fifteen-by-fifteen-foot space with pasteboard furniture and a lumpy mattress.

"You're kidding, right?"

"Nope. I occasionally watch movies on my laptop. If I had a television, I'd be tempted to channel surf through a lot of crap I don't need to watch. Plus, all the news is bad these days. A real downer."

"Well, can we get one?" I asked.

"No."

He didn't even apologize or explain why. Shouldn't he have been trying harder to win me over? Engrossed in his damn stir-fry, he didn't even look up.

"I guess I'll watch on my laptop," I said.

"You have a laptop?"

My face colored. I guess Frank assumed I wouldn't have nice things.

"It's Mo's old one."

"Oh. Nice kid. But if you ever need a newer model, just let me know."

"Well, I won't," I mumbled and turned my attention to his bookshelves. He'd arranged the books alphabetically by author. That was something I'd probably have done if I'd been allowed to keep books. Mom always said they were too heavy and slowed us down, and that I could go to a library if I needed to read.

"Borrow any books you'd like," Frank said. "Although I doubt we share the same tastes."

Maybe not, but I liked that he read. Book people were more interesting.

Within a few minutes, he'd cleared the small table of the architectural drawings for the house and set down two steaming bowls of shrimp and veggies over rice. There were a few textures I couldn't take, rice being one of them. Anything grainy like that, and slimy things like cooked spinach and ripe bananas.

Many days I'd just buy a milk shake or frozen coffee drink for lunch because at least I could choke down smooth, cold things. To ensure I was getting enough calories, I sometimes drank protein shakes intended for old people who didn't eat right, only those were awfully expensive.

"So how is it?" Frank's freckled skin seemed to rage against the spiciness of the food. Perspiration trickled down his forehead in impressive rivulets.

"Habanero or Scotch bonnet?" I asked.

"Thai chili. Sorry, I got carried away. I can make you something else if it's too hot."

"No worries. I can't taste it anyway." Although the rice grains were sure to tease my gag reflex, I gulped down a large spoonful in appreciation of his hard work.

"What do you mean, 'can't taste it anyway'?" He put down his fork.

I spent the next half hour explaining that I'd lost my senses of taste and smell following the explosion—except for the lingering chemical taste on my tongue and in my nose. But even that wasn't there all the time. Mostly it was just a numb sensation that made eating a miserable chore.

"That's awful, Arlie. Has a doctor said if it's permanent?"

I snorted. "Doctor? Too expensive. Besides, I never told Mom the full story."

Frank's face twisted with what looked like shock, anger, and sorrow in one messy stew.

"It's okay, really. I just couldn't burden Mom with another thing. She couldn't handle a lot of stress."

My uncle slammed his palms on the table, causing the spoon to jump from my bowl. I startled. The move reminded me of Lloyd and his hair-trigger temper. Then the hiccups started—probably a by-product of the Thai chili as well as shock at Frank's anger.

"Shit, I didn't mean to scare you. It's not like me." He shook his head. "I just keep hearing about all the horrible stuff that's happened to you. Things will be different now. Sarah may have failed you, but I won't."

"Where do you get off saying that? You don't know me." Hiccups peppered my reaction. I clenched my jaws to keep from saying more.

Frank put his bowl in the sink even though he hadn't finished. He stood looking out the small kitchen window.

"And you didn't know her." I looked down at my food, ashamed because I knew he was right. Mom *had* failed me. But I'd protected her for so many years that it was my go-to response.

"I used to know her," he said. "But you're right. I don't know a thing about your lives together. I just meant I'll try my best."

Frank handed me a glass of water to help with the hiccups. I chugged it and waited for him to sit back down.

"I don't need rescuing, you know."

When he didn't answer, I wondered if that meant he didn't believe me.

"I'm not really hungry." I pushed back from the table and returned to my new bedroom. As I closed the plastic accordion door behind me, Frank called out from the kitchen.

"You're going to see a doctor about that taste thing."

* * *

I must have dozed off because I woke shuddering from the cold, the edge of the bedspread pulled up over my shoulders. The Airstream must not be airtight. Might not have been a problem in Texas, but Colorado would be a different story.

I opened my door. Frank was on the sofa at the other end of the trailer, reading. He'd propped his beer bottle up against a throw pillow.

"A little cold for beer, isn't it?" I rubbed my arms and blew into my hands.

"Never too cold for beer," he said, putting down his book. "There's an electric heater in the far corner of your room near the baseboard. I meant to tell you earlier but didn't get the chance. Don't put anything in front of it or it'll catch fire."

He'd pulled on a large wool sweater, which made him look even stockier. And his socks didn't match.

I pulled a kitchen chair around so I wouldn't have to sit on the sofa with him.

"I didn't mean anything, you know…before," Frank said. "I don't know how Sarah was with you. Hell, I didn't even know where she ended up after she left Texas."

He tossed me the crocheted afghan that was draped across the sofa. I wrapped it around my shoulders.

"You didn't know where we were all these years?"

"Hell, I didn't even know I had a niece. Sarah fell off the face of the earth after Mom and Dad died. Car wreck. I was twenty and your mom was eighteen."

He took a swig of beer.

"That sucks," I said.

"Yeah, it does. So your mom never mentioned our parents? Not even that you're named after your great-grandmother?"

"I'm named after somebody? I always wondered. Mom never talked about her childhood."

Whenever I asked her about my grandparents, she'd change the subject so eventually I stopped asking. Suddenly I felt sad for the grandma and grandpa I'd never met and who had died without ever meeting me. Mom had kept her family a secret for some reason, even the brother who might have been able to help us.

"What's wrong, Arlie?"

"Just thinking my family tree is missing a lot of branches." The image of a Charlie Brown Christmas tree came to mind, a pathetic twig losing the last of its needles.

"Well, you can ask me anything. But I warn you, I'm not that interesting."

I wanted to ask questions about Mom instead. What she was like at my age. What music she listened to. Whether she had a steady boyfriend. I couldn't go there yet.

"You moved out here pretty quick. Didn't you have some kind of job in Corpus?"

"I was in construction. I built houses mostly."

"So you didn't go to college?" I asked.

"Oh, I went. Got a wildlife and fisheries degree, but I found out I liked using my hands more."

That explained why he thought he could build a house by himself, but how could he afford the lumber and materials? He didn't have a job and he'd just purchased a lot in a mountain resort town where real estate was outrageously expensive.

"I know this isn't any of my business," I said. "But you're going to have some major-league expenses if you plan to build a house here. What do you do for money?"

Frank's mouth tightened into a line. "I have the means to take care of you."

"I didn't mean it like that."

His chest heaved with a large sigh. "Sorry. Guess I'm still defensive after my 'interviews' with the social services people." He used his fingers to put air quotes around the word "interviews."

"What do you mean?"

"Let's say they were pretty thorough in checking out my

background. Couldn't let some loser be your guardian."

I hadn't given much thought to how social services tracked him down or what they'd talked about. When I'd made the decision to call the police after finding Mom's body, I'd been swept up in my own vortex of change. That same day I'd been assigned a foster family. Two days later I was enrolled at the high school. The day after that, I was in Jane's office for observation. I guess Frank had joined me under the microscope.

"So, they determined you weren't a loser? Even though you can't find a matching pair of socks?"

"They appreciated that I bathe and brush my teeth daily."

"No doubt," I said.

When he smiled, I got up from the kitchen chair and joined him on the sofa, aware that I'd been as tense as steel cable before.

"Back to your question about money…" he said.

"It's none of my business. You don't have to explain."

"I don't mind. You should know."

He said that Mom and he inherited a bunch of money after their parents died. "They had a lot of farm and ranch land, but Sarah and I couldn't manage it on our own. We sold it… for a good price. Let's just say I've invested wisely these past twenty years."

Frank didn't look like he had a lot of money. I pictured him living frugally in his Airstream, splurging on books instead of clothes. How expensive could Carhartts and T-shirts be? He didn't have a wife or kids to spend money on, but now I wondered what he might have been saving that money for and what plans I might have derailed.

"So Mom got half of the money?"

"Yeah, she got half. But it didn't last long."

Frank's shoulders slumped as he looked at the floor. I regretted that I'd put him on the spot.

"You don't have to tell me about it if you don't want to."

"Nah, it's okay," he said. "It was just a very painful time in my life. And in your mom's. We both made bad choices."

He described how my mother squandered her inheritance in less than two years. She'd hooked up with former high-school classmates who squatted in abandoned houses and gladly accepted her money to fund their drug habits.

"I literally kidnapped her and brought her home on several occasions," he said. "But she just ran back to the junkies. She said they cared about her more than I did."

I knew exactly what he meant. Too many times I'd felt Mom cared more about who could supply her next high. Those ever-changing, transient friends were more like family to her than I could ever be.

These memories were almost too much to absorb, so I left the room with the pretense of making some tea. Frank grabbed a bag of chips and ate them mindlessly, handful after handful, while I sat at the far end of the sofa, sipping the tasteless water and wondering if I dared ask any more questions about Mom's past.

My hand shook so I placed the hot mug on the floor near the sofa. "Mom was on drugs back then?"

"You look surprised," he said.

"No...it's just...I thought my stepfather turned her on to them."

Frank downed his beer quickly. "I should've tried harder. Back then, I mean." His full mustache almost hid the quivering of his lip.

I didn't know how to feel about this remorse bubbling up after twenty-plus years. It seemed out of place for someone who hadn't seen his sister in so long. Still, I didn't need Frank to process his shit in front of me.

"We can't fool ourselves into thinking we had any control over her," I said.

"How old are you again?" His smile was weaker now.

I'd figured out a long time ago that I couldn't change her actions. All I could do was manage the chaos that surrounded us to protect us in whatever way I could.

"Do you know how Mom ended up in Albuquerque?"

"I don't know when she moved. I couldn't take any more of the lies so I cut her out of my life. For good. Guess that's why she didn't tell me about you."

"Well, I didn't know I had an uncle. That makes us even."

"Yeah, maybe," he said.

We sat without talking for a couple of minutes before I spoke again. "Could I ask you why you wanted to help bury Mom? I mean, I thought the funeral home handled stuff like that."

"It's kind of a ritual in our family," he said. "That's what my parents did at my grandparents' funerals. And I did it for Mom and Dad too. I guess it's a more personal way of saying good-bye."

Frank got a faraway look in his eyes. I cleared my throat to end the awkward silence.

Without looking at me, he grabbed the book he'd been reading earlier. I took it as a sign we wouldn't be talking about Mom or funerals or anything more that night. He couldn't answer all my questions anyway. I'd never know who my real dad was, or why Mom and he didn't stay together, or how she hooked up with Lloyd. She'd deprived me of all those answers.

"Think I'll watch something on my laptop. Don't feel like

reading." I sloughed off the afghan and made my way to the opposite side of the trailer.

Frank looked up from his book. "I'm not going to buy you a TV so you'll like me more."

"Whatever. I can tough it out." As I shut my door, I heard him laugh.

CHAPTER 6

Over the next few weeks, Frank and I eased awkwardly into daily routines that sometimes clicked and sometimes tested our tempers. We both had zero experience in our new roles of guardian and orphan.

This morning, he blocked the door to the trailer, making me late for school. "What did I say to upset you?" he demanded.

"I said I didn't need any money for lunch, but you kept pushing it," I said.

"All I said was that you didn't have to borrow from Mo anymore. That I was happy to give you spending money." His cheeks flared and I could tell he was struggling not to raise his voice.

"It's fine, Frank. Really. Just let me go to school."

He followed me out the door and into the yard. "We'll talk later then?"

I nodded and waved him off. His hovering was suffocating at times, but I had to remind myself that for the first time in my life, I was not worried about money and how many odd jobs it'd take me to earn enough for groceries.

* * *

Mo met me at lunch. It was the one time of day we had time to talk since the only class we had together was American history. Today she was worried I'd back out of trying out for choral. I couldn't remember why I'd let her talk me into it in the first place. Now I sat with my arms wrapped around my waist, sure I was going to throw up before my audition, which was just forty minutes away.

"I don't know any of the students in choral," I said. "I wish you could be there."

"Cody from your English lit class is a member."

"He's in the choral society?" An odd mix of fear and excitement tightened my chest.

"Yeah, so you *do* know someone. Stop being so nervous." She flicked a piece of her sandwich at me and I batted it away.

Cody and I had spoken only a handful of times, mostly about homework assignments or other students who clearly hadn't done their reading before class. But he was one of the few people who'd been openly nice to me since I was forced to go back to school.

Mo usually called him "the hot blind dude" because she always described guys by their looks first: height, build, eye color, hunk factor. I saw so much more: the sureness of his steps in navigating the halls and classrooms at school, the way he'd bite his lower lip for an instant before he flashed a smile, the long strands of dishwater blond hair that fell across his forehead.

More importantly, he'd figured out a way to fit in despite being different and almost made it look effortless. I wondered if Cody's confidence was partly an act, and if he sometimes still felt as alien as I did.

* * *

At the choral audition, a group of ten or twelve students sat at the back of the music room, most too busy talking to notice I'd entered. They'd all seen me at one point or another during my first couple of months at school, so my disfigurement wasn't likely to cause odd looks and whispers. The absence of stares almost unnerved me more.

A girl with a hot-pink stripe in her hair called me over. Claire. She was also in my English class and clearly a friend of Cody, who was sitting next to her.

"Have a seat," she said, patting a chair.

"Good luck, and don't be nervous." Cody leaned across Claire's lap as if his words wouldn't reach me otherwise.

Miss Browning, the choir director, was petite and unassuming, but with a voice that had a wicked range. When she entered the classroom, everyone stopped talking. She motioned for me to join her by the piano before she spoke.

"This is Arlie Betts," she said. "She's joining us a little late in the year, but I'm sure we can bring her up to speed in time for the community concert in a couple of months."

Miss Browning had stumbled upon me singing with Mo in the gym parking lot one evening after a basketball game. She and Mo had double-teamed me, badgering me until I agreed to try choral. *Try*, I emphasized to Mo. As director, Miss Browning had final approval on who got in, but she liked the group to weigh in concerning the elite show choir. And that meant an audition.

Now, standing in the practice room, my throat dry with panic, I almost hated Mo for her zealousness in trying to make me fit in. Not that she resented being my only friend, but she worried I wasn't interested in connecting with anyone else.

I spotted Brittany, the girl who hated me. Mo hadn't warned

me that she too was in choral. I eyed the door, my escape should I really mess things up. I pictured myself running toward it in slow motion, then kicking it open with one push and running down the hall.

"So, are you ready to sing for us?" The choral director sat at the piano, waiting for me to gather my wits. She had the sheet music we'd chosen earlier in the week when we practiced the number. We'd settled on "Jar of Hearts" by Christina Perri, a song that would showcase my vocals. She'd done everything in her power to make sure I understood how much she believed in me. Her attention made me uncomfortable, yet here I was, sweating profusely and worried that I would disappoint her somehow.

I stared past the faces of the students in front of me, purposely blurring my vision and blocking out everything around me, including Cody. To squelch my nerves, I kept telling myself none of it mattered: not Miss Browning, not these students, and definitely not Brittany.

Being afraid of singing in front of a group was laughable considering all I'd been able to handle in the past. Like answering our apartment door at 2 a.m. when my stepdad's dealer friends and junkies came begging for a fix. Or hiding in a closet, clutching Lloyd's handgun, when an angry gang member stopped by to dispute the size of a meth delivery.

Even though I knew the song backward and forward, I started out shaky, my throat catching at the end of the line: *And don't you know I'm not your ghost anymore?* But then my voice grew stronger and stronger until I gave it my all during the chorus.

And who do you think you are?
Runnin' 'round leaving scars.

After a few more lines, I dared to look at the students. Most were smiling, moving their heads in time with the music. Cody swayed from side to side almost imperceptibly. His full lips stayed fixed in a soft smile for the entire song.

As I neared the end, my vocals were overshadowed by clapping and whistling so I just let the last few lines of lyrics drop. Miss Browning mouthed "Good job" as she too clapped.

I mumbled "thanks" a few times and sat down in the chair Claire had saved for me.

"Looks like we have ourselves a new mezzo-soprano, although I bet you could do alto too," she said. "Hope you can handle the classical stuff." She gave me a serious stare. Then a huge smile broke across her face.

"Yeah...I mean, I'll try my best," I said.

"You'll have to do better than that," Brittany said. "We're a competition choir. You have to look good and sing good."

"It's sing *well*, not sing good. And stop being such a bitch." Cody whispered the words, but everyone heard him anyway. Most chuckled, which made Brittany's face turn a raging red.

"Don't think we need a vote, right, Miss Browning?" Claire asked. "Arlie's in as far as I'm concerned."

The rest of practice was a literal blur. My eyes teared so badly that I kept my head down. I thought I'd feel only relief after finishing the tryout number, but emotion pounded in my heart and head. I wanted to be part of this group, but I wanted to run away. And Brittany. I already had to suffer through calculus class with her. Now, she threatened to ruin something good in my life.

Thinking about her and the audition was too much at once. When Miss Browning dismissed us, I was the first one out the door even though Claire and Cody called for me to wait up.

* * *

I met Mo by her car and asked her to drive me straight to Frank's.

"What's wrong? What happened at choir?"

I was crying so hard I couldn't find enough breath to talk.

"You're freaking me out. Tell me what's wrong," she said.

"I did great." My sobbing muffled my words. "I mean, they all said I did great. Well, except one, but I'm in. I…I'm just a little overwhelmed."

Mo threw her arms around me, shouting her congratulations. Her enthusiasm buoyed me instantly.

"I told you they'd think you were awesome."

For a moment, I remembered what it was like before the explosion, before people stared, before the ugly words and awkward silences. Today, I wasn't my scar. The students had listened to my music; they'd listened to *me*. Just plain Arlie. Not poor, disfigured Arlie. Not Arlie, the homeless girl whose mother killed herself.

"I feel like a crazy person," I admitted as we drove up North Main.

"No, you mean you feel normal," Mo corrected me. "This is how it feels when you don't have to worry about your mother getting high or if you have enough money for rent."

I winced at her words. She was wrong. It had been a messed-up sort of normal to be with my addict mother, sleeping in our car, living by our own rules. Sitting in classrooms all day, auditioning for a choir, making friends—those things didn't even approach normal.

"Let's not talk about Mom now, okay?"

She glanced over at me. "Sorry. You know what I mean. I want all this to feel normal now...for you to feel good."

"It's just been weird for me. All of it. Especially school." I fanned my flushed face, which felt taut from salty tears. "And on top of it, I'm living in a trailer with someone I just met."

"You haven't *just* met him. And from what you've told me, Frank sounds like a good guy."

"He is a good guy."

"It's only been a couple of months. Get to know him better and it won't feel weird."

Mo stopped the car in front of Frank's trailer, but I didn't get out.

"I'm trying," I said. "What more can I do? I feel like he watches my every step."

She hugged me fiercely and I remembered why I'd fought so hard not to push her away. I needed Mo.

"I know you're trying," she said. "I didn't mean anything. Except give yourself a break. You did something pretty courageous today. It's all about the baby steps, girlfriend."

"Frank should pay you instead of my therapist. I swear you do me more good."

"I think you need both of us." She licked her thumbs and rubbed the mascara smudges from beneath my eyes. "Now pull yourself together or Frank will give you the third degree."

"I'll text you later," I said and got out of the car.

"Yep, I want to hear what Cody thought of your performance," she said.

"Cody?"

"Don't play dumb. I know you like him. You just won't admit it. But now that you're in choral together, who knows what will happen."

I felt a new sensation in my stomach, one that was wonderful and unbearable at the same time. Yet I didn't want to admit to Mo how much he occupied my thoughts. She would just try to convince me that Cody and I could be more than friends. She'd try to tell me he wouldn't care about my physical scar.

But she could never convince me that Cody or any other guy would be able to look beyond my other scars—my mom's addiction, her suicide, and the ugliness of our lives these past years. Those things would be with me always, keeping my dreams small and unspoken.

CHAPTER 7
THREE MONTHS AGO — GOOD-BYE, MOM

Mom didn't have an off button. Asleep, drunk, or high, she made noises without even knowing it. Snorts, snuffles, mumbles, cries. Not today. Today, she was the absence of sound.

I'd been with Mo all day and had just returned from buying groceries to find Mom lying on the bedspread, her face to the wall. I stared at the bottoms of her feet, cracked and dirty from walking on the black asphalt in the motel parking lot. She rarely wore shoes, even in winter.

"Mom?" I placed the bags of groceries down on the table and sat in a chair. I didn't call out her name again because her body no longer rose with breath. Instead, I grabbed my phone to call Mo, but then set it down again. I didn't want Mo to see this. I was supposed to see this. No one else.

I took a few deep breaths and mentally went over my to-do list: flush anything flushable; throw the rest in the dumpster. Lately, she'd been smoking more than shooting up, but today a half-filled syringe and a spoon were on the bed. On the floor were her glass pipe and a small, open plastic bag of rock meth.

Why both and why so much?

I carefully wrapped everything but the meth in a pillowcase and then stuffed the bundle in a trash-can liner before tossing it in the dumpster. Next I flushed the meth.

I watched hundreds of dollars go down the toilet, wondering where Mom could have scored the cash needed for that amount or if she had a new friend who liked to share. But even that friend would have taken the rest of the dope once he realized Mom was dead. Had someone helped her end her life, or was this just an ugly accident?

Nothing made sense. For the first time in my life, I wanted someone to tell me what to do next. I could leave. Leave Durango. Someone would find her eventually. Other long-term motel guests would tell police she had a daughter, but no, they hadn't seen her in days.

If I called the police, I'd no longer be invisible. I'd be a sixteen-year-old who didn't go to school. A child without a guardian. I'd lose everything and nothing. Mom had always hoped Mo's family would take me in if something happened to her. Mo's mother might have agreed, but her dad would never welcome me into their home. After he found out Mom used drugs and that I didn't go to school, he thought of me as a bad influence on Mo. That wasn't giving either of us any credit.

The numbers on the digital clock challenged me to hurry up and make a decision. I closed my eyes, trying to ignore it and my mother's body.

"*Fuck!*" My voice rang out in the silent space.

Leaving was my only real choice. I packed a small duffel bag; a suitcase would have looked suspicious. Jeans, underwear, my Doc Marten boots, a map of Colorado, and the nonperishable foods I'd just purchased. Where did I think I was going with these basics?

I reached behind the television and groped for the envelope that was taped there. I opened it—only forty dollars remained in our emergency fund. I folded the two twenties in half and stuffed them inside the bottom of my sneaker. Maybe I should have kept the meth and sold it. I'd need more money wherever I was going.

I looked back at Mom. I couldn't leave her like that. In the bathroom, I ran the hot-water tap until it steamed the mirror above it. I held a threadbare washcloth under the stream until it burned my hands, then wrung it out.

My mother's body shifted slightly when I sat on the bed near her legs. Gently, I washed the grime from her feet, returning to the sink to rinse the cloth when it became soiled.

I turned her onto her back, straightened her arms at her sides, and pulled down her sleeves to cover the needle marks. I lifted her denim skirt and checked. Yep. Panties were in place.

Her mouth hung slack. I didn't want others to see her stained, crumbling teeth, so I pushed her chin up to close her mouth. It opened again, no matter how many times I tried. I smoothed her hair and tucked still-tangled strands behind her ears. She'd left a pair of gold hoops on the nightstand, so I fastened them to her lobes. I'd bought them from Walmart three years ago for her birthday, and she wore them almost every day. I think she knew I'd shoveled more than a few driveways to be able to afford them.

The clock read 4:30 p.m. when I'd finished.

I wondered if I should stay the night and set out in the morning. It'd be safer here than on the streets, but I couldn't bear the thought of falling asleep in the same room as my mother's body.

I could knock on Dora's door. Maybe I could stay with her a while. She could help me call the police and find out what had really happened to Mom.

I sat back down on a chair and my brain finally checked out.

When my head snapped forward, I sat bolt upright, headachy and disoriented. The clock told me it was 5:30 a.m. My neck ached from awkward sleep. Then I remembered.

She lay there in silence. No sighs or grunts or whispered dreams.

I was so tired. Too tired to run anymore. Too tired to hide.

I waited for sunlight, then picked up the motel phone and dialed 911. Whatever waited for me couldn't be as bad as what I'd already been through.

CHAPTER 8

My therapist stared at me so intently that I wanted to knock the glasses off her face and stomp on them. Not exactly the smartest move if I was trying to prove how well-adjusted I was and that life was now all sunshine and unicorns.

"I sense you're pretty angry today," Jane said.

"Wow. You're good at your job."

"Thank you," she deadpanned. "So, if I'm doing my job, why aren't you doing yours?"

"Which is?"

"To show up. Be honest. No matter how painful it might be."

Jane had spent the better part of an hour pressing me to tell her what had happened this past week to cause my anger. Didn't she realize it wasn't one thing? That perhaps it was the thousand-and-one things that had changed since Mom died?

"Nothing is the same," I finally said. "Mom had no expectations of me. Now I'm expected to suddenly be okay with living with my wacky uncle in a silver tube. I'm expected to go to school and be a normal kid. I'm expected to come to therapy and bare my soul so you can tell the courts I'm not a freakin' basket case."

"I've never asked you to bare your soul. And I've never thought you were a basket case," Jane said. "In fact, I've thought the opposite. That you've held everything together for so long you don't know how to ask for help."

I didn't really have a reason to hold it together anymore. I no longer had to worry about Mom getting beat up by her latest boyfriend or burning down our motel room by smoking meth in bed. I no longer had to slog to the food bank or shelter to get us food. I didn't have to pack up our things and load the car in the middle of the night so we could skip out on our past-due motel bill and find another Durango motel that'd take us.

Frank made me breakfast every day—a real breakfast that I couldn't taste, but that I still appreciated. Mo picked me up for school. I sat in class and took notes. I studied and got good grades. I sang in a choral group.

"It's make-believe. All bullshit," I said.

She stared, obviously wanting more. "What's real in your life, Arlie? Just name one thing."

I didn't hesitate. "Mo. She's never let me down."

I felt a stinging pang of guilt that I didn't trust my best friend enough to tell her I liked Cody. And, more importantly, that I wanted Cody to like me.

"What about your uncle? Do you trust he's here for you?"

This same question popped into my head from time to time, but I never let it linger there for long. Frank had given me plenty of reasons to believe he cared about me and that I could count on him. Yet a little part of me suspected that I'd arrive home from school one day and his Suburban and Airstream would be gone, leaving only an empty lot and my belongings in a heap. The image rarely stressed me out. Some days, I ached to be alone. I knew I could survive on my own again.

"Do you feel safe now?" she asked.

"Yes," I admitted. No Lloyd. No drugs. No worrying where I'd be sleeping.

"Does that feel good or scary?"

"Safe can be scary too." That sounded weird to say aloud.

"Can you tell me more?" she probed.

"Don't you think I'd be better off just getting on with my life and leaving the past as past?"

"Because it's too difficult to talk about?"

"No, because it won't change anything. I'm fine. I've always been fine."

As much as I liked Jane, I hated when she resorted to psychobabble. And I saw through her attempts to put me at ease with her casual stance.

"What do you want, Jane?" I asked. "Should I scream and tear out my hair? Do you want me to curse Mom for destroying my chances at a normal life?"

"I don't want anything, Arlie, except for you to have a full, happy life. But you've lost your mother. You have a new guardian and are experiencing all the normal stressors of teenage life, with the added stressor of being physically different. So, yeah, I think you have some emotions to sort out. Maybe ones you haven't even allowed yourself to feel yet."

I played with a hole in my jeans, avoiding Jane's stare. Mom had done the unforgivable in leaving me. And it frightened me to think I hated her more than I loved her.

"I think it's time for me to be going," I said. "I'll see you next Friday."

Before I could leave, Jane reached out and touched my elbow.

"Your mother didn't destroy your chances at a normal life," she said. "Only you can do that."

CHAPTER 9

Frank lugged a bundle of two-by-fours on one shoulder without breaking a sweat. When he saw me, he dropped the wooden planks to the ground and they bounced noisily.

"How was school?" he called out.

"It's Monday. What's there to say?" I mumbled and made my way over to the Airstream trailer.

"It's Monday. What's there to say," he mimicked in a high-pitched voice. "Get over here and tell me how your day went."

He sat down on the edge of the smooth concrete foundation. I sat down beside him and offered him the rest of the water in my Nalgene. He downed it and wiped droplets from his thick beard.

"It's a warm one for April," he said. "You wearing sunscreen?"

Both he and Mo were overprotective of my burn scar. Or maybe being a redhead made Frank unusually concerned.

"Yes," I said. "Want to inspect the tube I have in my backpack?"

"You don't always have to be a smart-ass."

I shrugged.

"Hey, I borrowed that new Karen Russell book from your room," he said. "I'm sure you're probably working on several others."

He was right. I usually had four or five books going at once. If I got bored with one story too easily, I liked to have choices. And since we didn't have a TV, I was reading more than usual lately.

"You almost done for the day?" I looked at the chaotic construction site. No matter how cluttered it seemed, by the end of each day, Frank always had his tools in order and locked away in a storage shed. Scrap materials found their place into the dumpster.

"I'm going to finish framing this wall and then I'll cook us some supper." He slapped his thighs with both hands and returned to his woodpile.

Besides recognizing his voracious appetite for books and an aversion to razors, I still knew little about my uncle, but we felt more and more comfortable around one another. He usually said what was on his mind, which kept things real. Sometimes too real.

"Can I do anything to help?" I asked. "Chop something?"

"Already done that," he said. "Relax or read."

I shielded my eyes and continued to watch him work. He assembled two-by-fours into a grid on the foundation. Within forty-five minutes, he had another wall lifted and braced into place. He'd designed the house himself. In fact, he'd drawn and redrawn the plans over and over for the past twenty years. He said he'd never gotten around to building it, but now seemed as good a time as any.

My stomach knotted in a weird way—happy and sad all at once— to know he was building the damn thing for me. I still doubted that sharing a house was enough for us to feel like a family.

* * *

I dropped my backpack on the floor and slipped under the thin blanket covering my bed. Although I'd lived in the trailer for more than two months, every day when I came home was like visiting someone else's house. Frank offered me money to buy whatever I wanted to make the room feel homier, but I'd never had stuff to call my own and didn't know what I'd even buy.

Every few days, something new would show up—a lamp, a clock, some throw pillows. Frank was trying his hardest to get me to feel some permanence, but I saw the trailer and all this stuff as his alone.

I heard Frank in the trailer's galley kitchen rummaging for a skillet, but the gnawing in my gut had already told me it was dinnertime. If I couldn't taste food, it seemed unfair my body could alert me to hunger in such an obnoxious way.

"I'm going to start the stir-fry now, okay?" he called out.

This Asian food rut would have to stop. If I wanted to eat something other than rice and slimy lo mein noodles, I needed to speak up.

"Sure, be right out."

Frank had made me see a doctor about my inability to taste and smell. The specialist couldn't find a medical reason and suggested it was a psychosomatic by-product of the trauma I'd endured in the explosion. He said that once my "mental state" improved, I'd likely regain those senses.

Frank wasn't patient enough to wait so he'd begun bizarre experiments with foods that were bitter, sweet, sour, salty, and savory. My taste buds wouldn't cooperate, no matter how many different combinations he tried.

I grabbed plates and utensils while Frank expertly juggled

two serving bowls, a bottle of soy sauce, and a tube of wasabi. He pushed the screen door with his butt and we headed to the cedar picnic table. Protected by a large canvas tarp overhead, this outdoor dining room served as our largest living space since Frank used the Airstream's living room as his bedroom and library. I sometimes did my homework at the picnic table after school while Frank continued his work on the house. On nights I'd come home late from Mo's, Frank would often be sitting at the picnic table, nursing a beer or reading by lantern light.

"Arlie, I know we can beat this. We just haven't found the right ingredient." Rice dribbled down his chin from talking with his mouth so full.

"Nothing to beat," I said. "Buy whatever's on sale. Lamb testicles. Cow tongue. Won't make a difference to me."

"You really do take snark to a whole new level," he said.

"I don't like to mince words."

"Whatever," he said and got up from the table. "I can't eat this crap. I made it spicy thinking you might finally taste it. I'm going to have some cereal. Want some?"

I shook my head. "I'll just finish this." What did it matter anyway?

* * *

Frank didn't like cell phones in general, and never when we were eating. This meant I often forgot to check messages until much later in the evening. Mo had texted several times in the last hour, which wasn't all that unusual except for the news she had to share.

Not gonna believe this, she wrote. Nick punched Cody. Busted his lip.

Can you believe Nick hit a blind guy????

Hellllloooo? You there?

Text me!

This is about you!

Nick was Brittany's pathetic lapdog, but I thought he and Cody were friends. My gut told me she had to be involved. What I couldn't figure out was how a fight with Cody had anything to do with me.

Get over here, I texted back. With the way my stomach was somersaulting, I just prayed Frank's latest stir-fry wouldn't come up before I got some answers.

* * *

Mo laid the Oreos package between us on the bed and pulled back its resealable top. She wore plaid pajama bottoms and a sweatshirt. Her blond hair spiraled around chopsticks in a messy bun. Comfort obviously mattered more than fashion after 7 p.m. on a school night, and I wished I'd changed out of my jeans earlier.

"Have one." She stuffed a whole cookie into her mouth and chomped, sending crumbs onto my blanket.

"I don't like cookie texture. And stop getting crap on my bed."

She huffed her displeasure. "Eat them for the calories at least. We weigh the same and you tower above me."

Her stalling wasn't funny. I needed to know what had happened with Cody. "Why do you think the fight had anything to do with me?"

"Jessica said she saw Cody get all up in Nick's face after school. Supposedly he swung at Nick. *Pow*, right in the eye. Must have honed in on Nick's voice."

I sat up. "Cody took the first swing? Your text said Nick hit Cody."

"He did. He hit him *back*." Mo's smile revealed a perfect row of teeth dotted with chocolate cookie bits. She was enjoying this way too much.

"Why are you smiling? You look insane."

"Because he was sticking up for you. Jess told me that Nick called you some name and Cody snapped. No words. No warning. Just fist to face."

Why would Cody come to my defense? Especially if I wasn't even around to hear the insult. My cheeks tingled with heat and confusion.

"That's not all," Mo continued. "When Cody fell backward after being punched, Brittany went all Florence Nightingale on him, and he just pushed her away. Then she screamed that he was stupid to care about a reject like you."

Reject. Yep, that sounded like Brittany. I'd never done a thing to her, but she made her dislike more than apparent. At school and in choral practice, staring her down instead of looking away took everything out of me, but I wasn't about to let her intimidate me.

"Brittany can't stand that Cody is interested in you."

"Huh?"

"She'd normally go for a dumb jock, but once Cody expressed an interest in you...well, challenge accepted," Mo said.

"Challenge? What are you talking about?"

"For some reason she's made you a personal target. She probably thinks that hooking up with him would somehow hurt you," she said.

"Why would I care?"

"Because you like him."

I started to object, but it was pointless to lie to Mo. I'd liked him for a long while now.

"And why are we talking about Brittany?" Mo continued. "This is about you and Cody. Wow. A blind guy who can fight. How hot is that?"

"I'll be right back." My hand shook as I slid open the plastic accordion door to my room and headed for the trailer's kitchen sink. Tap water would do. My mouth had gone dry, and I had visions of choking if I didn't have something wet immediately. I filled the glass and downed it, then filled it a second time.

"Where's the fire?" Frank sat on the sofa, reading the newspaper. Mo used to be the only person in my life who could say the words "fire," "flame," and "burn" without immediately apologizing for saying something inappropriate, but Frank was getting better at it too.

Mo pushed past me and plopped down next to Frank. She held out the package of Oreos and his eyes lit up. Suddenly, they were best friends.

"A boy likes Arlie and she's having some kind of weird reaction. I think she might faint."

This time both Frank and Mo smiled with chocolaty teeth.

"Figures it'd take a blind guy to be interested in me," I said to myself.

They frowned in unison.

"Oh, I know you didn't just say that. Don't make me slap you," Mo warned.

"Yeah," Frank added. "What she said."

"Mo got the story secondhand. Cody doesn't like me. We barely know each other." The trailer suddenly seemed smaller than it ever had. My racing heart began to make me dizzy as well.

"Cody?" Frank stuffed a third cookie in his mouth.

"A super-hot guy who's in Arlie's English class and the choral society," Mo explained. "Oh, and like she said, he's blind."

"Well, invite him over!" Frank's enthusiasm only egged on Mo who continued to describe Cody in great detail.

"Mo, go home. Frank, mind your own business." I needed time to think and to fight the urge to throw up.

"Oh my God, I can't wait to see what happens tomorrow in your English class," Mo said.

"Go!" I pointed to the door.

"I won't sleep a wink tonight." Mo's voice trailed off after I shut the door behind her.

"This is going to be good." Frank tittered like a little girl, then stuffed another two Oreos in his mouth. "Tell me more about this guy."

Their ribbing set my confused emotions roiling. Anger was the first to bubble up. "Shut up for once, Frank. Just shut the hell up!"

"Hey, now. What gives?"

He took a tentative step toward me, but I raised my arms, indicating I wanted him to back off. "Never mind. I just need to go to bed."

Frank took hold of my elbow before I could leave. "Sit down. Please."

The trailer walls closed in further, making Frank's concern too big for the space.

"One minute we're all joking, and the next you're mad as hell. Talk."

"Maybe I don't find the jokes funny," I said.

"Mo and I are happy for you. That's all. What's the big deal? Don't you like this guy?"

"You don't get it."

"Then enlighten me."

I didn't know what to say. *Stop being so chummy with my best friend? Stop thinking I have a freakin' chance in hell with Cody? Stop pretending this is how I envisioned my life after Mom?*

"You're not my dad. I wish you'd stop acting like one."

Frank stared at me. *Through* me. He didn't seem angry or sad or anything. Just numb.

"That line is getting pretty fucking old." He got up and went into the kitchenette while I sat there dumbstruck.

My skin felt too tight, and I didn't think I could remember how to breathe on my own. I wanted to be in my room, but I'd have to squeeze past him to reach it. So I remained on the sofa and watched him wash and stow away dishes, wipe down the stove, rinse out the sink, straighten the salt and pepper shakers on the table. His methodical, slow-motion movements freaked me out more than if he'd just yell at me and get it over with.

"Say something, would ya?" I asked.

After a few seconds, he turned to me, the same non-look on his face. "What do you want me to say? Something non-parenty?"

"I shouldn't have—"

"You're right. You shouldn't have." He grabbed his coat off the hook by the front door and yanked it on. "I'm going out. Don't wait up."

When he opened the door, the cold rushed in and traveled up the length of my body. It stole every breath, every word I might utter to stop him from leaving.

"And do me a favor. Figure out who you're angry at." The screen door slammed behind him.

CHAPTER 10

It had been past midnight when Frank finally got back to the trailer. He opened and closed the door as quietly as he could, probably to avoid waking me, but I hadn't been able to doze even a little. Sleep eluded me most of the night. I was grateful to finally hear Frank's morning sounds—his raspy cough, the clank of the kettle on the burner, the radio tuned to NPR.

He didn't say a word when I stole into the bathroom for a shower or when I popped back into my room to dress. By the time I opened the bedroom door again, he was stirring something on the stove top.

"Sit." He pointed to the table but didn't look at me.

I did as instructed. He handed me a mug of hot tea first, then a bowl of oatmeal. God, that texture was going to kill me, but I vowed to eat every last spoonful in a pitiful attempt at an apology.

He sat down with a larger bowl for himself. He'd added raisins and brown sugar and heavy cream to his.

"What? I don't get the good stuff on mine?" The joke came

out flat and I regretted that those were my first words after what had gone down last night.

"Didn't realize you could taste again." He gulped heaping spoonful after spoonful, rarely looking up from the newspaper. He wasn't going to talk so I stayed quiet too.

I had to follow every bite of oatmeal with a sip of hot tea to make it go down. When I scraped the bottom of the bowl, I almost raised my arms in victory—something Frank and I had started doing as a joke whenever I finished an onerous meal. Instead, I grabbed both our bowls and put them in the sink.

"I'll do the dishes," he said.

"It's no big deal." I turned on the hot-water faucet and grabbed the sponge.

"You can wash dishes tonight after dinner."

Once the dishes were done, I wiped my wet hands on my jeans, then picked up my backpack. Mo had pulled up and was already honking her horn, but I stood frozen. Why couldn't I just say I was sorry? Three simple words. Not so friggin' hard.

"It's all right," he said. "Go to school."

I nodded.

"And you look nice," he added. "Good luck today with Cody."

* * *

I walked through the halls of Durango High, my head down to avoid the intense stares that greeted me. The not-so-subtle glances had less to do with my scar and more to do with Cody and Nick's fight. It's not every day that the captain of the lacrosse team hits a blind guy, and the news spread more quickly than if it'd been blared over the PA system.

I made it to English in record time so I could get seated

before anyone else arrived. The last thing I wanted to do today was make an entrance.

"Why, hello, Arlie." Mrs. Sires didn't turn from the chalkboard to greet me, giving credence to the notion that teachers really did have eyes in the back of their heads. "You're early."

I sat down in my usual seat on the far side of the room next to the bank of windows. From that angle, my scar wasn't visible to the students who sat to my right.

"Just wanted to review my notes," I said.

"Uh-huh."

I sensed she didn't quite believe me, but was thankful she didn't ask the real reason I chose her classroom to hide out.

I had my nose in my Shakespeare anthology when I heard a familiar tap, tap, tap. *Cody*. Or rather, Cody's cane. I tried deep breathing to calm myself, but then decided my exhales were too loud.

"Ah, Mr. Jenkins. Another student eager for English class to start. Miss Betts beat you by two minutes."

Cody couldn't see the smile that spread over Mrs. Sires's face, but I bet he could feel the blush rising in his.

"Oh… Arlie. Hey."

"Hey," I said.

He moved toward me, or rather the sound of my voice, and sat in a desk adjacent to mine even though he'd always sat in the back of the room before. My throat tightened, the same sensation I'd had when I almost choked on Mo's retelling of Cody's fight. We each coughed nervously before he finally spoke.

"You've been doing great at choral practice. Are you glad you joined?"

"I guess." *Damn it, Arlie, what are you doing?* I pulled my hair over my cheek, wishing I could hide altogether.

"Well, this town turns out big time for the community concert. It's pretty cool. We'll start working on those numbers soon."

He fidgeted with his Braille notetaker, an assistive device that combined a computer, text recognition software, email, MP3 player, and more in a sleek rectangle the size of an iPad but thicker. Some time ago, he'd demonstrated its features to the choral group—and even recorded our practice for playback.

"I guess that cost as much as a new car," I said.

"Well, my parents won't be buying me a car for graduation. And since this thing doesn't run on gas, I'm saving them money in the long run."

I winced at my own insensitivity. "I'm…I didn't mean…I just think it's cool that technology allows you to go to a regular school," I said.

"Yeah, me too. I hate feeling different."

Short of a face transplant, there was no device, no technology, no amount of money that could help me assimilate into this student body. I wanted to tell him I understood. Yet my brain and mouth refused to work together to express something we had in common.

His gaze fell just below my shoulder. If he were sighted, I'd punch him for staring at my boob. Instead, I stared at his swollen lip. My hand lifted as if it intended to touch the bruised area. I pulled it back quickly and pinned it beneath my thigh.

"Does it hurt? Your lip, I mean."

"Not much. I hear Nick's in worse shape." Cody ran his tongue over the injury before a smile tugged at his lips.

"Well, you sure gave the school something to talk about today," I blurted out.

"At least until the next blind guy does something stupid, right?"

My heart sank. *Stupid?* Did he regret confronting Nick? Maybe punching him was a reaction against all bullies and not in my defense at all. Maybe I was the stupid one to believe that one simple act meant he felt something for me.

"Class is going to start in a bit. You might want to get to your regular seat." I turned back to my book, not seeing a damn word on the page.

Out of the corner of my eye, I could see he was staring at my lips this time, his gaze as direct as someone who could see. "Yeah, sure. See you at practice."

I longed to run, to hide, to close the door to my seven-by-seven-foot room back at Frank's trailer. I felt more on display than I'd ever felt in my life. I was just barely aware of Mrs. Sires's voice and the bustling of students preparing for class to start. I had the strange sensation that Cody was staring at me from the back of the room. He'd never know if I turned around and looked at him. Yet I sat frozen. I didn't hear another word Mrs. Sires said. I opened my notebook and started on the next day's homework assignment.

* * *

"Lipstick and mascara. Nice." Mo lay next to me on the cool grass near the baseball fields at lunch. "Did Cody notice?"

Mo might have been joking, but I was the dummy who'd put on makeup for a blind guy, a guy I had totally shut down and told to go sit in the back of the room instead of beside me.

"Yeah, well, it didn't go so well with Cody in English."

"What'd you do now?"

"Why do you say it like that?"

Mo raised her eyebrows. It was no secret that I could say the wrong thing when I felt cornered. Case in point: my flub-up with Frank last night.

"He made a crack that getting in the fight was stupid," I said.

"The fight may have been stupid, but that doesn't mean sticking up for you was stupid, or that he regretted it." Mo held my hand and we squinted up at the cloudless blue sky. Her long hair pooled about her head like a golden halo. She tethered me to this world, ensuring I didn't float away or disappear. I loved that she was never embarrassed to touch me.

"I wish you'd never told me," I said.

"Oh, like you wouldn't have heard about it at school. Don't make this about me," Mo said. "You're so afraid of people caring about you that you try to scare them off first. You're just damn lucky I didn't fall for that bullshit."

My lip trembled. "I don't know what to do."

"When you get to choral practice today, tell Cody 'thank you,'" Mo said. "Don't try to say anything else. Just let him know his busted lip was worth it."

I nodded. "Yeah. I can do that."

At least I had two more hours to find the courage it'd take.

"And what about Frank?" I asked. "Any advice there?"

"Same thing," Mo said. "Keep it simple. Say you're sorry and stop. Anything more than that and you might screw up."

* * *

Choral practice drew a motley crew of students who weren't on the swim, tennis, track, or other sports teams that met each afternoon. Some were part of established cliques during the school day. At practice, though, all hierarchies disappeared.

Each of us mattered equally and no one was singled out for his or her differences. Not even me.

I'd started looking forward to practice. We all laughed when harmonies didn't work out and high-fived when they did. Each time we met, I got a little bolder about expressing my opinions and not worrying when someone disagreed with me.

After last bell, many students gravitated to the convenience store across the street from the school for snacks or a Coke before practice, and sometimes I joined them. Most days, though, I preferred to get to the practice room as quickly as possible. It was the most peaceful part of the whole school day.

Today, I had a good reason to arrive early. Mo thought it'd be easy for me to thank Cody for sticking up for me, but I was freaking out and wanted time to collect my thoughts. No matter how much I practiced what to say, it all sounded stupid or inadequate. All I could think about was how I'd blown the conversation with him earlier in English.

As I neared the room, I was disappointed to hear someone had already arrived first. A female was singing a solo version of "The Blue Bird." Our choral group had practiced it several times for the upcoming community concert. Stopping outside the door to listen more closely, I recognized that voice. It was my own. I pushed open the door with my shoulder, accidentally dropping my backpack.

The practice room was empty except for Cody.

"Who's there?" He reached over and clicked a key on his laptop. The music stopped abruptly. He stood and stared in my direction. "I said, who's there?"

He'd recorded my voice. I grabbed my pack and ran from the room and down the hall.

My lungs burned as I sprinted past the other students who were heading to the practice room. Rounding the corner, I slammed into Brittany, knocking an iced latte down her shirt.

"You stupid bitch." She swiped at her soaked tee.

Other students had stopped and were now staring.

"Sorry. Didn't see you," I said, moving past her.

She grabbed my elbow and whipped me around. I jerked my arm back.

"Don't touch me," I hissed.

"Don't you see you're not wanted here? You should have died in that fire. That way we wouldn't have to look at you."

One of the students who'd stopped to gawk told Brittany to knock it off, and then two more chimed in. I didn't hear their exact words as I escaped through the door.

CHAPTER 11
SEVEN YEARS AGO—BURNED

Rosa said my stepfather, Lloyd, and his friends were bad men and I should be careful, especially when Mom wasn't around. That's why Rosa let me stay in her apartment most afternoons while she watched her stories on television.

Today she spoke to herself in Spanish and made the sign of the cross. Her face told me she was mad, but I could tell she wasn't mad at me. She quit talking for a second and leaned in to smell my hair. Then she started up again, pulling me down the hall and into the bathroom. She ran the water in the tub and motioned for me to put my head under the faucet.

I smelled fruit and flowers as she rubbed my hair into a thick pile of bubbles. I laughed, and then she laughed too. She never called me Arlie, but instead *cariña* and *mija*—her special names for me.

I wished Rosa was my mother or grandmother, but I never said so out loud. I just pretended Mom and Lloyd were moving away and asked Rosa if she would take care of me. Then they kissed me good-bye and never came back.

Rosa and I sat on the edge of the tub as she pulled at my tangles. She said I had beautiful black hair, like Snow White.

"Your hair...It smelled of death, *mija*," she said. "Now, you smell good, yes?"

I nodded even though I didn't know what death smelled like. My wet hair soaked the top of my T-shirt, but that felt good on such a hot day. Rosa didn't have air-conditioning so she kept her front and back doors open to let a breeze pass.

"It's so hot in our place," I said. "Lloyd covered all the windows with newspaper. I can't even see outside."

Rosa talked to herself in Spanish again, but the words seemed heavy and sad, not fast and angry.

"Your mama must take you away, *cariña*," she said softly. "A mother should not put her child in danger."

Rosa's words made my tummy hurt. "But I would miss you," I said.

"*Sí*, I would miss you too. But better to be safe."

Rosa stooped to wipe up the water that had dripped on the bathroom floor. I took the towel from her so I could help.

"Arlie, where in the hell are you?"

Oh no. Lloyd. Goose bumps covered my arms and I almost couldn't breathe. I wanted to hide in the tub and pull the plastic curtain around me. Rosa put a finger to her lips, then left me in the bathroom alone.

She shouted at Lloyd in the living room. "I will call police if you hurt this little girl. I know what you're doing in that apartment. I can smell it. Everyone in the apartments can smell it."

"Old woman, you better mind your own business. Or I'll make you sorry you didn't."

"I not afraid, *señor*."

A loud crack reached all the way to my ears. Rosa cried out. I ran from the bathroom and straight at Lloyd, pushing him. Rosa slumped on the floor crying, but I wasn't afraid of him.

"Stop it! Don't you hurt her!"

I screamed when he grabbed my wet hair. It was slick and almost impossible to grip, so he wrapped it around his hand like a rope and pulled me across the courtyard. I was crying hard by the time we reached our apartment. Once we were in, we both started coughing. The smell burned my nose and throat. My tongue tasted funny and I gagged.

Lloyd turned me loose and ran into the kitchen.

It really wasn't our kitchen anymore. Now it was like some science lab that I wasn't allowed to go in. Two of his friends worked there almost every day, their faces hidden by little blue masks.

He was angrier with those men than he'd been with Rosa. He used bad words and threw things: *crash*, *clang*, *bang*. They shouted back in Spanish. I should have gone back to Rosa's, but instead I took a few steps toward the kitchen door, covering my mouth and nose with the front of my wet shirt.

"Where's Mom?" I asked, but no one answered.

"Where's Mom?" I asked louder. "I want Mom."

Lloyd flew from the kitchen and shoved me to the living-room floor. "Shut the hell up!"

Before I could stand on my own, Rosa grabbed me from behind and held me like a baby against her chest. She pinned both my arms beneath hers and turned for the front door. I cried that I wanted my mom. I cried that my throat hurt. I cried when a blast of white-hot fire pushed us out the door.

CHAPTER 12

At the start of April, I began seeing Jane only once a week. Supposedly, I'd made it past some imaginary point of crisis that Mom's death could've triggered. Still, social services wanted to be sure I had all the support someone in my "situation" might need.

Mo couldn't meet me after today's session because of a dentist appointment. I'd grown so accustomed to our routine of going to the bookstore on Friday afternoons that I headed there by myself.

Durango was a small enough town that even if people didn't know my name, they knew of the "burned face" girl. Just as we all knew of the Rasta chick who carried a half-dozen hula hoops around town, sometimes selling them, sometimes just putting on a show. Just as we all knew of the lanky, homeless guy with the humongous backpack who rode the city's red trolley from one end of town to the other all day long. Would I ever get used to being so visible?

One place I didn't mind the attention was the Book Nook.

In one of my sessions, Jane had asked me to name something real in my world. I wish I would've remembered to mention James, one of the booksellers.

He was Cody's older brother, although I'd only learned that by accident one afternoon recently when Cody was doing his homework at the counter.

I'd known James a while, thanks to Mo's and my frequent visits, and he'd become an important part of my life. I counted on him to be at the Book Nook weekdays from 4 to 9 p.m. I counted on him to recognize me and greet me like a long-lost friend. He'd never once asked about my scar.

When he looked at my face, he looked directly into my eyes, making me feel like I was the only customer in the store and the only girl in the world. Although twenty-three, James looked more my age. A tall man-child with a sparse blond beard that never got its act together. I could see why Mo would crush on this guy.

I didn't admit to her that it was nice to see Cody at the store some days. I felt less self-conscious there than I did talking to him at school.

When I entered the store today, James was working on a window display. His brother wasn't around.

"Arlie! What's happening, girl? Where's your sidekick?" He had been juggling an armful of books but set them down when I walked in.

"Mo's at the dentist." I pointed at my teeth as if the words had been ambiguous, then I cringed at my stupid move. Hopefully, my embarrassment didn't show too much.

"My bro's not here," he said. "He went across the street to Magpie's for a smoothie. I could text him that you're here."

My face burned hot. "I'm not here to see Cody."

"Yeah, sure. Whatever you say."

To get him off the subject, I asked him about his window display on organic gardening and water conservation. While we chatted, a late-model Mustang slowed near the store, catching our attention. It was robin's-egg blue with dark, tinted windows. After a few seconds, the car peeled out. Customers turned at the sound of the screeching tires.

"What an ass," James muttered.

"You know that guy?"

"Nah, but he came by the store yesterday. Just looked through the window but wouldn't come in."

"How do you know it's the same guy?"

"He parked that sweet ride out front. I asked him if he was looking for someone. Then I tried to strike up a conversation about his car, but he just ignored me. Like I said, he's an asshole."

James turned his attention back to the display so I left him to his work. I made my way to the back wall and sat cross-legged on the floor, skimming through books whose covers caught my eye. Frank had mentioned he loved sci-fi so I decided to check out a few series he'd recommended.

Lost in thought, I barely noticed the pink Uggs standing in front of me.

"Cody only talks to you because he can't see how hideous you look."

There was no mistaking that voice. *Brittany*. Still on her personal crusade to make me feel like I didn't belong, although I don't know why she wasted the effort. I was more and more comfortable at school, so it was easier to ignore her and her friends now that I was making my own.

"Is there something you want?" I scanned the back cover of a book in hopes she'd leave me alone.

"You're pathetic to think you have a chance with him."

Mo had been right. Brittany was in some imaginary competition with me for Cody's attention. I ignored her and kept my head low.

"I bet you're a drug addict like your dead mom. Why don't you take her lead and put us out of our misery?" She toed my leg.

I exploded from the floor, knocking her against a bookshelf. In a flash, she scrambled to her knees and slapped viciously at my face. I covered my head to block her blows. When I managed to shove my knee into her stomach, she grunted and fell to her side, giving me a clear shot at her ribs.

James and another bookseller reached us within seconds and pulled me off.

"What's going on here?" James asked, holding my arm.

"*Bitch!*" Brittany struggled against the other bookseller, who wasn't about to let go. "I'm going to call the police."

"You started it!" I shouted.

"Arlie, why don't you leave. Now, please." James pointed toward the door of the shop.

I bolted, dodging a handful of startled customers and the looming shelves in my path. My lungs burned as I took off down Main, first one block and then another. I slowed to catch my breath, looking behind me to make sure Brittany hadn't followed…and hoping that James had. That's when I noticed the blue Mustang again.

It crept along so slowly that cars had to go around it. I quickened my steps and the car seemed to match my stride. I turned to get a look at the driver, but the windows were too dark. I could only make out that the driver was male and wore a ball cap.

When he revved the engine, I broke into a run and cut across the street, ducking into the alley that ran parallel to Main Avenue. The Mustang pulled a U-turn to follow me. Even though my legs felt like jelly, I kept running until I saw the entrance to the downtown parking garage. I climbed the stairs two at a time and hid near the railing.

From that vantage point, I saw the Mustang enter the alley, but it kept going, eventually turning back onto Main and heading south. The back license plate was partially caked in mud, but I could tell it was from New Mexico. I waited until the car was out of sight before leaving the garage.

Deep breathing couldn't stave off the panic attack coming on. *Get a grip, Arlie. It was just some jerk.* I turned north onto Main and began running again. I had to get home. *It can't be Lloyd. There's no reason for him to be in Durango. Don't be stupid.*

I slowed to a walk. It was hard to run and breathe and cry at the same time. I neared Buckley Park, jogging the last few steps to the trolley shelter.

Sitting alone on the bench, just a few feet in front of me, was Cody. He held two plastic cups filled with something pink like smoothies or maybe shakes.

Not this. I willed myself to back up slowly and run the other way. Yet my legs wouldn't cooperate. All energy had been expended on my escape from Brittany and then the Mustang.

"Arlie? Is that you?" He scanned my general direction.

"How'd you know it was me?" I wiped my tears and straightened my shirt.

"I recognized your perfume," he said.

"I don't wear any."

"Well, you don't have to wear perfume to have a certain

smell," he said.

"I smell?"

"That's not what…"

"Doesn't matter." I sat next to him on the bench and waited for the next trolley that would take me up North Main and away from the discomfort I felt.

"You okay?" Cody leaned in a bit too close so I slid a few inches down the bench.

"Why do you ask?"

"I thought I heard you crying when you ran up. And you're breathing really weird."

His super-acute senses unnerved me. I could lie and say no, but I was sure he'd sense that as well.

"No big deal," I said. "I was at the bookstore and Brittany decided to pick a fight. I guess the school day wasn't long enough for all the harassment she had in her."

"What happened? You all right?"

I wasn't all right. Adrenaline still sickened my stomach and weakened my legs. I was embarrassed by the fight with Brittany, but more upset that James had kicked me out of the bookstore. I didn't want to talk to Cody about it—and definitely not at a trolley stop near a busy park.

"Seriously. Tell me," he said.

"Nothing important. You waiting for someone?"

"Huh?"

"The smoothies. You have two of them. Unless you're just extremely thirsty."

"Oh, yeah. James texted that you were in the store so I thought I'd buy an extra and wait here for you. I hear you drink one almost every day for lunch. I figured you must really love them."

He handed one over and I took it, even though the gesture confused me. Who told him what I had for lunch?

"How did you know I'd be taking the trolley?"

Cody's cheeks colored. He took a long draw on the smoothie and wiped his mouth with the back of his hand.

"James also texted you weren't with Mo today. So she wouldn't be giving you a ride."

My world wobbled. Cody recording me singing, the fight with Brittany, and now this weird, planned encounter—I couldn't take much more and my shaking hands proved it.

"I hope I didn't creep you out. I wasn't trying to be stalky. I just wanted to talk to you somewhere besides school."

"I'm just a little overwhelmed," I said. "Give me a second."

We sat in silence for a minute or two, which was awkward, but a better kind of awkward than figuring out what to say to Cody.

"I'm sorry if I've upset you," he said weakly.

"No, no, it's okay," I stuttered. "I'm still shaken up by Brittany. James had to pull her off me. He probably hates me."

"Don't worry about my brother. He thinks you're cool. I just can't believe Brit got physical." His knuckles turned white from clenching the edge of the bench.

I looked up the street, half expecting to see Brittany coming after me to finish what she'd started.

"You hurt?" he asked.

"Just embarrassed I let her get in so many punches. Although I did get in one good blow to the gut and two to the ribs."

"When I get to school tomorrow, I'll talk to her. She can't go around bullying you."

"No, please don't!" I begged. "That'll make it worse."

Cody rubbed his still-bruised lip from the row with Nick.

"Fighting's not what it's cracked up to be, is it? Maybe we both need karate lessons."

His joking helped my breathing return to an acceptable rate. At least one that would allow me to speak if I could find the words.

"Your brother is something else," I finally said.

"Why do you say that?"

"Well, he's making all kinds of assumptions. Like you wanted to see me today."

"He didn't assume anything. I told him I wanted to see you."

My breathing accelerated again and the adrenaline-fueled nausea returned.

"I mean…you seemed kind of angry the other day in English and then you skipped choral practice. I don't have your phone number and I don't know where you live, so this was my best chance to talk to you alone," he added. "Hey, are you okay? You're breathing funny."

I reddened to think he could read my emotions by listening to me breathe. I held my breath but felt even closer to passing out. I cringed at the audible whoosh of air from my lungs.

"If you don't say something, I'm going to call nine-one-one," he joked.

I exhaled deeply a couple of times and managed to calm myself enough to speak coherently. "Nothing's wrong. I'm just having the strangest day of my life, and I have no idea how to act or what to say."

I slumped with exhaustion.

"Then let's not talk for now," he said. "Let's sit in the park and finish our smoothies."

He found my hand on the first try and led me around the

trolley shelter and onto the cool, green grass. We headed to the back edge of Buckley Park, which had the most sun. The angle of the grassy slope made it perfect for lying back and surveying what everyone else in the park was doing.

I placed my hand so close to his that I swore I could feel a charge between us. What would it take for him to reach over as confidently as he had in the trolley shelter? I kicked off my sneakers and pulled off my socks. The cool grass felt great between my toes.

"Do you like the smoothie?" Cody asked. "I didn't know what flavor you'd like so I went for boring strawberry banana. I had them add ice cream so it wouldn't be too healthy."

My gut clenched. My first instinct was to lie, but Cody deserved better.

"Yeah, about that…" I began.

"Oh. You didn't like it."

I noticed that his usually smiling lips had turned down.

"No, it's not that at all. It's hard to explain. Not a lot of people know…"

Cody sat up on his elbows. "Know what?"

I let out one long, low breath. "I can't taste or smell anything."

"What do you mean by that?"

"I have a medical condition of sorts. It's like my taste buds don't work. I can feel texture and sense temperature, but flavors? Nada."

"Jeez, that's horrible. I can't imagine how hard that must be." Cody cocked his head slightly more toward me as if he wanted to listen more intently.

"It can't be as hard as being blind," I said.

Cody went silent and I wondered if I'd offended him in

some way. I just didn't want him to feel sorry for me. I didn't do pity well.

"I don't know. I get by okay, but not being able to taste a cheeseburger and fries? Or pizza? Hell on earth." His playful smile told me I hadn't put my foot in my mouth after all.

"Let's just say we both got bum deals and leave it at that," I said. "At least my condition is the best diet aid ever."

Cody laughed heartily. "Yeah, James said you were slim."

"He did, did he?" I liked that James noticed and thought to comment on it to his brother.

Immediately, Cody turned purple. Not pink. Not red. Purple. At least I saw the full range of embarrassment the guy could feel.

"I…I…Well, it came up when we were talking about some-thing else. I mean, it wasn't like we were just talking about how you looked."

"Uh-huh." His discomfort amused me. At least I wasn't the only one mortified by our increasingly personal discussion.

"My face is red, isn't it?" He ran his fingers through the hair that fell across his face.

"Way beyond that."

We both laughed and returned to our lounging positions.

"I like coming to this park," he said. "So much going on all the time. Sometimes I just hang out here while James finishes a shift."

I listened to the sounds that Cody must be hearing: the guys playing Frisbee and laughing, the air brakes of the bus, a small child pitching a fit.

"I kind of picture you with superhuman hearing skills," I said.

"Nothing as cool as that. Over the years, I've just gotten good at paying attention. That's how I knew you'd been running when you got to the bus stop."

His beautiful full lips formed the widest grin I'd ever seen. I couldn't help but smile too.

"And it's green apples," he said.

"Huh?"

"You smell like green apples."

"I don't know what to say. Thanks?"

We fell into an easy silence as Cody picked at blades of grass, his hand still dangerously close to mine.

"I wish I could see your face," he said. "James said you're beautiful."

The lump in my throat grew bigger. I wanted to disappear.

He leaned in, just enough so my breath caught, and said, "I told him I already knew that."

I allowed the fight with Brittany and the weird footrace with the Mustang to slip from my mind. In that instant, only Cody mattered. I didn't want to be anywhere else.

CHAPTER 13

When I got back to the trailer, Mo waited for me on the steps. She tapped her watch to indicate she'd been waiting a while.

"What happened with Brittany? And why you didn't call or text right away?" she asked.

"Read something on Facebook, did ya?"

"No. James called me to check on you. He was worried after you ran from the store."

James. I'd left him there in the sci-fi aisle to clean up my mess with Brittany. He'd told me to leave, but I should've gone back to apologize.

"Why does James have your number?" I asked.

"Sometimes I have him special order a book for me. The store has my number on file." She smiled slyly. "Why else would I give him my cell number?"

"You're a flirt," I said. "Anyway, I'm surprised Cody didn't tell him I was okay."

"What's Cody got to do with this?"

"I ran into him at the trolley stop. It's a long story. And I didn't text earlier because you were at the dentist."

"I got out two hours ago." She gave me a look that told me I needed to give her every detail—and fast.

"I couldn't call. I've been with Cody this whole time."

Mo froze. Then she mouthed "Oh my God."

"I'm freaked out too." I reached over to pinch her lips closed. "My head is going to explode if I think about this anymore."

"Details. Now."

"Let's go to my room. It's chilly out here."

Mo followed me into the trailer. We nodded quick hellos to Frank, who was on his computer at the kitchen table. He seemed to want to ask something, but we rushed past. Other than my quick apology earlier in the week, we hadn't talked much, but Mo would have to come first.

Once in my room, we closed the door and lay side by side on the bed.

"So tell me already!" Mo's voice filled the trailer.

"Keep it down. I don't want Frank knowing my business. Okay?"

"Fine," she whispered. "Spill it."

As I expected, the fight with Brittany interested Mo less than Cody's scheming to meet me at the trolley stop.

"He apologized for being stalky," I said.

"It's not stalky. It's romantic," Mo said. "And James helped him? What a great guy."

"Cody or James?"

"Both, but let's concentrate on Cody for now. First, he punches a guy who insults you. Then he records and listens to you singing. Now this? He's in deep."

I could feel my face flushing, but I still found it hard to believe, even with evidence right in front of me. I wrapped my arms around my sick stomach and begged it to stop flopping for just an instant. Another part of me wanted this new and unbelievable feeling to last.

"I don't get it, Mo."

"What's to get? You're smart. You're beautiful. You both sing in choral. Maybe he's tired of all the girls who gush over him but in the end treat him like an imbecile."

"Yeah, he mentioned that people are always trying to help him navigate the halls or else they talk extremely loudly like he's deaf or stupid."

I thought about our conversation. He got it. He knew what it was like when people felt awkward around us and said stupid things—like somehow we were to blame for making them feel uncomfortable. How could we feel normal when we spent so much energy trying to make others feel okay?

But I *had* felt normal with Cody today. Once I got over my excruciating nerves, that is. And although I was comfortable around Mo, she couldn't help but try to protect me from anyone and anything that could hurt me. She saw the scar. She saw all my scars because I let her. I didn't know if I could reveal everything about myself to Cody. I still hadn't figured out how much I could share with Frank or Jane, for that matter.

"So he held your hand?" Mo lay down beside me and whispered directly in my ear. "Did he stroke it like this?"

I jerked away. "Stop joking. Yes, he held my hand, but only at the beginning. Then we just sat in the grass, close but not touching."

"You could've grabbed his hand." Mo turned over onto her stomach and rested her chin on her arms. "Don't expect a guy to always make the first move."

I had no clue how to make a move. Any move. I'd missed out on the middle-school and junior-high crushes other girls experienced. I'd spent those years recovering from the accident and then taking care of Mom. Only the wrong kind of boys had ever paid me any attention. And some of Mom's adult friends.

"So, you think I should kiss him first?" Saying that out loud caused my stomach to catapult through my throat.

"Definitely. What's your plan?"

I had no plan. I didn't think I could even sleep, much less plot my next interaction with Cody.

"I thought you were going to help me with geometry." I tugged at her backpack until she let go of it. I pulled out a textbook and spiral.

"How can you study at a time like this?"

"Um…because there's a test later this week?" I loved teasing Mo. Her faked annoyance made me laugh.

She snatched the book in my hand and stuffed it into her pack. "You make all As. You don't need me to tutor you anymore."

"Not all As. I have a B in geometry. Hence, the need to study."

"I'm not playing teacher anymore," she said. "Those days are done."

Starting the day after I'd met Mo, and every school day after that, she'd shown up with textbooks in hand, ready to teach me everything she'd learned. She even graded my homework assignments and made me take exams. Maybe those days had run their course, but the thought made me sad.

"I could tutor you in other ways." She puckered her lips.

"You look like a fish," I said.

"A fish who's kissed a lot of boys."

I didn't doubt her. Mo's mom already allowed her to go on dates.

"Tell me about your first kiss," I said.

"It was stupid. Fourth grade. Joe Parrish and I both had hall passes to go to the restroom. He sort of ambushed me."

"Not swoon-worthy, huh?"

"No, just a lot of spit. And he smelled like Doritos. You'll get to kiss the most luscious full lips I've ever seen on anyone, except maybe Sam from *Glee*. I'm almost jealous of what that will feel like." She buried her face in the bed and squealed like a girl with far less kissing experience than Mo actually had.

Did I really want this goofball coaching me through my first kiss? Well, my first real kiss. When I was only seven, one of Lloyd's friends had caught me off guard one night as I was sneaking a Coke from the fridge. He'd smelled of chewing tobacco and beer, not Doritos. When he forced himself onto my mouth, his teeth had clicked against mine and cut my upper lip. At the time, I thought it was the worst thing I'd ever have to endure.

"What's wrong? You got all quiet."

"It's nothing. Maybe I'm just a little freaked out," I said.

"Come on. You had to know someone was going to fall for you one day."

I'd seen the train wrecks Mom dated. Or rather, slept with. I never felt I could trust a guy's reasons for hanging out with me. She'd warned me over and over that they'd only end up hurting me.

"If you dare say you're not good enough for Cody, I will seriously smack you." When Mo leaned in for a hug, I couldn't hold back my tears. Crying for the second time that day.

* * *

After she left, I wanted to be alone, completely deprived of all stimuli so I could recover from the mind-blowing day I'd had.

My brain would surely malfunction if I had to interact with another human being. That, of course, meant Frank wanted to talk.

"Arlie? I'd like to come in." He shuffled his feet on the linoleum outside the door to my room.

"I'm really tired. Can it wait until morning?"

"No, it can't. I'm not trying to invade your space, but I'd like you to respect my request."

Oh brother.

I pulled back the door and made a sweeping motion with my arm. "Welcome to my abode."

The full-size mattress and its plywood platform took up most of the room. A one-foot-wide pathway wound around it, just enough to be able to scoot through to reach the closet. Frank stood awkwardly in the doorway like he couldn't decide where to sit.

"How 'bout the couch," I suggested. "We'll have more room."

I tried to look relaxed. But more than anything, I wanted to get on my bike and ride as far away from this conversation as I could.

"What do you want to talk about?" I asked.

"You get home from your therapy appointment two hours later than usual, then Mo shows up and you guys hole up in your room," he said. "I was worried something came up for you."

"I'm fine."

Frank picked at his fingernails, chipped and dirty from construction work. "I just want to know how you're doing. You made it clear you don't want me acting like a father, but you seem to be holding back more and more."

My uncle had uprooted his life and moved here to be my guardian. I had no idea who and what he'd left behind for me. He asked questions about my life but told me very little about his.

"I'm sorry," I said. "Not used to anyone checking up on me."
Stupid gut clenched some more.

"What about your mom?"

"What about her?" *Please stop, Frank. Not this, not now.*

"Didn't you guys talk? I mean, you haven't said much about what happened before her death."

What would I have to share to get Frank to back off? Every so often, he'd start these conversations…little investigations into what life was like with a drug addict. I was surprised he hadn't asked me if I'd ever used or was tempted to use.

"Mom wasn't really capable of that type of relationship. She had problems."

"That's obvious," he said. "But did she even act like a mother?"

"It was hard for her."

"Hard for her? What about the little girl she let get burned in a meth-lab explosion? I mean, what the hell? Who does that?"

I choked back my gasp. I couldn't even enjoy one of the happiest days of my life without talk of Mom ruining it.

"Well, shit. I've done it again," he said, quieter now. "I'm just so…I don't know…Oh hell."

When he stopped talking, I thought about taking his hand but changed my mind.

"It's okay. Nothing's black and white. She wasn't all bad, and she wasn't all good," I said. "I just don't see why I have to talk about it all the time. Isn't it enough that I see a shrink?"

"I want you to be okay."

"Do you think I'm not okay now?" I pulled back, more curious than defensive.

"Who would be okay with all that you've gone through? The accident alone was bad enough, but Sarah killing herself?"

I'd grown tired of everyone insisting Mom killed herself, but I resisted challenging them. They'd just say my hurt was keeping me from seeing the truth. They didn't realize it was actually scarier to think someone else might have hurt her.

"Why isn't anyone willing to admit it's possible she didn't kill herself?" I braced for the response I knew was coming by the look on Frank's face.

"The coroner declared it a suicide. For chrissakes, she had enough meth in her to kill a horse. It wasn't an accidental OD."

"I'm not saying she didn't OD." I'd pulled a thread that was now unraveling the safe, new world I'd just begun to build for myself.

"Then what are you saying?"

"Maybe someone—"

"Maybe someone what?"

"Someone could have killed her," I whispered.

"Murder? Really? Why do you keep protecting her? Maybe it's time you got angry."

Frank's wet eyes shone with pity or sadness or something close to it. I didn't need his pity, and I didn't want his advice.

"I *am* angry!" I shouted. "But it's not like I can fight with a corpse."

"Arlie, I'm sorry."

"Stop being so sorry for everything," I said. "I get it. She was worthless. She was selfish, but suicide doesn't make sense."

"Why not face the truth?" Frank asked.

"If you'd seen the room—"

"The motel room? What about it?"

"Mom was neat with her drugs. I mean, she kept things in order."

I told Frank about the day I'd found Mom dead and the

contradictions that still haunted me: her glass pipe near a half-filled syringe, the mind-blowing amount of meth left behind. It wasn't like her. Why shoot up if she'd just smoked? Or vice versa?

"Because she was an addict." Frank's expression was so hard that it hurt to look at him.

Frank, the police, Dora—all of them were so sure about the cause of death. They made me feel like a crazy person for thinking differently. I was feeling even crazier for thinking my stepfather could have been involved. Lloyd used to only occupy my nightmares. Now I was wasting energy trying to convince myself he hadn't tracked me down, that he wasn't the driver of that Mustang.

I decided against sharing these new fears with Frank. His anger at Mom was all-consuming.

"You've been angry at Mom for a while, haven't you?" I asked.

Frank chewed on my question and a ragged thumbnail at the same time. Then he looked me squarely in the eyes. "Yeah, I'm angry. For what she did to you. For what she did to me. For dying."

"You mean because you got stuck having to take care of me."

"That's not what I meant," he said. "I meant she checked out on me twenty years ago when I needed her most. After Mom and Dad died."

"I don't want to be this angry forever," I said. "And I don't want to hate her anymore."

"I don't want to hate her either."

"Maybe it doesn't always have to feel like this," I said. "Maybe we can help each other."

"Of course we'll help each other," he said. "Now can I give you a hug?" Frank showed respect for my boundaries in the weirdest ways. One was always to ask before touching me.

"Sounds good." I accepted the uncharacteristically gentle embrace of his massive arms. But I couldn't yet accept that Mom had made a conscious decision to leave me.

* * *

Back in my room, I peeled off my jeans and crawled under the bedcover. No matter the room temperature, I always pulled the sheet or spread over my head. The habit had taken hold during the times when Mom and I shared a motel room. She stayed up late with the lights and TV on. Only by covering my head would it be dark enough for me to fall asleep.

"Your brother is cool," I said softly, as if Mom was just on the other side of the covers. "But you should've introduced me to him while you were still alive."

CHAPTER 14
TWO YEARS AGO—A SURROGATE MOM

The water in Mo's parents' tub was just about as hot as I could stand it, and I usually liked it scalding. I placed my hand over the jet that circulated the foamy water.

Mo sat beside the tub reading and ignoring me, so I flicked water onto her with my toes.

"Don't. You'll get my book wet."

When I splashed her again, she slapped the water, spraying my face.

"Hey! You're getting soap in my eyes," I said.

"You're taking a bath. Stop whining." She returned to her reading.

The sunken tub was my favorite part of Mo's house. When she and I were younger, we could both fit in it at the same time. She always let me have the side with the plastic seashell pillow. We'd keep our feet pressed together like fins and pretend to be mermaid sisters.

I dipped beneath the surface, my hair fanning out around me. I could hold my breath for almost two minutes, which freaked out Mo. She rarely could wait that long before pulling at my arm for me to come up for air.

She tapped the top of my head and I gave up on setting a new record.

"You have a death wish?" she asked.

I had at one time, in the weeks after the explosion when I was in the burn treatment center. Many times, I'd begged the youngest nurse on the ward to kill me—and I meant it. My pleas only made her cry. After that, the hospital psychiatrist made regular visits.

"When I'm underwater, I can't hear your mom and dad fighting," I said.

Her parents had been arguing downstairs since I arrived. Although I couldn't make out their exact words, I suspected the fight was about me visiting Mo.

"You promised he wouldn't be here," I said.

"He came back early. Just don't listen. You know how he is."

I did know. Her dad had always objected to Mo being my friend. He said I'd just bring trouble. And maybe he was right. There was nothing I could do about Mom and the people she hung around, but I made sure Mo never visited me at the motel. We'd meet at the library or the Dairy Queen, or at her house when her father was at work. And I kept Mo's address secret from Mom. I wanted those worlds as separate as possible.

Her father's voice grew muddled until I didn't hear it anymore.

"You know Mom really loves you." Mo closed her book and tossed me a sponge.

"I know."

I dunked the sponge and then squeezed it over my head, sending streams of water down my face.

Last year, Mo's mother had added a cell phone to the family's plan so that I'd be able to contact Mo or her in an emergency. She slipped me money from time to time, urging me to buy fresh fruit and vegetables and vitamins. When I got my period, she bought me tampons and Motrin since she knew those were expensive.

"It's not that Daddy doesn't like you," Mo said.

"Yeah. I feel the love."

Mo pursed her lips. "He doesn't like that you don't go to school."

"I won't go to school," I said.

"I'm just saying you should think about it."

Mo got up and stood in front of the vanity. She opened her mother's makeup drawer and took out a tube of lipstick.

"If I went back to school, he still wouldn't like me," I said.

Mo lifted her long hair and struck a pose in the mirror, her lips a color between coral and tangerine.

"Not your color," I said.

"Yeah, maybe." She grabbed a tissue, wiped her lips, and tried another shade. This one was a frosty bubblegum pink.

"Your mom wears that color?" I asked.

"Impulse buy," Mo said.

I stepped out of the tub and wrapped a large bath towel around me. Mo gave up on the lipstick search. I sat on the stool near the vanity so she could untangle my hair.

"It'll be our freshman year. You could say you've transferred from out of state," she said.

"Without any records or transcripts."

"Say you were homeschooled," she said.

"I am homeschooled. Sort of."

"I'm not a real teacher." Mo began to braid my hair, pulling the strands too roughly. "You'd get a better education going to class."

"I don't need a better education."

"You do if you don't want to end up like your mom," she said.

I looked at our reflections in the mirror. "That's not fair."

"I'm sorry. I just want what's best for you."

"Would you rather not tutor me anymore?"

"It's not that."

The front door slammed so forcefully that we felt the vibration upstairs. When her dad started shouting again, Mo opened the bathroom door and looked down the hall.

A female—not her mom—shouted something back at Mo's dad. Before Mo could say anything, I recognized my mother's voice in the hall.

Mom stomped up the stairs and it sounded like Mo's parents followed.

"Where's Arlie? I know she's here!" Mom pushed past Mo and into the bathroom.

"Please go home, Mrs. Betts," Mo begged, then yelled for her parents not to come in, that I wasn't dressed.

"Well, isn't this fancy. Just like your fancy friend here." Mom stumbled forward and I caught her. "So this is where you sneak off to."

"Oh my God, Mom. What are you doing here? Please go. Now."

"I'm your family. You shouldn't be here." She slurred her words and found it difficult to stand. "You've betrayed me, you little slut."

I slapped her. Hard. I wanted her to shut up. I wanted to keep hitting her until there was nothing left of her or our life together.

"You don't get to call me that," I said. "I've never let anyone touch me."

"Get them both out of my house!" Mo's dad raged on the other side of the door.

"It's not the girl's fault. Let's go back downstairs." Mo's mom coaxed her dad away from the bathroom while I held my breath.

Mom pressed her hand against the cheek I'd slapped. She'd stopped babbling. Mo gently took her arm and helped her sit on the vanity stool.

"Get dressed," Mo said to me. "You should go."

I put on my T-shirt and shorts, not bothering with my underwear or bra. I slipped on my flip-flops.

"I'm sorry, Mo." Tears rolled down my cheeks. Her dad was right. I'd just brought trouble to their house. How long would Mo keep fighting for our friendship after something like this?

"It's okay. Just take her home."

This was definitely not okay. It'd never be okay. I pinched Mom's elbow, digging my fingers into the bony joint, and led her downstairs hoping we wouldn't run into Mo's parents on our way out.

CHAPTER 15

The last thing I wanted to hear on a Saturday morning was the screeching of Frank's table saw. Where were the outraged neighbors who should be putting a stop to the madness? Frank's cluelessness could be charming at times. This wasn't one of those times. I pulled on some sweatpants and a hoodie and marched outside.

"Ah, good. I need your help." He hoisted a piece of plywood over his head.

"Does it look like I came out here to offer my assistance?" I shielded my eyes from the sun, but hoped he could see my put-out expression.

"I don't care what it looks like," he said. "Now that you're here, I need another pair of hands."

I opened my mouth to protest, but he turned back to his work, seemingly uninterested in what I had to say about the sanctity of Saturday morning sleep-ins.

"Let me get my shoes," I mumbled in defeat.

"And sunscreen," he added. "We might be out here a while."

I huffed around the trailer for a few minutes but then gave in. After chugging a vanilla protein drink so I wouldn't faint from hunger, I joined my uncle in the wooden skeleton he'd assembled.

"What are we doing?" I asked.

"Putting the plywood sheath around the structure," Frank said, lost in the rhythm of his work.

He held up large expanses of plywood and instructed me to attach the sheets to the studs using a nail gun. Soon, the skeleton had skin and the interior spaces darkened as walls blocked out the sunshine.

While I went in to fix us sandwiches for lunch, Frank cut away pieces of the wall to reveal where the windows would go.

I peered into one of the openings. "Hungry?"

My uncle removed his tool belt and grabbed the plate I held out to him. "Thanks. How's it looking?"

He beamed. Working with his hands suited him. I guessed finally seeing his endless drawings take physical shape stirred a pride that couldn't be suppressed.

"It's amazing. Really. It looks like a real house. I didn't think one person could build a house by himself."

"This is your room, you know. The closet's kind of small…"

"It's perfect. I don't have a lot of clothes anyway." My throat constricted. This burly, kind-hearted man had changed my life irrevocably. By realizing his own dream, he was introducing me to ones I'd never dared to have.

"Just because you'll have your own room doesn't mean you and that Cody kid can hang out in there without some rules." His laugh revealed a mouthful of sandwich.

"Oh, please." I blushed at his assumption but didn't mind his teasing. Cody in my room. Was that even possible?

"Aha! There is something to this Cody. Your cheeks don't lie."

I brought my palms to my face.

"Is that what you and Mo were talking about last night?"

I took a large bite of my sandwich to buy some time before having to answer. Was this what kids talked about with their parents? Did I want Frank to act like a parent?

"Tell me if it's none of my business," he added. "But I can always get the deets from Mo. She and I are buds."

"Mo's version would be exaggerated," I said. "She has a flair for the dramatic."

Frank crawled through the opening and sat on the ground next to me. "What's your version then?"

"He was waiting for me at Buckley Park, near the trolley stop. He just wanted to talk."

"So that's where you were?"

I nodded. "He seems nice. I mean, he is nice."

"The other night, Mo mentioned you and he sing together, right?"

"Uh-huh. In choral." My heart rate quickened as I remembered the recording Cody had made of me singing.

"So he's nice, huh?"

"Seems that way."

"And he can sing?" Frank asked.

"Yep. He's a great singer."

Frank and I laughed at our awkward exchange.

"Think I can meet him sometime?"

I hadn't even thought of next steps like Cody meeting Frank. Did that mean I'd have to meet his parents? What would they think of me?

"Why the storm clouds over your head?" Frank asked. "You

don't want me to meet him? I promise not to fart or pick my nose."

"That's not it at all. You'd like him. I was just wondering if he'd want to introduce me to his parents. In any case, we're nowhere near the meeting-the-parents stage."

"Oh, so I'm your parent now?" Frank winked.

"I haven't figured out what you are," I said. "I'd say you're cooler than a parent but stricter than a friend."

"A hybrid. Awesome!"

Frank got up and dusted off his carpenter jeans. He let out a trombone-like belch.

"Pardon me," he said. "I promise not to fart, pick my nose, *or* burp when I meet your young man."

"Cody's sense of smell and hearing are exceptional, so definitely no farting and burping, but he wouldn't be able to see you pick your nose," I said.

"Whew. I was starting to feel the pressure."

My uncle squinted against the midday sun. Dusty, a little rumpled, and definitely in need of a haircut and beard trim, but he was growing on me.

"This house isn't going to build itself," I said. "I have a few more hours before Mo picks me up. Put me to work."

Frank draped an arm around my shoulders, this time without asking. I didn't mind.

* * *

Bits of sawdust clung to my sweaty skin, and the tops of my shoulders radiated from too much sun. Frank and I had worked nonstop for several hours, lost in our weird new relationship of master craftsman and apprentice.

I found myself working harder, *faster*, as if the completion of this house had been my lifelong dream instead of his. Frank's musings on recycled insulation, bamboo flooring, nontoxic paints, and energy-efficient windows started to fill out my mind's hazy picture of what the place would eventually look like.

His words broke into my daydream. "Hey, weren't you meeting Mo this evening?"

"Oh hell! I completely forgot." I shed my carpenter's belt and gloves. "I need to take a shower before she gets here."

"Too late," Frank said, pointing to the street. "And she's not alone."

My legs, already fatigued from the day's work, almost gave out. Mo emerged from her mom's car and rushed to the passenger side. She held out her elbow and Cody grasped it so she could help him navigate the uneven yard.

"Is that your boyfriend?" Frank teased.

"Shut up or I will kill you. Seriously," I hissed at him.

Mo spoke first. "Cody, I want to introduce you to Arlie's Uncle Frank."

Cody held out his hand and Frank shook it vigorously.

"Nice to meet ya. Heard a lot about you, man," Frank said, even though I'd told him very little.

"Same here," Cody offered.

I shot an angry, questioning glance at Mo. "So, this visit is a surprise."

"Don't be mad. I sort of invited myself along," Cody said. "I ran into her at the Book Nook. She said you two were going to hang out and I asked if I could join you."

I guess Cody heard the tension in my voice.

"No worries. It's a nice surprise. Just unexpected."

"Duh. That's what a surprise is…unexpected." Mo snorted and then exchanged googly eyes with Frank. My discomfort brought them loads of enjoyment. Frank was right—they'd become buds.

"I've been working on the house all day," I said. "I could use a shower. Give me a few minutes?"

"You girls head inside," Frank said. "I'll show Cody our progress."

I almost blurted out that he wouldn't be able to see it anyway, but between Cody's directional sense and Frank's vivid descriptions, I suspected Cody would get a pretty good idea of the layout.

"Say, man, grab my elbow," Frank said. "Don't want you tripping over all these bits of lumber."

Before Mo and I had even made it into the trailer, Frank had begun his tour with a boisterous rant on green building methods.

"What were you thinking?" I asked Mo when we were inside.

"They get along great. Don't worry."

"I'm not worried about Frank. I meant, why did you invite Cody over at all?"

"Just shower," Mo ordered. She lounged on the couch with her feet up against the trailer's wall.

I stripped out of my dirty work clothes and left them in a pile on the floor while I stepped into the cramped shower stall of the Airstream. The cool water stung my sunburned shoulders so I washed hurriedly. I also didn't want Cody stuck with Frank for too long. No telling what well-intentioned damage my uncle could do.

After I'd dressed in jeans and a black tee, I called Mo over to braid my hair so I wouldn't have to blow-dry it.

"You should be thrilled," Mo said, tugging my hair a bit too tautly. "Quit wigging out and try to enjoy the attention. He wants to be with you."

"I need to throw up," I warned Mo.

"No, you don't. It will pass. Let's find you something awesome to wear. You're not wearing that ugly T-shirt."

"I don't even know where we're going," I whined.

Mo rummaged through my things until she found my tight black jeans and a sky-blue halter top.

"It's April."

"So? Bring a sweater."

"It's too revealing," I protested.

"You're sixteen. You sound like your mother." Mo brought a hand to her mouth. "I'm sorry. Didn't mean to mention your mom again."

"She never cared what I wore. Maybe that's why I do."

"Please, Arlie. This is so pretty. The pale blue looks awesome with your dark hair. You obviously liked the top enough to buy it at some point. Why not wear it?"

I'd spotted the halter at a consignment shop a few months ago. The owner had pestered me until I tried it on and then wouldn't let me leave without it. She even gave me fifty percent off so I'd have no excuse.

"Isn't this a little dressy? Where are we going?" I pulled the cool, satiny top over my head.

"To a dance."

* * *

Mo practically dragged me from the trailer to where Cody and Frank were sitting at the picnic table. *Dance? Hell no*, I told her under my breath.

"We're ready!" Mo exclaimed.

Frank let out a low whistle. "You look great. Way to scrub up."

Heat traveled up my neck and into my face. I gave him a crusty stare.

"What am I missing?" Cody asked.

"Well, she's wearing this shiny, blue halter thing and black jeans," Frank began. "And her hair is all twisted up with braids."

"Stop, Frank. Please." I was going to die of embarrassment before I even had the chance to kiss Cody. *Where did that come from?*

"So, what's the plan?" Frank asked.

"We're going to a dance at the high school," Mo said. "If it's lame, we'll probably head to the movies."

"The place will be crowded, right?" Frank asked.

"Dances usually are," I said. "Why?"

"Just be safe."

Was all this fatherly concern for Cody's benefit?

"Of course we'll be safe. Stop being so weird," I said.

"And there will be teachers around?"

I gave Frank my angriest stare and mouthed the word "stop."

"Yes, plenty of adults," Mo said. "No drugs, no alcohol, no sex."

"God, Mo. Just shut up," I said. "Let's go already."

We made our way over to the car, and Cody climbed into the backseat so I could sit in front with Mo. My face flushed. What the hell was Frank thinking?

As Mo pulled away from the curb, Cody leaned forward so his lips were near my right ear.

"It's cool your uncle looks out for you," he whispered.

"Yeah, right," I said.

"And by the way, you smell nice."

I shivered and hoped Cody didn't notice how my breathing had changed.

* * *

The high-school gym pulsated with strobe lights, pounding

music, and a mass of kids all moving as one organism. Mo took my hand and I grabbed Cody's, and we snaked our way along the wall until we reached the bleachers.

"I'm going to talk with Mindy a bit," Mo shouted above the music. "I'm sure you two will be fine."

Cody and I sat on the first row of the bleachers, pulling in our feet so we wouldn't be trampled by students moving to and from the dance floor.

"You can't even tell what song this is with all that techno garbage in the background," I shouted to Cody.

"That's how they can stretch a four-minute song to twelve minutes," he said.

Even though I'd just labeled it techno garbage, I tapped my feet against the wooden floor in perfect rhythm.

"A percussionist, I see." Cody leaned in closer. "Or are you hinting you'd like to dance?"

"I...uh...I don't..."

"Mo said you're a great dancer, so no excuses. Or do you think I'll embarrass you?"

Mo and her big mouth had been sharing way too much lately.

"If I step on your feet, don't say I didn't warn you," I said.

"There's a better chance I'll step on yours...and everybody else's. Don't let me drift away from you in the crowd or I'll never find my way back."

I laid my sweater on the bleacher seat and took his hand. We pushed our way onto the dance floor. Sensation after sensation assaulted me: the music ringing in my ears, the press of bodies around me, the heat of Cody's sweaty palm, the stares of people who stopped to gawk at the burned girl who dared to show up at a dance—and with her hair swept up off her scar.

The scene could have been straight out of a teen movie where the unlikely couple moves in slow motion as their stunned classmates part and allow them to enter the dance floor. The only thing missing was a spotlight.

Suddenly, Mo eased up beside me, dancing her heart out with a guy I didn't know. She winked, her arms waving above her head. I could no longer ignore the music and began to move my body. Soon, my movements mirrored Cody's. He closed his eyes and leaned forward, pressing into me slightly. I touched his hand, letting him know I was still near. He smiled at the contact.

"Close your eyes," he shouted.

"I can't. I'll get sick," I shouted back.

"Take my hands. I won't let you fall."

I reluctantly closed my eyes. Cody's confident grip held me in place. Without the sense of sight, everything felt bigger, louder. Even Cody's touch felt more intense, as if our skin was fused. Laughter erupted from deep in my belly.

"It's great, right?" Cody pressed even closer. "I'm so glad you're here."

The music stopped abruptly and I swayed, feeling unbalanced. I opened my eyes and found Cody looking at me, *through* me.

Jay-Z's "Empire State of Mind" rang out from the speakers, slowing the movement of the crowd, which instinctively lowered its energy to match the easy piano rhythm behind the lyrics.

Cody pulled me against him. He placed one hand on my bare back while the other pinned my hand at my side. When I put my arm around his neck, he gasped softly. I closed my eyes again, willing myself to stay present, to feel the electricity as his thumb moved down the curve of my back.

I began to sing the Alicia Keys parts of the song and Cody

answered by singing Jay-Z's parts. We sang softly enough that only we could hear ourselves. Someone looking at us might have thought we were just talking.

The song merged directly into another with a much faster beat, breaking the spell between us.

"I want to go outside," Cody said above the music. "Take me outside."

The frantic tone of his request set my teeth on edge. I led him back through the crowd and out the front doors of the gym, not bothering to go back to the bleachers to retrieve his cane or my sweater. The night air chilled the perspiration trickling down my back.

"Is there anyone else out here?" he asked.

"Just a couple of kids leaning against a car and smoking. A few others sitting on the steps. Why?"

"Let's go around the side of the gym." He used our conjoined hands to point in the direction he wanted me to lead us. As soon as we rounded the corner, he asked me to stop.

"I want to touch your face. It's how I'll be able to see you." He reached for my scar, but I pulled his hand down to his side.

"No, don't," I whispered. As much as it hurt to deny him, I couldn't bear the thought of his hand brushing the disfigured skin and the ridges left by the grafts.

"Please, Arlie."

His breath tickled my neck.

"I don't want you to," I said.

"You can trust me."

He didn't know what he was asking. If he recoiled in disgust, I wouldn't be able to bear it.

"It's not that. Let's just go inside." I walked off without him.

"Wait up. I don't have my cane." Cody held out his arm and I had to scramble back to him.

We didn't speak as we walked back into the gym. I led him over to the bleachers, unsure what to say. My face burned with shame. *You're an idiot. He wanted to kiss you.*

"I'm going to talk to the guys." Cody grabbed his cane. "I'll see you later."

I watched him maneuver expertly through the crowd. I had to find Mo. I had to go home.

* * *

"I don't understand. Did he do something to upset you?" The music almost drowned out Mo's question.

"No. I just want to go home. Can you drive me?"

"What happened?"

"Never mind, I'll call Frank." I turned on my heel.

Mo struggled to keep up. I was already outside on the gym steps when she finally tugged at my shoulder.

"Arlie, what the hell?"

"I'm fine. Let's talk tomorrow." If I tried to explain, I might never stop crying. "Please go inside. Frank will pick me up."

I walked through the gym parking lot and onto Main Avenue, trying to shake the last thing I saw before leaving: Cody and Brittany dancing.

CHAPTER 16

If I dared to walk all the way home, Frank would kill me so I stopped at the Exxon station and called him. With any luck, the fact that I was waiting in a well-lit public place would make him forget the several blocks I'd already walked alone. After being tailed by the Mustang yesterday, I should've known better, but I wasn't thinking when I bolted from the dance. Shivering, I sat on the curb at the far end of the gas station's parking lot and waited.

Frank's Suburban rounded the corner and came to a halt directly in front of me. He left the engine running and hopped out before I could get up.

"We're going back to the dance. I'm going to kill that little turd. I don't care if he's blind." Frank stood fuming, red-faced, ready to pummel a teenager half his size.

"God, no! Cody didn't do anything."

"Then why did you feel you had to walk home from the dance in the dark?"

"It's complicated," I said.

"I'm an educated man. I can follow."

"Let's just go back to the trailer. We can talk there."

Frank hesitated but finally got back into the truck. He alternately gripped the steering wheel and hit it with his palms.

"Holy hell. I can't believe you were walking alone. Something could have happened. What if—"

"What if what?"

"Nothing. It's just that someone could've grabbed you and you'd never be heard from again. You said you'd stay safe."

His wild eyes made him look like a crazy person.

"You're being a little melodramatic. I used to walk alone at night all the time. No big deal."

"It's a big deal. A very big deal."

I stared straight ahead, worried that he wasn't being melodramatic after all and that I'd been stupid to risk walking alone at night.

* * *

I changed into sweatpants and a hoodie before joining Frank outside. He'd lit a small fire in the chiminea to ward off the night's chill. He'd brought the thing from Corpus. He said lots of people in the south used the earthenware urns as outdoor fireplaces.

I pulled my chair back several feet from the crackling flames.

"I'm sorry about the fire," he said. "I wasn't thinking. Do you want to go inside?"

"No, I'm fine. I'll just stay back here." I wasn't fine, but there was only so much I could deal with in one night. Fire seemed less dangerous than talking about Cody.

Frank pulled his chair next to mine.

"I'm still furious you walked to that gas station in the dark, but first I want to hear what happened with Blondie."

"Don't call him that."

My breath quickened as I thought about Cody's thumb on the small of my back and his lips so close to my neck before I essentially rejected him.

"Fine. What happened with *Cody?*" he asked.

I exhaled. "He tried to touch—"

"I knew it. I'm going to kill him."

"Calm yourself. He tried to touch my face, Frank. My *face.*"

Frank relaxed back into his canvas camping chair. He rubbed his bearded chin. "Oh man. I get it."

My uncle did understand. We'd only known each other a short time, but he respected the rules that kept my world upright. One was that no one touches me, at least not without my permission, and definitely not my scar.

"So, he was going to kiss you then, huh."

"Are we really going to talk about this?" I slumped down in my chair, grateful the darkness of night hid my embarrassment.

"I know this is between you and Cody, but it seems you really like this guy. And he's probably completely clueless about what went down between you tonight."

"Clueless?"

"How much have you told him about the accident?"

"Well…I…It hasn't come up like that. I mean, he has to know about my face, right?"

Frank stood and poked at the tiny fire. His stocky frame blocked most of its light and heat. "He may know about the physical scars, but not the most important ones."

A retort caught in my throat. I wanted to tell him he didn't know what he was talking about. I wanted to tell him to mind his own business, but he *did* know what he was talking about. And

Mom's death made me his business now.

"If he's important to you, then you need to tell him how you feel. And that means sharing what you're going through."

"But I don't want to tell him about Mom."

"He probably already knows a lot of the story because of the way people talk, but you can correct any rumors. You're your own person. You're not a reflection of your mom and the way she lived."

Cody rejecting me outright wouldn't hurt any more than the pain I felt right now. Pain was pain, no matter what the cause. Tonight I'd shut things down before even trying.

"So, when did you become an expert on relationships?" I hoped he heard the joking in my voice.

"That's a long story for another night. I do know there's a point of no return and regret is a bitch," he said, not turning from the fire. "Now get some sleep. And don't you ever walk alone at night."

I waited for him to turn around. When he didn't, I went to my room, but I doubted sleep would come.

CHAPTER 17
SIX YEARS AGO—UNMASKED

I stood very still while Kiki, my foster mom, removed my compression mask. She screwed up her face, but then her normal blank expression returned. I looked straight into the bathroom mirror and tried to remember what my face had looked like before the accident.

"Does that hurt, Arlene?" She called all six of us foster kids by our given names: Theodore, Ignacio, Joanne, Elizabeth, Corrine, and Arlene. She said nicknames weren't dignified.

"No, ma'am. It don't hurt," I lied. We were only allowed to call her "ma'am," not "Mom" or "Kiki" or even "Mrs. Campbell."

"*Doesn't* hurt. Use proper English."

As she dabbed medicine on my bright red skin, Theodore, who was eleven and the oldest of us kids, rushed into the bathroom and snapped a photo of me without my mask on. Kiki ran after him, screaming for him to stop or the punishment would be much worse. I hoped he'd get the whooping of his life.

He'd taken my picture once before, the first night I'd arrived at the foster home. I had just gone to bed and covered my head with my blanket because Corey—I mean, Corrine—talked so loudly in her sleep. I didn't even hear Theodore sneak into the room. He pulled back the blanket and blinded me with the camera flash. I didn't stop screaming for an hour.

Tonight, it was Theodore who screamed somewhere on the first floor. Kiki must have caught him. The crack of her special belt was loud enough to hear throughout the house, which usually ensured the rest of us behaved.

I didn't wait for Kiki to return to pull on my mask. I was old enough to take care of myself. The mask was the same color as skin and had holes where my eyes, nose, and ears were. "You look like a bald alien or a bank robber," I said to my reflection, then made my hand into a gun and started shooting into the mirror. "*Bang-bang. Bang-bang-bang.*"

Later, as I walked down the hall, I opened the door to the first room and peeked inside. "Good night, Joanie and Lizzy," I whispered.

"Good night, Arlie," they called back.

When Kiki wasn't around, we used our nicknames because they felt like real names to us, and we didn't care about seeming dignified.

Next, I peeked into the den that served as Ted's and Iggy's bedroom. While Ted was downstairs getting an ass-whooping, Iggy snored like a fat pig on the sofa that unfolded into a bed at night. I walked over to the desk the boys shared and fumbled around for a Magic Marker. I uncapped it and breathed in, but I could no longer smell one of my favorite smells.

As quiet as a mouse, I walked over to Iggy and drew a mustache on his upper lip. It must have tickled because he swiped his hand across his face, smearing the wet ink into an even larger mustache. I put the cap back on the marker and placed it on Ted's pillow.

As I left the room, I changed my mind and grabbed the marker. I rushed back into the bathroom. I drew hair over my compression mask including some bangs. I resisted the urge to give myself a mustache.

I heard Ted climbing the stairs slowly, whining like a baby the whole way. I made a beeline for my room and shut the door behind me.

Corrine was fast asleep in her twin bed, talking nonsense that involved kick ball, butterflies, and creamed corn. Her dream talk always gave me the shivers, and I sometimes wished she'd just dream about regular old monsters. Scary I could take. Weird I could not.

The room was very dark, but I didn't turn on the light. She was outside again and I didn't want her to see me. She was out there every night, sitting on the curb, smoking smelly cigarettes—not that I could smell them anymore. I could almost feel her staring up at my window.

I knelt on the floor and raised my head to the windowsill so that just one eye looked outside. There was no moon and someone had knocked out the streetlight again, but a tiny orange dot glowed every once in a while, giving away her location.

She never came to see me in the hospital during all those months when the pain made me forget who I was and where I came from. She didn't hold my hand and tell me Rosa was still alive, that everything would be all right, that she was going to leave Lloyd and take us somewhere new.

I imagined the nurses whispering those things behind the white paper masks that protected me from their germs. I imagined the doctors telling me the police had found Lloyd and locked him up in a jail and thrown away the key.

Watching Mom hide in the dark was boring so I crawled into my bed, covering my ears against Corey's one-sided conversations. The rest of the house was quiet. Even Ted had stopped his crying.

I ran my hand over my head, feeling the fine, mesh-like fabric. I couldn't feel the fake hair I'd drawn, but I imagined it there anyway.

Tomorrow, I would think about packing my little suitcase. When Kiki was finally asleep, I would creep through the house on tippy-toes, whispering good-byes to my foster brothers and sisters. I'd walk across the street toward the little orange point of light. If Mom held out her arms, I'd hug her and tell her I forgave her because that's what a daughter was supposed to do. And then we would run away together.

CHAPTER 18

I dressed as quietly as I could and slipped from the trailer before Frank woke up. He slept in on Sundays so my stealth wasn't that impressive. My note said I was meeting Mo for breakfast and that he shouldn't worry. She'd texted me after the dance, threatening to give up on our friendship if I didn't meet her at Denny's by eight. While she was joking, she had every reason to be angry. I should've confided in her about Cody, but I'd run. As I'd done time and time again.

My cruiser bike carried me down a mostly deserted Main Avenue. The sun warmed my face even though my breath escaped in white puffs. I made a point to detour off Main and into the neighborhoods so I wouldn't have to pass the Animas View Motel. I didn't want to risk Dora spotting me. I hadn't talked to her since before Mom's funeral. I felt horrible that I'd cut her out of my life so completely, but maybe Mo had been right. Contact with Dora kept me chained to a past I needed to bury.

Mo beat me to the restaurant. Sherri, the hostess, hugged me and said she'd given us our favorite booth at the back. Mo saw me enter and waved me over. The scolding I expected didn't come, but neither did a warm hello.

"Here's your sweater, Cinderella. You left it behind at the dance." Mo tossed me the sweater without giving me a hug.

"I shouldn't have left last night without explaining," I admitted.

"You're damn right about that," she said. "Now drink this. Then you can apologize a few hundred times and I'll think about forgiving you."

Mo handed me an iced latte. Her standard way of making sure I got enough calories was ordering smoothies, lattes, and shakes with cream instead of milk.

"And you're going to eat, right?" She wasn't asking. She was insisting.

"Sure. Maybe pancakes? Something soft." Choking down a stack of pancakes wouldn't kill me. And I'd do anything to make up with Mo.

"I talked to Cody last night," she said. "I know what happened."

My stomach lurched at the thought of her interrogating him. "Well, you have Cody's version of what happened. Do you want to hear mine?"

"I can guess. It doesn't take a genius to figure it out."

I shouldn't have been surprised to hear Mo's assessment or to learn that she was taking it upon herself to fix something she thought was broken.

"So you freaked, huh," she said.

"Essentially."

"Cody said he just tried to touch your face and you suddenly didn't want to be around him. He thought he'd read your feelings all wrong. So I set him straight."

I closed my eyes, too scared to even ask what she meant.

"Don't freak out again," she said. "But he deserved to know a little more about your accident. I told him you're self-conscious about the scar, that you were probably afraid it would gross him out and he wouldn't like you anymore."

"Oh shit, Mo. You didn't."

"That's the truth, isn't it?"

"Well, yes, but you didn't have to put it that way." I slumped down in the vinyl booth. "Did you have to use the word 'gross'?"

"There's no other way to put it. You don't see how beautiful you are, inside and out. Your scar is part of you. If he loves you, he has to love your scar."

"Love me? Where did you get that idea?"

"It's obvious, if you'd open your eyes," she said. "I'm going to order breakfast at the counter since our waitress seems to be missing in action. Be right back."

I had just gotten used to the idea that I *liked* Cody. Now, Mo was talking love. And what did that even mean? Kids declared their love for each other from third grade on—yet I had somehow missed out on feeling even the one-sided version.

"Lookie-loos at the far table." Mo sat back down in the booth. "Want me to have a chat with them? Teach them some manners?"

While Mo was away, several customers having breakfast tried to sneak looks in my direction without being noticed. I always seemed to catch their eye. Mo used to say I had radar that could pick up curiosity at a hundred yards.

That's exactly what I chalked it up to: curiosity. Deep down I knew my facial scar wasn't grotesque, but a person would have to be dead not to notice it. People had always stared. And that would never change.

"They don't matter, Mo."

"No, but Cody does."

"Is this whole breakfast going to be about Cody?"

"It doesn't have to be," she said. "Just tell me you'll talk to him."

Ignoring Mo, I made a funny face at a toddler who stared at me. She giggled and hid her face, prompting me into a game of hide-and-seek. Children were always curious, but the smallest ones were never cruel.

"Well? Will you talk to him today?" she persisted.

"He was dancing with Brittany—last night when I left," I said, wincing at the memory of his hands on her hips.

"It was a dance. They're friends, although I don't know why. Brittany stopped being interesting a long time ago. Now she's just mean."

The dance might not have meant anything to Cody, but it would have meant something to Brittany. I hated that I let her push my buttons like no one else could. It had felt personal ever since the day I met Mo and she told me Brittany had warned her away from being friends with "white trash."

"Fine, fine. I'll talk to him," I said, hoping Mo would drop the conversation.

If I let her continue to be a go-between, I'd be engaged by midweek or Cody would be running for the hills. Our relationship—or whatever it was—couldn't go forward or end without a conversation. And limbo sucked. I had no choice but to explain my actions to him.

The waitress arrived with more food than two people could eat. Mo had ordered me a full stack of pancakes, scrambled eggs, grits, and juice. At least the conversation would stop while we filled ourselves with carbs.

"What happened to the idea of a little food?" I asked.

"I'm glad I ordered so much," she said. "Here comes your uncle. He can eat your eggs if you like."

Dressed in plaid shorts and a contradictory plaid shirt, Frank marched purposefully around the tables to reach us. His hair was plastered down on one side and his eyes wet with fury.

"Why in the hell did you go out on your own? Weren't you listening to me last night at all? Jesus Christ." His hoarse whisper went beyond our booth. Diners turned in our direction.

"Sit down. You look and sound like a crazy person." I slid over and patted the booth seat.

He sat and shook his head as if in a private conversation.

"I left you a note," I said. "Why are you so wigged out?"

"I'm supposed to be your guardian. That means you listen when I ask you to do something."

Mo arched her eyebrows at Frank's over-the-top agitation. I shrugged my shoulders in answer. I'd never seen him like this.

"I ride my bike all the time," I said. "And before I lived with you, I took care of myself and my mother all on my own. I think I can manage to get across town without falling off my bicycle."

"I'm going to get a coffee refill and let you guys talk." Mo left me alone with Frank, but I wished she hadn't. He scared me.

"This isn't like you, or at least the 'you' I've come to know," I said. "What's up?"

I wanted to be the type of person who could reach out and smooth down his crazy wiry hair, or hug him to take away the fear on his face, but I just sat there unable to process his mood.

"I don't want to scare you...but your dad showed up," Frank said. "Day before yesterday."

"My dad?"

"I mean your stepdad. He must have figured out where you live."

"Lloyd's in Durango." Saying it out loud didn't help dissipate the fear taking over me.

I let Frank's words sink in. Then I vomited into his lap, giving everyone a better reason to stare at me.

CHAPTER 19

Mo said she'd check on me later and stayed behind to tell the waitress about my mess. Frank and I needed some time alone. We couldn't talk freely at Denny's, especially after I spewed latte over my uncle, the table, and the booth.

While Frank loaded my bike in the back of his Suburban, I sat in the front seat, shaking. My reaction freaked me out as much as the confirmation that Lloyd was in town. My body acted on its own accord, trying to convince my brain to panic more.

"I won't let anything happen to you." Frank concentrated on the road, his demeanor calmer now.

"Why do you think anything could happen to me?" Now my brain was catching up, frantically analyzing Frank's concern.

"I didn't mean it like that," he said. "But your stepfather was a meth cook and dealer. That spells trouble on its own. He has no right to contact you for any reason."

If Frank worried about my safety, did he also worry about his own? "What did you say to him?"

"I said I'd kill him if he came near you."

"And?"

"He laughed. So, I picked up a sledge hammer to prove my point. After he left, I called the police."

Frank confirmed that Lloyd had been driving a '67 Mustang, the same one that followed me from the Book Nook. Once we arrived back at the trailer, I couldn't help but scan the street for the Mustang, believing he'd be waiting for me.

We went inside quickly. I sat on the sofa, which was still made up as Frank's bed from the night before. He pulled the sheet and blanket around my shoulders.

"You're shaking," he said. "Do you want some coffee or tea? Something hot?"

I drew my knees up to my chin. "I don't want any friggin' tea. Why didn't you tell me about this? And don't say you were trying to protect me."

"Well, that's the truth. I didn't want you to be afraid." Frank joined me on the sofa, a cup of instant coffee in his hand even though I'd said I didn't want anything to drink. "For now, don't go anywhere alone. I'll drive you to school and choir practice, and to your therapy appointments."

"Were you ever going to tell me?"

The muscles in his neck tightened, but he didn't answer.

"You weren't, huh? You demand our honest little chitchats, but you keep something this important from me?"

"Why didn't you tell me you thought he was following you Friday?" Frank asked.

"I didn't know for sure it was him, but you did. You saw him. You *spoke* to him."

"I understand you're angry…" he began.

"You have no idea."

"I do now," he said. "I was wrong. I thought I was doing the right thing. I was sure the police would handle it and that you wouldn't have to deal with one more thing."

"The police can't help," I said. "He hasn't done anything yet."

"The man's wanted in New Mexico. That's reason enough for them to look hard. I gave them the make and model of the car and the license plate number. I also gave them a physical description."

I hadn't seen Lloyd since I was nine. My mostly hazy memory of him had clear enough edges to form an image for my nightmares, but not enough to know him if I saw him on the street today.

"What did he look like? I didn't get a good look because the car windows were so dark."

"What does it matter?"

"Maybe so I can recognize him if I see him again." Part of me wanted Frank to paint a picture of someone so wholly pathetic and unassuming that I couldn't possibly be afraid of him. Yet Frank was afraid. His anger proved it.

"He was tall, thin. His hair was pulled back in a ponytail," Frank finally offered. "And he had a mustache."

A shock wave went through my body as I remembered Lloyd kissing me good-night, the edges of his mustache tickling my chin until I had giggled. I raised my hand to my mouth.

"You okay, Arlie?"

I nodded but choked back the urge to vomit for a second time. "He had a large tattoo across his chest, all letters," I said. "The first letter was an *A*, but I don't remember anything else."

"I think you should talk to the police," Frank said. "You might remember some details that would help them."

"Was he burned?"

"What do you mean?"

"He was in the same room as me and Rosa when the explosion happened. He'd have been burned as well."

"I didn't notice anything, but then again, he wasn't around for long," Frank said. "But we should tell the police about it. A visible scar might make him easier to spot."

Mom never mentioned if she'd been with Lloyd the year I was in the hospital and rehab. Her fear had seemed so great that I suspected she'd had nothing to do with him after I'd been injured.

"I'm sorry, Arlie."

"What for?"

"I shouldn't have let him drive away. I should've…I don't know…detained him."

My heart sank at the thought. "You could have been hurt. I'm glad you didn't do anything."

It was hard to hold on to my anger at Frank for keeping this from me. All I felt now was jealousy that he'd been the one to see Lloyd. I didn't get a chance to look him in the eye, to tell him he'd rot in hell for Rosa's death even if the criminal justice system wouldn't do anything, to tell him he never meant anything to me and Mom.

Frank got up and leaned over a stack of books. He pulled out a leather-bound Bible and opened it. Just as I was about to make a wisecrack about him being religious, I realized it was one of those fake books with hollowed-out insides. Frank had hidden a gun in the secret recess.

He pulled out the gun's clip and then clicked it back into place.

"It's fully loaded. Just in case."

"A gun?"

"I'd like us to go to the shooting range today. I'll show you what to do," he said.

"You're scaring me." I sloughed off the blanket and stood next to Frank. He grabbed me by the shoulder and squeezed.

"I'm not trying to, but it's better to be safe than sorry. I've already lost my sister. I'm not going to lose you."

* * *

Frank and I spent most of the afternoon at the range. He went on and on about handgun safety for so long that I finally had to tell him I was ready to shoot, but I wasn't. The kickback startled me more than I expected and I failed to hit the target, time and time again. He'd assured me that I'd get better with practice, but with Lloyd in town, I really didn't have any time left.

When we got back to the trailer, Frank wanted to work on the house. He said he needed the physical exertion and I understood. I'd witnessed the Zen state he entered every time he picked up a hammer or turned on a power saw. He asked if I wanted to help, but I sensed he needed the time alone.

I hoped reading a book would calm my mind, but it didn't. I cleaned the trailer's bathroom and straightened up the living area, which took all of thirty minutes. Finally, I fired up my computer. Earlier in the week, Miss Browning had asked me to recommend a number for the girls' group to perform at the community concert in two weeks. Strangely, the task did calm me. Perhaps it was because music made me feel stronger.

I texted Claire and two other group members and asked their opinions. We finally arrived at "Rumor Has It" by Adele because it was high energy with strong backup vocals, perfect since we had seven girls. And I'd heard that other choral groups had used the song in competitions with good results.

The director asked Cody to choose the duet that would be performed. He had the strongest male voice in choir. I believed

I had the strongest female voice, but I'd only been a member a short time—and it didn't seem quite fair to share the spotlight with Cody. Now with my muddled feelings, I doubted my ability to stand next to him sharing something as intimate as a song, something almost more frightening than a kiss.

I put in my earbuds and listened to several Adele tracks, but I couldn't connect with her breakup album. I'd never been in a relationship that ended badly—or had I?

The slamming of a car door got my attention. I looked through the curtain to see Mo running across the yard toward the trailer. She was in my room within seconds.

She flopped onto the bed. "So, what's up with Frank? That was freaky, even for him."

I filled her in. Mo's jaw dropped when I told her about the gun.

"This is serious. What are you going to do?"

"Frank wants me to talk to the police. He thinks I might remember something about Lloyd that would help them find him faster."

"Maybe he left town already. Isn't that possible?"

Mo moved strands of hair from my forehead, worry apparent in the gesture.

"I kind of want to see him."

"What?"

Maybe it was closure I wanted. Maybe I just wanted to know why it was so important for him to see me. I regretted, though, that I'd spoken the words out loud to my friend, who was probably going to worry herself sick.

"I just meant it'd feel good to tell him to 'fuck off' once and for all," I said.

"Let the police tell him that. While they're putting him behind bars."

Mo rolled over and grabbed my phone from the nightstand.

"What are you doing?"

"James gave me Cody's cell number. I'm putting it into your phone in case you want to text him later."

"He can't read a text," I said.

"No, but his phone speaks his messages. Kind of like Siri on the iPhone. So don't text anything inappropriate."

"Have you been listening to me? I've had a rough day," I reminded her. "The last thing I need to think about is Cody."

"He's exactly what you should be thinking about. Don't let your stepdad take something else from you."

My stomach muscles contracted and the queasiness set in again. Was I really using Lloyd to avoid dealing with what happened last night? *Last night.* It seemed a decade ago. Had I really shut Cody down when all he wanted was to connect with me in the only way he could? I placed my hand over my scar and felt the ridges and pits I couldn't bear for him to "see."

"I'll talk to him at school."

Mo saw straight through my evasive maneuver. "You really want an audience for something so important? Wouldn't it be easier to call or text him tonight?"

Neither option could be described as easy.

"Let me think about it. And if a day makes a difference, then Cody's feelings aren't as strong as you believe."

"Your decision, girl, but if it were me, I wouldn't wait another second to let him know how I felt." She kissed the top of my head. "Got to get home for dinner. Call or text if you need me."

Mo crawled across the bed and stood in the doorway. "And

don't worry about your stepfather. They'll find him and then he'll get what's coming to him."

Frank had said the same thing earlier. They both seemed so sure.

So why wasn't I?

* * *

After another hour, my head was pounding and my nerves were raw from the whine of the table saw and the thwack of Frank's nail gun. I decided to ask him to stop for the evening.

Nothing about the outside of the house had changed, but Frank had been busy creating a maze of interior walls. I walked from one room to the other by sliding my body sideways through the studs that hadn't been covered with drywall yet.

"You ready to call it a day?" I asked.

Frank turned to me and wiped the sweat from his face with the front of his T-shirt, revealing a bulging, hairy belly. I grinned.

"Hey, Budweiser and I worked hard to get this body. Don't make fun." His joke couldn't lift the worry that cloaked us.

"You've been out here since this morning. Want to take a break? Maybe get a burger and shake at Sonic, and then Putt-Putt?"

My uncle removed his tool belt and sat down. "Out two nights in a row? My, how social you've become."

I sat down next to him. The concrete foundation was cool compared to the air inside the half-finished structure.

"You holding up?" he asked.

"Sure. I guess. Maybe I'd feel better if we went out. It might take my mind off things."

"And you'll eat a burger and not just drink a shake? You'll eat a real meal?"

"Fine. I'll eat a burger too, but let's just get out for a while. I can't take much more of that nail gun. I might be tempted to use it on you."

* * *

Frank kept the windows of the Suburban rolled down as we drove up to the college soccer fields on the mesa overlooking downtown. The evening air whipped my hair around my face, and I struggled to keep it out of my mouth. He parked near the railing on the edge of the road and killed the engine.

"Much better view for dinner." He rummaged through the Sonic bag to find his burger.

"Agreed."

"Sorry about the wind. I'm just a little rank from sweating all day," he said. "Thought we needed the fresh air more than you needed a perfect hairdo."

I tapped my finger against my nose. "Can't smell a thing, remember?"

"Jeez. I don't think I'll ever get used to that. I can't wrap my head around it."

Sometimes even I forgot. I'd had this chemical sensation for so long that I thought of it as normal—at least for me. "Right now I wish I could smell those fries though. Must be pretty damn delicious for you to attack them like that."

Frank flashed me a greasy, potatoey grin. "They're pretty awesome."

I told him Cody had said he couldn't imagine giving up the taste and smell of pizza and hamburgers and fries—that grease was the primary food group in his diet because nothing tasted as amazing.

"He's right. The taste, the mouth feel, the aromas. But even more importantly, memories attach themselves to food."

I understood mouth feel because textures were the only way I related to food right now. Taste, aroma, and memories definitely had no bearing on my food choices.

"What's your favorite food memory?" I asked.

"Now that's a tough one." Frank put down the fries. He seemed to rifle through the files in his brain until he could hit on just the right memory.

"If I had to choose one thing, I'd say my grandmother's pecan pralines," he said. "They weren't chewy like caramel, but soft and buttery. She'd make them for Thanksgiving and Christmas so I associate them with family. The times when everyone is together."

I couldn't identify with the idyllic scene he'd painted. Mom and I had spent the holidays alone. And before the accident, when we lived with Lloyd, it was just the three of us. The last Thanksgiving that I remember with Lloyd, we ate pizza from a gas-station deli and then went to a movie.

"The way you described the holidays sounds nice."

"Jesus, I'm sorry. I guess you didn't have any family except your mom and stepfather."

"It is what it is. You have to stop worrying about saying the wrong thing."

I slurped my shake and soaked in the last of the warmth the sun could muster. Sunsets in Durango were rarely fiery red because the air was too clear, but tonight a slight pink haze tinted the clouds that streaked across the skies to the west. I loved this town, even when Mom and I stayed at the women's shelter or in our car when we couldn't afford the motel. I could walk almost everywhere, and the free trolley could take me to the farthest edges of town I couldn't reach by foot.

Our time at the Animas View Motel was the happiest because

we had hot water and television and a door that locked, but also because of the easy access I had to the Animas Mountain Trailhead. I often hiked up the steep path to the highest point overlooking the Animas Valley and the winding Animas River. Or I'd take the cutoff to the Sailing Hawks Trail and wind down the rocky path shielded by pine trees. Lloyd was not welcome in a place I'd finally come to see as home.

"When we're finished with the house and you have some time on your hands, I'd like to show you my favorite trails," I told Frank. "Some exercise might help with that belly. You could eat more fries that way."

"Genetics are to blame, not inactivity or french fries. You're just lucky to have your mom's and your granddad's genes. Both were string beans. You could just as easily have ended up a squat, female version of me."

He laughed at the image in his head. All I could picture was a hobbit.

I dutifully took another few bites of my burger before wrapping up the remainder and stuffing it back into the bag. I put my bare feet up on the dashboard and sucked down the rest of my shake.

"The other night when you said, 'Regret is a bitch,' was that from personal experience?"

Frank dug into the bag and retrieved my unfinished burger. He tore it in two and handed me a portion. He took a bite from his half.

"It's a boring story," he said, his mouth full. "Now eat some more of that burger, or I'll puree it at home and force you to drink it."

"Seriously, Frank. I'd like to know." I drew my legs onto the seat and leaned into the passenger door.

"I had a girlfriend. It didn't work out. And yes, it was my fault."

He took another bite of the burger I'd tried unsuccessfully to discard. His curtness told me I should've dropped the conversation.

"There are usually two sides to every story," I said. "Seems like you're telling me her side and not yours."

Frank grinned. "Who's the grown-up here?"

"I'm old enough to know that right and wrong are pretty subjective. And old enough to know we take on guilt for things we can't really control."

I patted his shoulder. I'd come to really care about Frank, and I was interested in his life before Durango.

"Lily was the executive director of the Habitat chapter in Corpus. I met her on a build. I'd volunteered to be the main contractor for the framing portion," he said. "We started dating and were together about five years."

"That's a long time. What happened?"

"Um...you don't really want to hear this stuff."

"You and I are family now, right?" After withholding so much of myself these past months, I should've known to stop pushing, but I wanted to hear more about Lily.

"If I say more, I might upset you."

"I don't understand."

"Lily wanted to have children and I didn't. So it was my fault. That was a deal breaker for her, and I wouldn't change my mind."

"I see." He gave up the woman he loved because he didn't want to be a father, and yet he was now stuck parenting a teenage girl with a complicated past and possibly a very complicated present because of Lloyd.

"Those dark eyebrows betray you all the time, Arlie. When you worry, they dip down in a vee."

"I'm fine. Really. I'm sorry it didn't work out."

I turned to face the windshield. The sky had grown dark and the night had taken on a chill. We'd been spoiled with the warm April days that made us hope winter was long past. I wished I'd brought my hoodie.

Frank must have noticed because he turned the key in the ignition so he could raise the automatic windows.

"Lily and I broke up twenty years ago. My reasons for ending our relationship have nothing to do with you and me now. It's completely different."

He'd had the freedom to make a choice about Lily. When social services tracked him down about me, he probably didn't feel he had a choice. He was too good a man. Not the type of guy who'd allow his niece to stay in the foster care system until she turned eighteen.

"If Mom hadn't died, and you didn't have to take care of me, what would you have done with the money?"

"First, I don't *have* to take care of you. I want to. And second, I don't even know what I was saving up for anymore. I'd tell myself I needed the money to one day build a house and retire comfortably, but before I met you, I'd done nothing to make that happen except draw house plans over and over."

The plans that had only existed in Frank's mind and in his sketch pad were now taking shape and form: windows and doors and rooms and a roof. Our home.

Frank nudged my chin so I'd have to look at him.

"Sometimes things happen exactly the way they're supposed to happen. I may never have considered Durango, but it's beautiful here. And I have family again after not having family for a very long time. It's all good."

I nodded. Speaking would have just led to tears, and I just didn't have any more energy after what I'd been through in the past twenty-four hours.

"Let's skip Putt-Putt and head home." Frank put the truck in gear. I nodded again and turned to look out the passenger-side window.

As we made our way down the winding mesa road and back into downtown Durango, I struggled with a new and troubling feeling. I was relieved that Mom was no longer in my life and Frank was.

CHAPTER 20

ONE YEAR AGO—PLAYBOOKS

Mom sat cross-legged on the bed facing me. Between us lay a green plastic tackle box of cosmetics, although most of its contents were strewn across the bedspread.

"Did you know you can curl your eyelashes after you put on mascara? Just be sure the mascara is dry or you'll yank them out," she said.

I blinked uncontrollably as my mother moved the crimper toward my eye. She'd given me this same advice every time we completed our Saturday afternoon ritual of hair and makeup.

"There. You're a masterpiece." Mom snuffed out her cigarette in a Styrofoam cup of coffee sitting on the nightstand. "Now it's my turn. And make it dramatic."

She didn't have to instruct me. I'd been doing her makeup for years and knew Saturday nights meant heavier makeup and twice the amount of hair spray.

I rummaged through the rainbow assortment of Maybelline and Cover Girl eye-shadow compacts Mom had accumulated over the years. She'd figured out it was easier to shoplift from

Walgreens than Walmart. Each time she came home with a pocketful of goodies, I'd leave an envelope with money at the cashier's the next day. My note always said the same thing: "My mom forgot to pay for her recent purchase. Enclosed is full payment." Who knows? Maybe they continued to let her get away with it because they knew I'd always make good.

"Blues or greens?" I asked. "Green makes your eyes look larger."

"Just make me look beautiful."

"You're already beautiful."

Mom gave me her public smile, the one where she pulled her lip down over her top teeth to hide their decay. She'd started using it more and more with me.

I dabbed foundation on a triangular sponge and swept it across my mother's gaunt face. She looked older than thirty-eight, and heavy makeup only magnified the rapid aging brought on by meth use.

"Arl, I was hoping I could borrow some money. You have any stashed away?" Mom kept her eyes closed while I applied a shimmery gold base to her lids.

"I have a little."

Mo held on to most of my money so I wouldn't have to carry it on me. If I hid it in the motel room, Mom would ferret it out. She had before.

"You're still working, right? I mean, rent's due soon and I'm short this month."

"Don't worry, Mom. Keep your eyes closed so I can finish."

I cut grass in the summers, raked leaves in the fall, and shoveled snowy sidewalks and driveways all winter. Two older women who lived alone in massive Victorians on Third Avenue paid me to run errands and buy groceries. Sometimes they paid me to just sit with them and read aloud. I took whatever jobs paid invisible money, the kind that didn't require Social Security numbers and home addresses.

"You'll have to curl your own lashes," I said. "That thing creeps me out."

Mom scooted off the bed and stood before the dresser mirror. While she worked on her sparse lashes, I combed through her tangled hair. The boxed bleach had made it yellow and brittle, not supple and shiny like the model's on the label. Sometimes, I'd rub baby oil into her hair to add shine, but then she'd complain it looked thin and lifeless. She looked thin and lifeless regardless of how she wore her hair.

"I wish you wouldn't go out. I could find jobs that paid better." I rested my chin on her shoulder.

"I'm just going out with friends. I won't be late."

The lies were also part of our Saturday ritual. I wouldn't see her again until Sunday afternoon at the earliest, and we both knew it.

I could barely look at the mask she'd painted over my face. Deep plum and lavender shadow swept from my eyelids to my brows like butterfly wings. The powder blush wouldn't adhere to my scar, but the other cheek had a slash of color from my hairline to the edge of my mouth. Spidery blue lashes framed a sadness Maybelline couldn't hide.

"You're a real looker, Arlie. Especially when your hair covers your scar. You need to be careful around boys."

She was like a broken record, warning me about this over and over. The wrong kind of boys would try to take advantage of me because they'd assume no one else would want to date me.

I'd fall into casual sex as a way to build my self-esteem. She'd described her own playbook, not mine.

"Don't worry about me," I said.

"I'm your mother. I'm supposed to worry."

I turned from her to put the liners and shadows and polishes in the tiny compartments of the tackle box—my mother's jewels, stowed away for safekeeping.

As she dressed, I could barely stand to look at her emaciated body. She hadn't been good to it, and it had returned the favor. Her tightest jeans sagged around her hips, and the filmy black blouse failed to hide the sharp edges of her collarbone.

"If you won't be going out, I thought I'd borrow your boots." She pulled on one, then the other without waiting for me to say it was okay. The exertion caused audible wheezes.

"I'm going to take a shower, Mom." I kissed her cheek and then checked to make sure I hadn't left lipstick behind. "Be careful."

I closed the bathroom door behind me and leaned into it, eyes closed. Her knock came only a second later.

"Arlie? About that money…"

CHAPTER 21

It was well past midnight when a tiny chirp and a blinking red light alerted me to a text message. Mo was a night owl but respected that I wasn't. A diffuse, half-asleep panic roused me. I didn't turn on the lamp so Frank wouldn't see the light peeking out from under my door.

The message wasn't from Mo. When she gave me Cody's cell phone number earlier in the evening, she failed to mention she'd also given him mine.

Hoping we can talk tomorrow, Cody texted.

When the phone chirped again in my hand, I almost bounced from the bed.

I mean today, he added.

If I didn't answer, maybe he'd just assume I was asleep or that my phone wasn't charged. Mo had taken it upon herself to explain to Cody why she thought I'd acted so strangely when he tried to touch my face. I had nothing to lose in talking to him. It wouldn't be easy, but I wouldn't die from being honest. And if I botched things up royally, it's not as if I'd had him to begin with.

I'd like that, I texted back. How about during lunch?

The few seconds it took him to answer felt like an eternity.

On campus or off?

Off, I texted back immediately although I hadn't formulated any sort of plan. Privacy from student busybodies was my main concern. That Cody even proposed off-campus as an option made me think he felt similarly.

Great. Hope I didn't wake you. See you tomorrow.

I didn't bother to answer because I didn't want an extended text session with a volley of good nights and smiley faces.

I did, however, text Mo. Need to borrow your car at lunch. Okay?

Her response was immediate, as I expected. You don't have a license. Why are you up this late?

I know how to drive. Need to talk to Cody and want to do it away from DHS.

Hells to the yes then, but only if I get deets after. Now go to sleep.

Sleep wasn't going to happen for too many reasons to count.

* * *

The impact of Frank's knuckles on the plastic accordion door to my room made more of a creaking sound than a full-fledged knock. I appreciated his gentle attempt to ease me from sleep rather than just shouting for me to get my butt in the shower.

I groaned into my pillow to let him know I'd heard him. My foggy head told me I'd dozed, but not for long. I was physically wiped out. Too much emotion followed by a chaser of adrenaline.

"Arlie? You up?"

"I said yes."

"That pitiful moan didn't sound like a yes to me." Frank was rarely this persistent, but then again, most mornings I didn't sleep in so late. "I'd like for us to go to the police station this morning. I'll write you a note for school."

I swung my legs over the side of the bed and rested my elbows on my knees. *Lloyd.* I didn't want to think about my stepfather. I wanted to think about Cody. Well, not really. My nerves could've used a break from both stressors, but now that didn't seem likely.

"I'll be out in a minute."

* * *

The orange plastic chairs in the police-department waiting area must have been standard issue from the official law-enforcement furnishings catalog. I'd seen identical ones at Albuquerque police stations—cold and uncomfortable and clipped together at their metal bases. Mom had dragged me along on more than a few occasions when she had to bail out Lloyd for some minor offense.

I'd sit on those chairs, feet dangling. Even though I was only five or six years old, I feared they would take one look at Mom and consider her unfit to be a parent. What did they think of her greasy hair and crumbling teeth, her unwashed clothes? Sometimes, I'd ask her to wear a coat even if it wasn't cold outside. Or I'd comb her hair on the ride over to the police station or jail.

"You okay?" Frank patted my thigh. "You were a thousand miles away."

"I'm fine. I just don't want to miss too much school."

"That's funny," he said. "Most kids would kill for a day off."

"I have something important to do at lunch, so let's make this quick."

"What could be more important than this?" Frank seemed agitated so I let it drop, but yes, in this instance, Cody was definitely more important than Lloyd. Mo was right. I wasn't about to let my asshole stepfather take up this much space in my mind or keep me from being happy.

An officer finally emerged from behind a heavy steel door. He introduced himself as Officer Chris Daugherty and shook Frank's hand. I put mine in my pockets before he could extend a hand to me.

"We're glad you called, Mr. Betts. I've asked a detective to meet with us," the officer said. "The preliminary info you gave us over the phone has raised some alarms."

I didn't know exactly what Frank had told them, but the word "alarms" had my attention.

Detective Monroe's desk was bare, although his credenza and the tops of two file cabinets were crowded with bulging files set so precariously that a door slam could knock them over.

"We ran the New Mexico plate you gave us," Monroe said. "The guy it's registered to said he loaned his car to an acquaintance named Lloyd Hanson several days ago and hasn't heard from him since."

"Because he's still here," I mumbled.

"Mr. Betts, you gave Officer Daugherty a physical description, correct?"

"Yeah, but it wasn't much. I chased him off my property pretty fast." Frank looked as if he'd failed me.

"Then perhaps your niece could give us some details about her stepfather."

"Yoo-hoo. I'm sitting right here so you can talk directly to me," I said. "And the last time I saw him was when his meth lab exploded and killed my friend Rosa and gave me this lovely facial."

Officer Daugherty cleared his throat and grinned ever so slightly. I liked him much more than Monroe.

"But he followed you just a couple of days ago. Did you see anything then?"

"There was nothing to see," I said. "The car windows were too dark."

Monroe sighed heavily as if I hadn't tried hard enough.

"I understand it's been a number of years since you saw him, but could you tell us what you can remember?" Office Daugherty took a gentler tone. "Any distinguishing marks?"

I told them what Frank had already told them. I remembered my stepfather as tall and thin. He almost always had his hair in a ponytail. And he had fancy script letters tattooed across his chest.

"And you don't know what the tattoo said?" Monroe asked.

"I already told you no. It's not like I saw his chest that often."

Frank leaned in and whispered, "They're trying to help."

"How long had your parents been together?" Monroe continued, ignoring Frank's plea for me to behave, but the longer I sat there, the angrier I became at Lloyd for reentering my life.

"Lloyd wasn't my parent, but he'd always been around…as long as I can remember. They got married when I was seven."

"And your biological father?"

"I don't know anything about him." Mom made sure of that. She'd deflected every question I'd thrown at her over the years and had instructed her friends not to talk about him. Maybe she thought I'd desert her and try to find him.

"Can you remember anything else about Mr. Hanson? His friends or hangouts?" Monroe scribbled in his notebook instead of looking at me.

"I was only nine when the accident happened. I don't remember much about that part of my life."

"Uh-huh." He took an awful lot of notes even though I said very little. Still no eye contact.

"I really have to get to school now. Is that all you need?"

"We've verified the warrant on Mr. Hanson," Monroe said. "He's wanted for three counts of manslaughter in addition to drug-trafficking charges. We're taking this seriously, Miss Betts."

Three counts of manslaughter. That meant his two cooking buddies died in addition to Rosa. How did Lloyd survive? I was alive because Rosa had followed me back to the apartment...because she'd scooped me up and held me like a swaddled child, pressed tightly against her chest. My sopping-wet hair had covered most of my face and neck. She'd saved my life in two ways that day—by washing my hair and then by being brave enough to come after me despite Lloyd's threats. I shivered to think that Rosa's daughters and grandchildren blamed me.

The detective's assurances that Frank and I would be safe fell on deaf ears. No amount of police surveillance could deter Lloyd. He'd avoided the law for close to eight years. And he'd been brazen enough to walk straight up to Frank and demand to see me.

Lloyd wasn't hiding anymore. And there had to be a damn good reason for it.

* * *

The rest of the morning crept by at an excruciating pace, leaving me plenty of time to mull over excuses not to meet Cody during our lunch break, but at 11:45 a.m., he was waiting for me at my locker. He grabbed my elbow and we made our way down the hall and to the parking lot. A stealthy exit appeared unlikely, especially since I was leading one of the handsomest guys in school to my best friend's car.

"You're lucky you can't see all these assholes staring," I said.

Cody's pace slowed just slightly, but enough to wake me to the fact that I'd just put my foot in my mouth.

"I'm sorry. I didn't mean you're lucky to be blind," I stammered.

"No offense taken," he said. "But I don't care who sees us. Why do you?"

"Almost to Mo's car," I said. "Just a few more steps."

I opened the passenger-side door to let him in and then ran around to the driver's side.

"Are you embarrassed to be seen with me?" Cody pressed.

"God, no," I said. "It's just that I don't want people giving you a lot of grief for hanging around with me."

His easy laugh offended me.

"It's not funny," I said.

"No, not funny. Just stupid. Why would I care what people think? I want to be with you. It's nobody's business."

The ringing in my head drowned out all his words except, "I want to be with you." Did he mean that literally, as in be with me in this car at this moment? Or be with me as in boyfriend-girlfriend?

I struggled to insert the key in the ignition. I winced to think the jingling of the keys gave away my nerves.

"Where are we going?" he asked.

I hadn't thought that far ahead, but I needed time to clear my head after the meeting at the police station. This hour was for Cody alone. I drove down El Camino.

"You turned left out of the parking lot, so I can tell we're headed south. Are you kidnapping me and taking me to Albuquerque?"

"Funny, but no. We're going to Santa Rita Park. Won't be too cold for you?"

"Not a bit," he said.

When we arrived, Cody waited by the passenger side of the car until I could offer my elbow. He slipped his hand in the crook of my arm and I led him to the paved trail that ran parallel to the Animas River. The trail was busy with cyclists, runners, and walkers—but definitely not other high-school students, who stayed closer to campus.

"You don't have to be nervous," he said.

"I'm not. Why would I be?" *Charming, Arlie. Start out on the defensive.*

"Things didn't exactly end on a high note for us at the dance."

"Yeah, I know."

I spotted a bench and suggested we sit. Cody stretched his long legs. He pulled the hood of his sweatshirt over his head and put his hands in his pockets. Despite the chill in the air, I perspired profusely. I unwound my scarf and wiped the back of my neck. Had I forgotten my deodorant in my rush to get to the police station? Without being able to taste, I didn't even know if I had bad breath. *Breathe, Arlie.*

"Mo explained—" he began.

"Mo shouldn't have explained," I interrupted him. "She means well, but she can't know exactly how I feel."

"About your scar?"

"About everything."

I stared at the muddy river. Snowmelt from the mountains had churned up the river floor. In six weeks or so, the river would be at its peak flow, and rafters and kayakers would clamber into their wet suits to take advantage. I'd always wanted to try rafting, but Mom and I couldn't justify the expense. Maybe Frank and I could try this year.

"The river's up, huh?" Cody cocked his head slightly. "Sounds like a murmur. A little softer than the sound of the wind."

"Yes, it's running red. Lots of silt."

Cody couldn't see the yellow-green glow of the cottonwood trees starting to bud. He couldn't see the cloudless sky, a blue so intense it made every other color seem washed out and drab. I couldn't imagine being blind, not being able to experience the expansive palette in nature. Moving us to Colorado was one thing Mom did right.

"It's beautiful out today," I said. "Just incredible."

"Yep, incredible." Cody took one hand out of his pocket and laid it on my thigh, palm up. I accepted his invitation and looped my fingers through his. The fleece of his sweatshirt had warmed them. His hand wasn't rough, but it wasn't as smooth as mine. The difference made it easy to feel where our fingers and palms touched.

Sitting there in such a perfect moment, I swore to myself I'd gladly do without taste and smell to feel the warmth of his hand, the pressure of his fingers; to witness the split second before his lips opened into a smile; to hear his voice in choral practice and imagine the words he sang were only for me.

"Surely you know that your scar doesn't bother me," he said.

"It's so much more than that. My mom... The way we lived..."

"None of it matters."

"But you're wrong. Do you know where I was this morning? At the police station because my insane, drug-dealer murderer stepfather is in Durango looking for me."

"Your stepdad killed someone?"

I'd stupidly offered up the details I'd planned to keep from Cody, the details that would surely drive him away. Like some sort of perverse self-sabotage. Still, he deserved to know everything, no matter what the outcome was.

"Lloyd killed three people. They died when the meth lab in our apartment blew up."

"Your scar."

I touched the rippled, taut skin on my left cheek. "Yeah. I was there when it blew."

"How'd you survive?" Cody's voice trembled with worry even though we were safe, sitting in little Durango and years away from that horror.

I told him about Rosa, the woman I'd considered a surrogate grandmother. How she'd tried to protect me from Lloyd. How she ran into the apartment without regard for her own safety. How Rosa's body absorbed the fire and blast that should've ended my life.

"Jesus, I'm sorry. I can't even imagine."

I stopped myself from explaining more. Really, what else could I say? Mom and Lloyd had broken the law. They'd hurt people. Even though I wasn't technically guilty by association, I bore a stain of guilt that would never wear off.

"I'm going to say it again, Arlie. None of this matters."

How could he sit there and sound so assured?

"Everything matters in high school. The kids judge me for my past. And they'll judge you too."

"You're not a victim. You shouldn't act like one."

I pulled back my hand. "I've never been a victim. I'm a survivor and I'm stronger than most."

"Exactly. Then what they think of you—or us—shouldn't matter."

His argumentative tone drove home the point. If I backed down—didn't allow myself a normal relationship—I was giving others power over my life. That was the last thing I wanted to do. Especially where Cody was concerned.

"Now, are you going to give me back your hand or what?"

He wanted to be with me, and I'd done my best to talk him out of it. Maybe it was time to believe him.

"What happens next?" I asked.

"We'll figure it out as we go along. Just be honest with me. And don't run away again."

"If I ran away, you'd have a hard time getting back to school."

"I meant don't run away *ever*."

I'd always looked to some arbitrary point in the future that would magically make my life perfect. *Just wait until I'm eighteen and on my own. Just wait until I can leave Durango and start a new life.* But my life had started—right here next to the river on a chilly April day with Cody's hand in mine.

"So…are you going to help me or what?" he asked.

"Help you how?"

"I want to kiss you, but if you won't let me touch your face, I'm going to aim and miss and then get all embarrassed. You're going to have to kiss me first."

I took a moment to let his words sink in and summon my courage. I grabbed both his hands and placed them against my cheeks, against my scar.

"It's okay," I whispered as his fingertips traced the rippled, taut skin. Then I pressed my lips against his for the first time.

* * *

Mint. I tasted mint. "Oh my God," I whispered.

"Yeah, exactly."

"Not that. I mean, yes, the kiss was great, but I tasted you."

I pushed the hood off Cody's head, grabbed the back of his neck, and pulled him toward me. I was hungrier for this second kiss. A joyful, fearless kiss. Nothing else mattered but the softness of those lips, the way they parted and closed around mine, the delicate rush of breath.

He pulled away sooner than I wanted him to. "Whoa, whoa, whoa. What do you mean you tasted me?"

"Something minty." I leaned my forehead against his. "Can you believe it?"

"I had a peppermint Life Saver in the car. I was hoping…"

"Yeah. Me too."

I giggled. I hadn't giggled in… I couldn't remember how long. How could I suddenly taste again? Maybe the doctors had been right that it had all been in my head. Frank had researched brain chemistry and trauma. He'd found that our brains could induce changes in our physical bodies in reaction to both positive and negative events. If the fire had taken my senses away, maybe finally being this incredibly happy could bring them back.

"You should probably see if it was a fluke or if you can still taste me." He kissed me again slowly, then nipped at my bottom lip before pulling away.

"Yep, minty fresh," I whispered. "But we need to know for sure."

"Anything you want." He moved in for another kiss, but I pulled away.

"You mentioned you wanted to get a burger on the way home. Well, now I'm going to join you."

* * *

Mo's donkey laugh never sounded so good. To be able to

share my incredible news with my best friend was almost as good as Cody's kiss and the amazing burger and fries I'd eaten—well, almost.

"Holy shit, Arlie!"

"I know! I know!"

We jumped and twirled, our arms tangled in a celebratory dance. Only when we grew breathless did we drop to the grass, sucking in air as we continued to laugh.

"What do you want to eat next?" Mo asked. "Ice cream, maybe. Or something chocolate. Chocolate chip cookies! That's it."

"I'll explode if I eat another thing. I'm not worried this is a fluke. We have plenty of time to pig out together."

"Then tell me more about Cody."

Twirling around with Mo after eating a greasy burger upset my stomach. Kissing Cody definitely added to it. The physical symptoms of love were killer. My heart beat wildly, my head pounded, my gut twisted and churned.

I unbuttoned my jeans and laid my hands across my belly. "I feel sick. I can't take this stress."

"You've dealt with a lot more stress than this," Mo said. "Now tell me about the kiss."

"Kisses. Plural. And they defy description."

"Cop out."

Mo didn't press me further. She sensed when I needed to keep my world small. Giving Mo a play-by-play would feel like releasing dandelion fuzz into the wind. I'd never get back the magic of this second. Plus, she knew I'd confide in her later. We'd likely be lying on my bed in the dark, listening to our favorite music. She'd ask me to describe the moment over and over, and I'd oblige.

"You going to tell Frank?"

"Not yet. First, he needs to hear about my taste and smell coming back. And we probably need to talk about Lloyd. That problem won't go away just because I finally got the courage to kiss Cody."

I'd kissed Cody. It would take a while for that sink in. It wasn't something that needed analyzing now. I just wanted to feel the topsy-turvy, nausea-inducing joy that came from finally connecting with someone.

"Do you need a ride, or is Frank still insisting on picking you up?" Mo's grin couldn't get any wider and that somehow intensified my happiness.

"I'm meeting him by the ball fields. You go on," I said. "I promise we'll talk later."

After sharing something so important, it pained me to lie to Mo, but I had somewhere to go and I didn't want her to try to talk me out of it.

CHAPTER 22

I gave Mo a few minutes to exit the school parking lot before I jogged up to the bus stop and caught the North Main trolley to the Animas View Motel. I took the stairs two treads at time to Dora's second-floor room.

Breathless, I pounded on the door. She opened it, leaving the chain on until she recognized my face.

"Arlie? Is there anything wrong?"

"Nope. For the first time in a long while, something is very right." I didn't know at what point I had decided to tell Dora about Cody, but once the thought took hold, there was no going home before I did. Even if that meant defying Frank's edict that I not go anywhere alone until Lloyd was apprehended.

"You've got me curious. Come in," she said. "I don't think I've ever seen you smile so much."

"I have a couple of reasons to smile today. And I couldn't think of anyone I'd rather share the news with than you." The tremble in my voice surprised me. It *had* been a big day, one I now found difficult to describe. "It's all so crazy…it's going to sound crazy…"

"I'm an old woman. Spit it out before I grow any older."

"I can taste again…and I kissed a guy. Well, first I kissed him and then I could taste. Really he kissed me…well, technically we kissed each other." I was right; it sounded crazy, but I managed to convey the important details.

Dora brought her hands together in a loud clap. Her laughter bubbled over both of us.

"Oh, Arlie. I don't know what to be happier about."

When she hugged me, I lifted her off the ground. "You don't have to decide," I said. "I can't myself."

She asked for details, just as Mo had, but for some reason, I freely gave them to Dora when I hadn't to Mo. I explained about the choral group and being with Cody at the dance and my fear of letting him touch my scar.

"For a second I was afraid I wouldn't know how to kiss him correctly, but it didn't matter. It all happened so naturally, and once it was happening, I couldn't think at all."

"You let him touch your face!" She brought her own palms to her cheeks.

"I did."

"And it didn't kill you," she added. "And he didn't run away."

No, it hadn't and he hadn't.

Over the past few years, I'd fought off the advances of drug addicts; I'd counseled Mom about her choices in boyfriends; and I'd driven her to Planned Parenthood for two abortions. Sitting here with Dora, though, I gushed like any girl who'd just had her first kiss. She made it easier for me to feel like a normal kid, just as Rosa always had.

"And you can taste? How?"

"I wish I could tell you. As soon as our lips met, I tasted him.

I tasted mint. Maybe it doesn't matter how."

"That must've been some kiss." She winked. "I bet you're ready for a follow-up. Yes?"

I didn't mind her teasing. I welcomed it. Sitting with a woman I wished had been my mother or my grandmother. A woman I'd naturally share a milestone with, instead of sharing with a therapist or an uncle first. It occurred to me that even if Mom were still alive, I'd have probably gone to Dora first. Well, after Mo.

"I hope this means you'll be eating. A lot," Dora said. "All these years, I've worried so much that you didn't get enough to eat."

I hadn't become this thin on purpose. Eating truly had been torturous. Every day I'd had to pump myself up. "Eat to live," I'd say over and over again.

"I'm certain Mo is going to make me try anything and everything with chocolate in it," I said. "And I bet Frank will help me overdose on fried food."

"Eat a vegetable now and then, okay?"

My phone rang. I hated that someone was interrupting this joyful time with Dora. My stomach flipped when I saw that the number was Mo's.

"I have to take this," I said.

Dora motioned that she'd be outside having a smoke. I nodded and gestured that I'd be right out.

"Hey, what's up?" I asked.

"I could ask you the same," she said.

"I don't understand."

"I couldn't stand waiting until tonight to hear more about you and Cody, so I dropped by the trailer. You could imagine how surprised Frank was that you weren't with me."

"Oh, shit…"

"Yeah, that's an understatement."

"I can explain," I said.

"To me or to Frank?"

"To both."

"Well, I'm parked outside," she said. "I think I calmed down Frank enough that he won't kill you later."

I ended the call just as Dora walked back in. "Your friend is out in the parking lot. Were you expecting her?"

"Definitely not." I kissed Dora on the cheek and left.

* * *

I got in Mo's car. She made no move to start the engine.

"Frank's literally freaking out. I didn't realize the seriousness of your stepdad being in town until today. Why would you do something that could make Frank feel worse?"

I hadn't thought about his feelings. Only getting to Dora as quickly as I could. Especially since I'd ignored her for a while.

"I'm sorry. I wanted to tell Dora about Cody…about being able to taste again."

"Why is this woman even important to you? I thought you'd be glad to leave this all behind."

Anger replaced any remorse I felt for scaring Mo and Frank. I'd listened to both of them remind me over and over how great my new life was and how I should be more thankful that things had been different since Mom's death.

"You and Frank almost seem happy that she died…like it was my big break."

"I'm not happy she died, but I'd be lying if I said you weren't better off now."

Her words hit like a stinging slap. "Better off?"

"If she hadn't died, what would have happened? Would you have gone back to high school or met Cody? What about when you turned eighteen…would you have applied to college or stayed behind to continue taking care of her?"

I hated that I knew the answers and I hated Mo for knowing them too. Tears traced my cheeks. She reached over and wiped them as they dropped off my chin.

"It's been hard being your friend." Mo looked out the windshield. Her chin quivered as she spoke. "I worried about you every day. Worried that you lived in a motel and didn't go to school. Worried that one of your mom's friends might hurt you, but when Frank arrived, I could breathe again. And it felt great. I'm not sorry for that."

"Then why didn't you stop being my friend?"

"That's not how friendship works, dummy. I thought you were interesting and smart and real. I wanted to hang out with you. I still do."

Through the years I'd often thought of myself as Mo's charity case—a pet project to keep her occupied, or even a surrogate sister since hers had died so young. I rarely allowed myself to think I brought something to our relationship.

"Do you know what today meant to me?" she asked. "I experienced the same mind-blowing joy you did when you got your taste back. And I got to be the first one to hear about you and Cody kissing. I almost cried that you let yourself be loved."

"Cody doesn't—"

"Shut up, Arlie. Yes, he does. That's how it works. You feel sick at your stomach not knowing, guessing, hoping. Then the person you love—yes, that *you* love—admits he feels the same."

"Love, huh? If you don't stop talking, I'm not going to be able to stop crying."

Mo released her seat belt and leaned across for a hug. "You made me cry too."

I swiped at my face and managed a smile. "I want you to understand that I love Dora too. Today wouldn't have felt as real if I didn't tell her."

"I guess I understand," Mo said, refastening her seat belt. "You just have to make your uncle understand."

CHAPTER 23
FIVE MONTHS AGO—ESCAPE

The bus station in Durango was sandwiched between a junk shop and a liquor store. The narrow building held only a ticket counter and one bench, so I waited outside on the curb.

"Spare some money for a fellow traveler?" The old man reeked of beer and he'd pissed on the front of his pants.

"Do I look like I have any money?" I pulled my backpack closer to my chest, although he was probably too drunk to cause me trouble. When he walked away, I breathed a sigh of relief.

I'd raked leaves in three yards to earn enough for the bus ride to Albuquerque. I would have to save the rest of my cash for food until I could find my dad.

The Sonic Drive-In directly across from the station was busy for a weekday afternoon. I hadn't eaten anything in a while, but I wasn't about to spend that much money on something I couldn't taste.

Instead I stared at the guy on the edge of the road who was about to play Frogger with the traffic. He looked in both directions a number of times before sprinting across.

He placed his fountain drink and bag of food on the ground next to me and then shrugged off the overstuffed army duffel he had strapped to his back.

"Impressive," I said. "Especially with that load."

"Nah, just lucky."

He had smooth, tan skin and wore his hair in one long, black braid like Lloyd used to sometimes. He could've been fourteen or twenty-four.

"Headed to ABQ?" he asked.

"Yep. You?"

He jammed two-thirds of a corn dog in his mouth and nodded.

"Name's J. R." He held out his hand. "You headed home for the Thanksgiving break too?"

"Sort of," I said. "My dad's in Albuquerque."

I didn't know that for certain, but saying it to another person made it feel real. I appreciated that J. R. didn't press for my name.

"My folks live in Bernalillo. Haven't seen 'em since August so I figured I better make an appearance."

"Do you go to college?" I asked.

"Yeah. Second year at Fort Lewis," he said. "You?"

"I'm not in school." I didn't bother to specify high school.

From my backpack, I pulled out a small paperback of Allen Ginsberg poems Mo had given me. I read while J. R. finished eating.

"Mind if I ask about that?" He pointed to his own cheek but meant my scar.

"Happened a long time ago."

I didn't offer any other details and he didn't probe further. He slurped on his drink while I continued reading.

Late November and it hadn't snowed once. I didn't mind. The drought and above-normal temps meant I wouldn't freeze in Albuquerque if I couldn't find a place to sleep. If I got desperate, I'd go to the women's shelter. I could pass for eighteen and an adult. Mom and I had gone there a few times after she'd broken up with Lloyd. We never stayed long because they required a sobriety pledge that Mom always ended up breaking.

If I got really desperate, I could call one of Rosa's daughters and hope they didn't still hate me because of how she died.

Yesterday, Mo and her parents had driven to Denver to visit her grandparents for Thanksgiving. I used Mom as the excuse why I couldn't tag along. By then, I'd already decided to leave Durango. With Mo gone, the decision became less complicated. And it wasn't like I'd never see her again. Plus, Dora would take care of Mom.

If I could find my real dad, I could convince him to help Mom get clean. He was my last hope. In the past month, Mom had been high more often than not. She'd all but stopped eating.

"Hey." J. R. touched my arm. "I think that lady's trying to get your attention."

Mom had parked our Subaru on a side street behind the liquor store, almost out of view. She stood by the driver's side door, waving at me to come over.

"Damn it," I mumbled.

"Not someone you want to see?" he asked.

"Not today. No."

I stood up and grabbed my backpack.

"Enjoy Turkey Day with your family," I said. "And don't rely on luck when crossing busy streets."

J. R. laughed. "Will do."

I walked over to the car and threw my pack in the backseat before joining Mom in the front. She didn't start the car but lit a cigarette instead.

"How'd you know I'd be here?" I asked.

"All your things were gone. You weren't at your little friend's place, so I figured you might be skipping town."

"Her name is Mo. And you promised you'd never go back to her house."

Mom's hand shook as she brought the cigarette to her lips. They were cracked and peeling, as if every bit of moisture had deserted her.

I propped my feet on the dashboard and stared at J. R. as he waited for the bus. I pictured him arriving at his own house later today, his mom and dad hugging him. What smells would be coming from the kitchen? Maybe pumpkin pie or homemade bread or fresh tortillas? I couldn't guess what those things would smell like, but it fleshed out my idea of a holiday homecoming. I wondered if he had a grandmother who looked like Rosa. Would they have turkey or ham tomorrow, or both?

"You promised you'd never leave me." Mom's shaking grew worse. If I thought she could control it, I'd have screamed at her to be still just for one goddamn minute.

"You and I break promises all the time," I said. "Roll down your window a bit, would you?" While the smell couldn't bother me, I was tired of Mo saying my clothes always reeked.

Mom ignored my request and took another drag.

"I'm doing the best I can," she said.

The car filled with smoke. I stayed silent because I didn't feel like small talk.

"I got a job," she said.

No one in his right mind would hire my mother. "Yeah, where?"

"The motel. I'll be helping the housekeeper strip and wash linens some mornings. In exchange for rent. Dora convinced the manager."

For a very brief moment, I felt hope. It was a queer feeling in my stomach, almost like butterflies, that I'd experienced more often as a kid. As I got older, I only felt foolish for thinking things could be different. Here I was, sixteen, and I still hadn't learned.

We sat for a long time—long enough for the Greyhound to pick up a handful of passengers and leave the station. J. R. waved and I placed my palm against my window.

"Your dad's not in Albuquerque," she said.

"I didn't think he was."

Deep down, I knew how foolish it was to pack up and head to a city of eight hundred thousand people to find a man who may not even exist. Maybe this was just my exit strategy and I'd broken my promise to Mom after all. I did want to leave.

Mom continued smoking until the cigarette was just a nub. They were too expensive to waste.

"He wasn't worth knowing," she said.

"Then why was he worth sleeping with?"

At least she knew who my father was. It made me ill to think I was the random outcome of one-night stands with strangers.

"I never regretted having you. That's why I had to get you away from the foster home," she said.

If she dared to cry, I was going to walk home. I'd just wasted fifty-nine bucks on a bus ticket that was now worthless, and I wasn't in the mood to make her feel better about herself.

"Tomorrow we're going to the community Thanksgiving dinner with Dora," I said.

"That's for poor people."

"Anyone can go. And we're going."

Mom started the car and pulled into traffic.

"I don't see why. You won't taste a thing anyway," she said.

I didn't care. Like Mo in Denver and J. R. in Bernalillo, we were going to be like any other family on that day—eating turkey and dressing and pumpkin pie until we thought we'd burst.

"And you're not getting high before we go," I added.

Mom didn't say another word the whole way back to the motel.

CHAPTER 24

After confronting me at Dora's, Mo drove us straight back to the trailer so I could apologize to Frank. As we pulled up to the curb, she pointed out the dark sedan parked at the end of the block. The threat from Lloyd was real if the police were watching the trailer. Frank waited on the picnic table until I got out of Mo's car. Then he took three long strides and wrapped his arms around me.

"I'm glad you're okay." His whispered words were hot on my neck.

"I know you're angry..."

"Yeah, but I'm trying not to be."

He let his arms drop so I stepped back.

"I was at Dora's."

"Mo suspected that. She called me once she found you there. She asked me to quote 'chill' while she talked to you."

Mo's mediation tactic made me smile.

"I had to tell Dora...something important."

"Mo told me you had a big day. Let's go inside."

I took one last look at the police officer before following Frank in. We both sat on the sofa. I kicked off my sneakers and rubbed my bare feet against the worn nap of the carpet.

"Dora doesn't use drugs." I wanted to ease any suspicions he might have.

"Mo told me. She said Dora's special to you."

"So, you know everything that happened today?" The knot in my throat almost cut off my air. What had Mo shared?

"Yeah...she said you guys were having lunch off campus. That she convinced you to have a burger and that your sense of taste came back. Just like that. *Bam*. No warning."

"That's it?"

"Isn't that enough? It's incredible," he said.

"Yep, incredible. I never tasted anything so good."

Mo hadn't mentioned Cody. Thank God I didn't have to talk about that on top of everything else.

"I guess I understand why you wanted to tell Dora the good news first." Disappointment flashed across his face.

"It wasn't like that, Frank. I just thought I'd stop by there on the way home from school. I didn't ask Mo to take me there because she's not exactly fond of Dora. Or, rather, the life she thinks Dora represents."

Although it made me love Mo even more that she'd gone out on a limb to convince Frank that I had my heart in the right place, even if my brain wasn't engaged.

"No, I get it. I really do," Frank said. "But we don't know if your stepfather is still around. I thought I made it clear that I didn't want you going anywhere alone. Is that so hard to understand?"

I twisted a loose of piece of yarn from the afghan thrown over the sofa's arm. "No, it's not. I'm really sorry."

"You could've texted me...I mean, after lunch," he said.

"I know, but I wanted to tell you in person." I couldn't believe that Frank wasn't reaming me out. I had braced for the worst. As the adrenaline wore off, I slumped into the sofa cushions. I'd never felt so physically and emotionally exhausted at the same time.

Frank got up and started rummaging around the kitchen cabinets. "Well, this means you've got to have something special for dinner."

"It's okay. I'm really not hungry."

"Let's go out. No expense spared. Maybe I should change into something nicer." He smoothed his wrinkled shirt.

"I'd rather stay in. I'm pretty wrung out." I also wanted to stay home in case Cody texted or called. Or if I got the courage to call him.

"Coke and chips, then?"

I nodded. "Absolutely."

* * *

A long swallow of Coke softened the chips I'd stuffed in my mouth. I couldn't get enough of their saltiness and the tang of vinegar. "This is better than the burger and fries."

"Sometimes it's the simple stuff that's best." Frank opened a second bag and handed it to me. "Just don't make yourself sick. Take baby steps...er, I mean baby bites."

We laughed comfortably as if junk food could wipe out Lloyd's existence.

"How could I not remember how Coke tasted?" I asked.

"It's so damn good, it's addictive," he said. "So watch out."

My smile faded at the mention of addiction even though he didn't mean anything by it.

"I just don't get what changed today," Frank said, oblivious to my mood change. "It's so weird. After all this time."

"Maybe the docs were right. It was all in my head."

"I know, but what happened today specifically," he mused. "Do you think talking to the police about Lloyd set you off? Were you especially emotional after I dropped you back at school?"

Emotional. Yeah, but not because of Lloyd. My heart raced as I replayed the kiss over and over in my mind. What would Cody taste like the next time I kissed him?

"I didn't feel any different today. Does it matter why?" I shouldn't have snapped, but I didn't want to share the real reason with him. At least not yet.

"Of course not. Sorry. Let's not look a gift horse in the mouth."

"Gift horse?"

"Never mind. It's an old-person thing." Frank laughed deep and low. He seemed as happy as I was to have those senses back.

"Hey, we should try making your grandma's pralines," I said, changing the subject. "That way I could taste one of your memories."

"You give me way too much credit in the kitchen. Stir-frying is the extent of my culinary talent."

I'd eaten dozens of his stir-fries, choking down the rice and ignoring the sliminess of overcooked broccoli and green pepper.

"Hey, don't be too sure it's a talent until I actually taste one," I said.

Frank grabbed the open bag of chips from my hand. "Enough of the junk food. Let me make us some real food."

I couldn't eat another thing. My belly roiled from the burger and fries, and now the greasiness of chips. "*No más, por favor.* I'm about to bust."

"Didn't know you could speak *español*."

"I can't really. I picked up some from Rosa."

Memories of my old friend had stayed fresh in my mind all these years. Unconditional love cemented them so they couldn't fade with time and distance. Rosa had allowed me to be a kid. Mom had loved me, but she wasn't the adult I needed. And Rosa gave the best hugs, rivaled only by Mo's.

"The bastard will pay for killing your friend and for hurting you. It won't be long before the police grab him. I'd put money on it."

Frank was either extremely confident or a fabulous actor. Still, his assurances squelched some of the rising panic I felt. We had no idea where Lloyd was, but he knew exactly where we lived. He had the advantage.

* * *

After overdoing it with the chips, I hoped lying down would help. It didn't. All I wanted was to fall asleep and not wake up until tomorrow, which couldn't be as mind-blowing and exhausting as today.

"You okay in there? Need some Pepto-Bismol?" Frank was having too much fun at my expense.

"Your concern is heartwarming, but I think I'll live."

Frank opened the door to my room, grinning like an idiot. When he sat down on the edge of the bed, my stomach heaved with the motion. "I'm going to pick up some tacos for dinner. Get up. You're coming with me. We can bike over for some exercise."

"Watch it or I'll barf all over you."

"Not like it'd be the first time. Oh, and you'll really like that smell and taste."

"I'm glad you're in a better mood," I said.

"How can I not be happy for you?" He leaned over and planted a fatherly kiss on my forehead.

"I'm happy for me too, but I feel like crap and don't want to go out. I'll be fine alone. Plus, the police have eyes on the trailer."

"Yeah, but..."

"Frank, get on your bike and get your damn tacos. You can't watch me twenty-four seven."

He got up and walked into the living room, returning immediately with the fake Bible. He placed it on the nightstand.

"Don't open the door for anyone. I'll be back in fifteen minutes tops."

As soon as Frank shut the front door of the trailer, I opened the Bible and withdrew the gun hidden inside. My attempts to hit a target at the range had been worse than pathetic. Frank's advice was that if I found myself in danger, I should keep shooting until there were no bullets left. I guess that method would improve my odds of stopping someone, but stop them from doing what?

Part of me wished I'd gone with him to get tacos. My skin prickled as I strained to hear anything but the silence of the trailer. Would the front door hold if someone really wanted in?

Get a grip. You're freaking yourself out.

I laid the gun on the bed beside me and opened my laptop to watch a sitcom on Hulu. Maybe a little humor would calm my nerves. It didn't. Instead, I obsessed on how thin my bedroom curtains were. Earlier, I'd stripped down to my sports bra and some pajama bottoms, but now I was self-conscious. At night, I couldn't see out, but anyone could see in if they stood in our yard. I turned off the lamp and closed the laptop, feeling more at ease in the dark.

My eyes were slow to adjust, but it still seemed unusually dark. Why weren't the streetlights on? Usually their light streamed into my room so that I had to sleep with the covers over my head. An odd sensation of vertigo took hold. The dizziness in my head teased the queasiness in my gut. I stumbled from my room and into the restroom. I flicked on the light and lifted the toilet lid just in time. Heaving and heaving, I emptied the contents of my stomach. My throat and nose burned from all the soda I'd consumed before.

The tiny bathroom left little space to sit on the floor, much less stretch out my legs. I stood and rinsed my face with cold water. When the vertigo passed, I leaned over the sink, cupping my hands beneath the water. I swished the sour taste from my mouth. Frank was right. Not something I wanted to taste or smell again.

I turned off the light before making my way to the living room. Those windows had mini blinds that could be closed tight.

Frank would have a field day with my paranoia. I smiled to think of how he'd tease me when he got home and found me in the dark. From the sound of it, he was already in the front yard, chaining up his bicycle.

I pulled the blinds back to peer outside. The police car was gone.

Something clanged against the metal side of the trailer. I lost my balance and knocked over a pile of Frank's books, landing on the sofa.

Another clang and then a heavy thud sent me scuttling back to the bedroom to get the gun. The trailer had only one entrance, both a good and a bad thing. No one could sneak in a back way, but I couldn't escape either. If I exited through the front door, I'd be on full display and less safe than if I just stayed inside.

Before I could formulate my next move, a huge thud rocked the trailer.

"You're going to pay, you son of a bitch." Frank's booming voice overshadowed another male voice, a weaker one that kept shouting, "*Stop! Stop!*"

I ran through the dark trailer, not caring as I bumped into the kitchen counters. I fumbled with the lock on the front door with one hand. The other gripped Frank's gun.

Once outside, I aimed at the two men rolling on the ground. "I swear to God I'll shoot!"

I recognized the broad-shouldered man on top as Frank. He rolled away from the scuffle at the sound of my voice. The man who had been on the bottom curled into a ball.

"Put down the gun, Arlie! Put it down. *Now!*" Frank approached the figure on the ground but with outstretched arms.

"Aw, man, I'm so sorry," he said. "I didn't recognize you." He put his arm around the other man and lifted him to his feet. Even in the darkness, I could make out that the man was considerably smaller than Frank.

"What's going on?" I cried out.

"It's your friend from choir."

* * *

Frank helped Cody to the sofa in the trailer's living room, then went into the kitchen to fill a plastic freezer bag with ice.

"Where are you hurt?" I helped Cody pull off his hooded sweatshirt. He winced as the shirt came over his head.

"I'm okay, really."

I held his chin tentatively, moving his face from side to side. No bruises there. I flashed back to the times when Mom came back to the motel room after a long night, her face or arms darkened by someone obviously stronger than her.

"You don't seem okay," I said, shaking off the memory. "What hurts?"

"Frank got in a few good punches to my rib cage and shoulder, but I covered my head. I'm a born fighter." Cody's lightheartedness did nothing to assuage Frank, who grimaced with remorse.

"I thought you were Arlie's stepfather." Frank rubbed his forehead. "It was so dark, and you were creeping along the side of the trailer."

"My brother was running a quick errand on this side of town so I asked him to drop me off. I'm sorry. I tried texting Arlie, but she didn't answer."

Cody took my hand. The move wasn't lost on Frank. His eyes narrowed as he cocked his head to one side.

I shook my head and mouthed, "Not now."

"I used the side of the trailer to guide me to the front door," Cody continued. "I remembered Arlie saying the ground near the construction site was uneven. I didn't want to fall and hurt myself."

I chuckled at the irony.

"We should take you to the ER," Frank said.

"I'll be fine, Mr. Betts. Really."

"It's Frank. Just Frank. We should be on a first-name basis considering I just tried to break all your ribs."

My uncle allowed himself a small smile before becoming serious again. "I'm putting up motion-detecting lights tomorrow morning first thing. And I'm going to give the city hell about the streetlights being out."

I nodded my head toward the door, hoping Frank would leave us alone for a bit.

He narrowed his eyes once again, but complied with my pantomimed request. "I dropped a bag of tacos outside when I lunged for Cody. I'm going to go find my supper before the raccoons do."

As soon as the door closed, I hugged Cody.

"Hey, watch the shoulder," he said. "Your uncle should've been a MMA fighter. I think he kicked me a few times."

"Yeah, that stumpy physique was made for mixed martial arts."

I scanned Cody's body again. He was gritting his teeth. "You're not fine. I can tell."

"I will be…in a few days." He extended his left arm and moved it in a large circle. His shoulder popped and he winced through his smile.

"It's not funny." I placed the bag of ice on his shoulder.

"You can't blame Frank. It was an honest mistake, considering how worried you are about your stepfather being in town."

"Worried is an understatement." We both sank into the back of the sofa. I ran my hand through his hair and then let it rest on his uninjured shoulder. "Now he'll never leave my side. I'm going to be a prisoner in this place."

"Did you really have a gun?"

"Yes. And I could've killed you." My body shook, trying to release the earlier adrenaline overload.

Cody leaned toward me so that I met his lips. I shuddered when he brushed them against my chin and nose. He pressed his forehead against mine and cupped my face in his hands.

"I don't like that you have a gun," he said. "There are other ways for you to be safe."

"I feel safe with you."

"A blind guy doesn't offer much protection."

I pulled away, taking his hands in mine.

"My *heart* feels safe with you," I said.

A loud rap on the door interrupted our next kiss. Frank walked inside, the crumpled taco bag in one hand. He wiped his mouth with the back of his sleeve. "Your brother's waiting outside. I told him what happened. He was good enough not to kick my ass for hurting his little brother."

"I'll walk him to the car," I said.

"Sit tight. I got this." Frank helped Cody from the sofa.

"I'll see you in school tomorrow?" he asked, looking back in my direction.

"Yes. See you then."

* * *

As instructed, I sat still, waiting for Frank. If I played the events of the day over in my mind one more time, I'd go certifiably crazy. I longed for a bathtub filled to the rim with scalding hot water. When I lived with Mom in the motel, I'd often submerge myself so my ears would be underwater, canceling out any noise from the TV or the neighboring rooms. The trailer didn't have a tub—just a dark, cramped shower that Frank could barely turn around in. Maybe I could stay over at Mo's soon and use her parents' huge sunken tub. I missed those times we'd play in the tub until the bathwater went cold or ended up all over the floor.

"Wake up, Arlie."

Frank walked in to find me with my eyes closed, daydreaming of an escape from our inevitable talk.

"I'm resting my eyes. Everything okay?"

He sloughed off his plaid shirt and handed it to me. "Here, put this on. You're half naked."

"My sports bra has more fabric than a bikini top."

"It's not appropriate attire for when that kid is here."

Frank sat down next to me. His T-shirt rode up his belly so that he had to keep pulling it down.

"Cody's blind. And I wasn't exactly expecting company," I said.

"He can still use his hands."

"Jesus, Frank. Why are you so down on Cody?" I pulled his shirt tighter and crossed my arms. "What has he done to upset you?"

"Nothing. I'm just…Tonight could have ended badly. I wanted to keep punching and punching until there was nothing left of him. Lloyd, I mean."

"But you did stop. And Cody will be fine."

"The police have to find your stepfather. I can't bear the thought of you in danger."

"Speaking of police, why weren't they here earlier?" I asked.

"They're back now. The squad car pulled up when I was talking to Cody's brother. They said it was a shift change, but they'd been delayed by a bad traffic accident. Great timing, huh?"

I walked over to the fridge and grabbed a beer. I twisted off the top and handed it to Frank.

"Here, you need this."

He motioned for me to sit down next to him. He took a long draw and then set the beer on the floor.

"So, you and Cody. Are you together or something?" Frank picked up the beer again and nearly downed the rest of it.

"Yeah," I said. "We're together…or something."

"It's the 'something' part that has me worried," he said.

"It's not like that. We only kissed for the first time today." *Where was my filter?*

"Kissed, huh? Was that before or after you got your taste back?"

I turned purple and didn't offer any details.

"Well, he seems to have fallen pretty hard for you," Frank said.

"Why do you say that?"

"His brother, James, told me. Said you're all Cody has talked about since you started school."

My stomach somersaulted again. Thank goodness it was empty so there wouldn't be a repeat of my earlier retching.

"You have a goofy grin on your face," Frank said.

"Do not."

"Do so."

I pinched my lips together with my thumb and forefinger, but burst out laughing.

"I like him, Frank."

"Really? I couldn't tell."

I punched my uncle in the gut that still peeked from beneath his tee.

"I need another beer and we both could use some sleep. How about we talk more tomorrow?"

I nodded and made my way to the bedroom, then turned and faced Frank again. "He's a good guy, you know."

"Yeah, yeah." He dismissed me with a wave.

CHAPTER 25

Even though Cody could navigate from class to class on his own, he often allowed friends to help him. It was faster because they could blast through the throng of students. Claire was today's guide. She now sported a purple stripe in her hair in place of the pink one. I wondered how often she changed the color.

"Hey, Arlie. This guy wouldn't stop bugging me until we found you. He's all yours now." She winked. I hoped it meant she approved of me.

"Claire knows about us?" I asked.

Cody looped his hand in my elbow and I led him down the hall toward English.

"She knew about us before I even knew about us."

"What do you mean?"

"Claire guessed right away that I was interested in you. She wouldn't let up until I promised I'd let you know my feelings. She was at Magpie's when I was buying our smoothies. You know, the day I met you at the bus stop."

"Do you think I could forget that day?"

We walked a short distance before Cody asked me to stop. "About last night..."

"Frank still feels terrible," I said. "How do you feel?"

"Scared. For you." He moved so close that I felt his breath.

"Peppermint again? Isn't that a bit obvious?"

Cody pressed me against the locker closest to us. His aim was off and he connected with my chin first. Then, his lips opened slightly and our tongues met. I could've stayed lost in that moment except for the crowd of students that hooted and whistled its approval.

"No public displays of affection in the hallways," I reminded him.

"You going to turn me in to the principal's office?"

"Not a chance," I said and kissed him again.

* * *

Mo caught up with me at lunch. It'd been less than twenty-four hours since we last spoke, but it felt like a week. I gave her all the details about Frank's boxing round with Cody.

"I'm sorry I didn't text last night. After Cody left, I fell into a dead sleep. Frank had to shake me awake this morning."

"It wouldn't have mattered. I lost my damn phone," she said. "Mom is so pissed. She spent the better part of the evening harping about how I should be more responsible at my age. That she expected more of me. Whatever."

The metal picnic table soaked up the midday sun. Lying against the warmth of the bench, I fought to stay awake. Mo lay on the other bench. She reached across to hold my hand beneath the table.

"Sorry about your mom," I said.

"I'm okay. It's you I'm worried about."

"Everyone is worried about me these days," I said. "It's both heartwarming and annoying as hell."

I let her hand drop and placed my arm over my eyes and scar to shield them from the sun.

"I agree with Cody that you shouldn't have the gun. It could do more harm than good. What do you think your stepdad wants?"

I couldn't answer her question. He'd said very little to Frank before that sledgehammer persuaded him to leave.

"I almost want to get it over with...just hear what he's come to say," I said.

"Oh, hell no." Mo swung her legs around and sat up. "We've already been over this. The best thing is for the police to pick him up. *They* can ask him what he wants."

"He's made a career of avoiding the police. I have a feeling he won't trip up."

"Well, it's still not a good idea for you to offer yourself as bait. Let the police protect you."

If Mom were still alive and suspected Lloyd was in town, we'd have packed our bags and gotten the hell out of Dodge. We had an unspoken agreement that running meant safety. But I didn't want to run. Safety meant something completely different to me now. I wanted to stay in Durango. With Mo and Frank. With Cody.

Why wasn't I more afraid? Maybe my brain had somehow reshaped the fear into something manageable—something existing only in the shadows, a boogeyman who hadn't yet stepped into the light.

* * *

When I arrived home from school, Frank was in the front yard lounging in a camp chair, sunglasses shading his eyes. He wore shorts and sandals even though the high was only sixty degrees.

"Hey, not working on the house?" I asked.

"Everyone deserves a day off now and then."

The curtness of his answer made the hairs on my neck stand.

"I agree. You've been working too hard. Maybe tomorrow I'll play hooky with you." The smile I hoped for never came.

I sat on the ground next to Frank's chair so I wouldn't block the sun.

"They found the Mustang," he said. "It'd been parked in the Hermosa Creek campground and set on fire."

"So Lloyd gave up his sweet ride. He doesn't strike me as the type to take public transportation," I said.

"This isn't funny."

"Am I smiling? Tell me why you're in such a funky mood."

Frank motioned for me to follow him into the trailer. Once inside, he pointed to the table in the kitchenette. On it sat Mom's suitcase and the green plastic tackle box she kept her cosmetics in. The small red suitcase, faded and scuffed, was missing its handle and one wheel. It was always light enough to carry tucked under one arm though.

"The police brought this stuff by today. They said they should've returned her personal effects sooner. Especially since your mom's death was ruled accidental."

Personal effects? Evidence, more like it. They never even considered another theory. *Meth addict commits suicide or overdoses accidentally. Either way, who cares? Case closed.*

"Did you look inside?" I asked.

"Nah. Not my place."

I retrieved a pencil from the kitchen drawer and used it to fasten my hair into a bun. Then I sat down at the table and opened the suitcase.

"You want me to leave?" Frank asked.

I touched his hand. "Stay. I'd like you to."

Mom's clothes looked both familiar and foreign. Small, almost child-sized shirts and tees. Faded jeans. Bras and panties in bright colors and animal prints.

Frank's cheeks colored when I pulled a leopard-print bra from the suitcase's zippered, mesh compartment. I tucked it under the clothes. No brother wants to see his own sister's underwear.

"She shoplifted clothes from Walmart mostly," I admitted. "She liked pretty underthings. Said they made her happy."

Happy wasn't something I associated with Mom. I'd never seen anyone exude sadness like she could. The weight of her own life seemed to crush her—and me by proxy. That's why I could never judge her for stealing. Any relief from sadness was welcome, even with the threat of jail time if she got caught.

Frank shifted in his chair. He looked like he wanted to ask me something.

"The thrift stores have voucher programs for women and children staying at the shelter. I got my clothes for free," I said.

"I didn't think you'd shoplifted. I was thinking that I wished it'd been different for you growing up."

My uncle stated that wish over and over. He wanted so badly to rewrite history. What he saw as horrific was just my idea of normal. It had to be, but then again, he had to deal with the misplaced guilt that he hadn't helped his sister, that he hadn't known about me.

"Things are different now, Frank. The past is the past."

"I know, I know. I just..."

My focus now was on my mom's things, not Frank. I removed

each article of clothing, refolded it neatly, and added it to the growing stack on the table. At the bottom of the suitcase lay a pocket-sized spiral notebook. Its pages were warped and water-stained as if it'd taken an unintentional swim at some point.

"What's that?" Frank asked.

I didn't know. I'd helped her pack and repack many times over the years but never ran across the notebook. I opened it. The scribbles were almost illegible. Names, phone numbers, but also nonsensical phrases. Had she been writing poetry or was she just rambling during a high?

I handed it to Frank. He flipped through the pages slowly, rubbing his beard from time to time. "I don't understand... seems like gibberish." He handed it back to me.

What she'd written on the notebook's cover caught my attention:

Ask Dora. She'll know what to do.

Know what to do? About what? I placed the notebook in my backpack and made a mental note to ask Dora what Mom could've meant.

"I'll bring the suitcase and clothes to the thrift store later this week," I said. "I don't need any of these things to remember Mom."

Frank gingerly placed all the clothes back in the case and closed it. "I can do it."

"I *want* to." I snatched the suitcase from the table and placed it in my room before returning.

"And this?" Frank pointed to the tackle box.

"Makeup, fingernail polish. We can toss it."

"Don't you want to look?"

"Not really."

We stood looking at each other. "Well, do you mind if I do?"

"Be my guest."

I leaned up against the kitchen counter and chewed on a hangnail while Frank rummaged through the contents.

"There's jewelry."

"It's not real," I said. "Completely worthless."

Frank turned away from the tackle box. "You're upset. What's up?"

I shrugged.

"Not an answer," he said. "Tell me what's wrong."

"Do we have to do this?" My tears were searing. I hated the police for bringing back these pieces of my mother's short life and the memories that the cheap cosmetics brought up for me.

"I'm only trying to help." Frank moved toward me, but I pushed him back.

"I don't need help. I need to be left alone."

"That's the last thing you need." He easily restrained my arms and pressed me against his chest. I buried my face in the soft nap of his flannel shirt that smelled of sun and sweat. Between sobs, I cursed the afternoons I painted Mom's face, giving her a vulgar new identity that made it easier to sell her body for grocery money.

"You both made choices so you could survive," Frank whispered. "You did the best you could."

I wanted to remember Mom teaching me to ride a bike or frosting sugar cookies at Christmas or helping me pick out school supplies, but those memories belonged to other daughters and mothers. They'd never be mine.

Frank used the cuff of his sleeve to wipe my face. "Why don't you lie down for a while before dinner?"

"Yep. Sorry. You'd think I'd be done with tears by now." I blew strands of hair out of my eyes.

"Arlie, we're never done with tears. We can just hope laughter balances them out over time."

Even though I said I didn't want the tackle box, I closed it and took it with me to my room. There I opened it and took great care to sort the items in the trays: eye shadows, lipsticks, eyeliners, various colors of mascara. Without thinking, I dumped it all back on the bed and started making piles of different color combinations that would work together. Each pile had an eye-shadow trio and liner, with lipstick, nail polish, and coordinating blush.

I'd painted Mom's face and nails with these palettes time and time again. Each time, I'd wait anxiously for her reaction. Her smile was always my reward. Sometimes, she encouraged me to try wild combinations, but I took my job seriously and wanted her to look nice.

When I was much younger, I believed her when she said I could be a makeup artist for celebrities and movie stars when I grew up. That's when I still believed anything she told me.

* * *

I leaned in the doorway, watching Frank chop onions. Even standing a couple of feet away didn't protect me from their pungency. My eyes watered, but I didn't mind. Now that my taste buds cooperated, I looked forward to trying different spices and flavors.

"Wait until I add the garlic." Frank winked and added the onions to a pan of sautéed Italian sausage.

"It smells so good. What have I been missing?"

"I can't even begin to tell you. I'm a little jealous though.

Every food you try will be a new experience."

"Don't be too jealous," I said. "I'll become a food snob and expect everything to taste phenomenal. You won't be able to stand the pressure."

Frank and I laughed. It amazed me that we could experience such pain going through Mom's belongings, then two hours later such lightheartedness. Our brains were friggin' remarkable.

"I expect you to start cooking some meals now. I don't mind if you experiment. Might be fun to see what you come up with."

While Frank worked on the sauce, I filled a pot with water and put it on the stove to boil. I'd break it to him later that my idea of cooking was anything that could be heated up in a motel microwave.

The cramped kitchenette didn't hinder us as we pulled together a simple meal of Italian sausage with whole wheat pasta and garlic bread. I consciously breathed in the aromas, noticing that they came together perfectly. We spoke only a handful of words as we ate. Mostly I just grunted with my mouth full. I was going to need larger jeans before long.

"I guess I should've made a double batch," Frank teased. "With enough time and training, you could qualify for competitive eating."

I threw my paper napkin at him, but it drifted harmlessly to the table. "I'm sure I'll slow down…some day."

The rest of the evening passed quickly. Frank read the paper and I watched a TV show on my laptop. Despite the number of times he looked over my shoulder, he wasn't convinced he should buy us a television. As the episode neared its end, I jumped up and headed back to my room.

"Hey! I want to know what happens," Frank called out.

I smiled and shut my door. The odds of getting a TV were looking better and better.

* * *

Back in my room, I pulled out Mom's spiral notebook and reread its contents. Nothing made sense except the phone numbers. I couldn't make heads or tails of what she wrote, but I did wonder what she meant by "Dora will know what to do." I wrapped a rubber band around the notebook and tucked it under my mattress. I was too tired to figure out anything.

When my phone beeped, I lunged for my backpack to retrieve it. Since Mo had lost her iPhone, it had to be Cody.

Urgant. Need to meet you in the a.m. Dennys. Back tabel. 7:30.

Weird. The message was from Mo, but Mo had never misspelled a word in her life. Even in texts.

Glad you found your phone. What's so important? I texted back.

Talk in person. Just you.

Pick me up? I asked.

Can't. Just meet there.

I texted xxoo, but she never texted back. I reread her message over and over, and grew more anxious with each reading. Mo had seemed fine earlier at school. Maybe a little pissed that her mom had scolded her for losing her phone, but now that she'd found it, they couldn't still be fighting. And why would she ask me to come alone? Who else would I bring?

I dialed her number, but it went to voice mail.

Something was very wrong. I had to see her. Tonight. I went to the living room to ask Frank to drive me, but he was already fast asleep, the newspaper blanketing his belly.

It would have to wait until morning after all.

CHAPTER 26

Even though I sprinted to the bus stop, I barely caught the trolley that would take me downtown. Out of breath, I used the short ride to calm my aching lungs. I couldn't shake the bad feeling that Mo was in trouble. Nothing about her message last night made sense.

Once the trolley stopped, I pushed past the other passengers and hurried into the restaurant. Sherri, the hostess, recognized me as soon as I walked in.

"Hey, Arl. Where's your best girlfriend? Better yet, why are you here on a school day?" She looked at her watch and then at the large clock on the wall.

"Mo's meeting me. She should be here by now. In the back."

I craned my head around the diners seated at the counter but couldn't see the far corner of the restaurant.

"The only one back there is some creepy guy who won't take off his sunglasses. Asshole. Let me find you girls another table."

Some creepy guy. My confusion over last night's texts began to lift.

"Hon? You don't look well." Sherri put a motherly hand to my forehead.

"I'm… I'll be okay. I think I know that guy. Let me see what's up." I did a crappy job of steadying my voice, but Sherri seemed to believe my lie.

"Shall I bring you some coffee then?"

"No. No, I'll wait for the waitress. Thanks though."

Sherri went about her job, but my sneakers stayed glued to the floor. This couldn't be happening. Why would Lloyd want to meet me in a public place? Only when Sherri looked back at me with worried eyes did I finally move.

I'd never taken so long to walk such a short distance. I assessed everything in my sight as a possible weapon: a pitcher of ice water, a tray of dirty dishes, the fire extinguisher on the wall, but it was a child's guessing game. I wouldn't be using a weapon. Not here. Not today.

A man with long, black hair and a baseball cap sat with his back to the wall. He wore aviator sunglasses as if the interior lighting blinded him. I couldn't see his eyes, but I felt his stare. When I reached his table, I stood waiting for my stepfather to speak.

"Been a while, Arlie."

None of the other diners looked familiar, but I scanned the crowded room anyway. Wouldn't someone think it odd for a schoolkid to be having breakfast with this sleazebag?

"Waiting for someone?" he asked.

"No. Just wondering why you picked this place. You could be recognized."

"Only you and your uncle know what I look like, and the police haven't been trying very hard. Sit down. You're attracting attention."

I obeyed his order, just as I had done as a child. Although I tried to steady my shaking hands, the sweaty water glass almost slipped through my fingers. No amount of water could quench the dryness in my throat.

"How did you get Mo's phone?"

"Is that so important?"

It was important to me. He'd obviously been following her. Following us. He'd gotten close enough to steal her phone.

"Stay away from her."

Lloyd laughed. I'd erased that sound from my memory, but now I remembered how it made my skin crawl. His laughter was revolting, never joyful.

"Always giving orders. You were a pain in the ass then, and you're still a pain in the ass. Your mom was too easy on you."

My heartbeat slowed considerably. I felt weirdly at ease, almost grounded. I finally had what I wanted: the chance to face Lloyd.

"You killed her."

"You're kidding me, right?" He scoffed at my accusation. "She was a drug addict. Stupidity killed her."

He removed the aviator sunglasses, revealing spiderweb wrinkles that circled both vacant eyes and inched down his cheeks. His face was tan and leathery but had no burn marks.

"I don't… I don't believe you," I said.

His sigh conveyed a fatigue that extended beyond his worn-out body. "How could I kill her? I hadn't seen her in years. Thought she took you to Texas. She had family there."

Lloyd must have known about Frank then. I didn't understand why Mom couldn't have told me if she shared those things with him.

"Then how did you know she died? That I was in Durango?"

"Some guy your mother knew here ended up in Albuquerque. He talked about a woman who OD'd and left behind a daughter. A teenager with a burned face. Figured it had to be you."

This couldn't be. My brain tried to wrap itself around his denials. I needed for him to be responsible for taking both Rosa and Mom from me.

"You know, you could've tracked me down when she died," he said. "I would've come to the funeral."

"Seriously? You think I'd seek you out on purpose?"

"I loved your mom," he said. "And she loved me."

"She was afraid of you."

"I took care of her," he said. "Both of you."

"Sounds like you're trying to rewrite history." I glanced at the wall clock. It'd be another thirty minutes before Mo realized I wasn't in school. She didn't have her phone so she couldn't text or call. I hoped she'd just wait to hear from me instead of checking with the school secretary or, worse, Frank.

"Hon?" The waitress had to tap my shoulder to get my attention. "I asked if you wanted coffee."

"Um…yeah. Thanks."

She topped off Lloyd's mug before filling mine. She said she'd be back to get our order in a minute.

I leaned in, my eyes trained on Lloyd's face and neck. "Why aren't you burned?"

"My scalp and back and legs were burned. Nothing that shows," he said. "My hair never grew back. Too much scar tissue."

I hadn't noticed before how unnatural his hair looked: matte black with no highlights, just like a doll's. His ball cap held a cheap wig in place. Judging by its length, it was a woman's wig.

Still vain about his appearance. I remembered Mom washing his hair in the kitchen sink and then untangling the long, black strands outside on the front steps while he sat between her legs. I'd always been jealous of those times he had with her.

"I'm sorry about your face, but you're still a looker," he said.

He took a sip of coffee. His hands were aged and rough for a guy in his forties. He looked ancient compared to Frank, who was about the same age.

"You're the reason I have this face," I said.

"It wasn't my fault. Dumb-ass *pendejos* messed up the cook, and you and I ended up paying the price."

"We're not in this together." We shared nothing now that Mom was gone.

"It was a goddamned accident, but Sarah wouldn't forgive me," he continued, lost in his own thoughts. "I saw it in her eyes. She blamed me."

"You saw her again after the explosion?"

"Who do you think took care of me? Couldn't risk the police finding me. She knew the state would take care of you."

My head swam. Mom didn't visit me while I was in rehab, but she'd gone back to the man responsible for hurting me and killing Rosa.

"You're lying." I clenched my teeth. *Don't cry. Not here. Not in front of him.*

"Believe what you want. I asked her to get you out of foster care. I said we could start over. Anywhere she'd like."

I looked around the room at the normal families having breakfast. Mine had been a twisted, drug-tinged version. It didn't matter that Mom was dead or if Lloyd disappeared forever. I'd never be able to erase the past or move on from it.

"Everything all right over here?" Sherri was suddenly at my side, one hand on my shoulder. "I can get the manager to ask this guy to leave if he's bothering you."

Lloyd ignored Sherri and stared at me instead. "I'm Arlie's father. Haven't seen her in a while. We're just catching up."

"Is that true?" she asked.

"Yes, this is my stepdad."

"All righty, honey. I just want to be sure you're okay. Does your uncle know you're here?"

"Yes, I told Frank where I'd be," I said. "Why don't you tell our waitress we'll have two Grand Slams?"

Sherri had been around long enough to recognize a meth head. His fractured, yellowing teeth and inflamed gums, his jerky movements. Just like Mom's. She turned around with some hesitation but left us alone.

Lloyd pulled at his collar, exposing even more of the tattoo. He noticed me staring before I could look away.

"It says '*Advertencia*,'" he said.

"'Warning' or 'beware,'" I mumbled.

"That's right, *cariña*. You know your Spanish."

I wish Mom had heeded that warning before hooking up with him. So much could have been different.

"You're not here to reminisce. Tell me what you really want," I said.

"At first, I was just curious."

"About?"

"About where you ended up after your mom died," he said.

"Well, now you know. There's nothing left to see."

A barely perceptible smile told me there was more to his appearance in Durango than just making sure I was all right.

"I decided you might be able to help settle a debt your mom owes me," he said.

"What debt?"

Lloyd explained that she'd run through most of his money during the year after the accident. He suspected she used the money to pay some of my hospital bills and then to buy the beat-up Subaru she used to get us out of Albuquerque.

"We had nothing, you asshole. She left nothing behind," I said.

"Oh, I know," he said. "But I got to thinking…your brand-new daddy must have money if he's building you that fairy-tale house."

"You're insane. Why would my uncle give you a dime?"

"He wouldn't, but you will to keep him safe. To keep your little friend safe. And then I'll be out of your lives for good."

Lloyd's expression turned from one of menace to panic in an instant. He stared at the entry to the restaurant so I turned to look. A police car had parked in front. Two officers entered the restaurant and stopped to chat briefly with Sherri.

"Stop staring at them." Lloyd grew even more agitated and more conspicuous than my stares. He reached one hand behind his back. I feared he had a gun tucked in his waistband underneath his shirt.

The officers sat down at the counter so I turned back to my stepfather. "Please. Please just leave town. I won't tell Frank or the police that we met."

"I'm not leaving without fifty-K."

"Fifty thousand?" The warmth of the dining room brought on a wave of nausea. "I can't get at Frank's money, especially that amount."

"You're a smart girl, Arlie. Or else you and your worthless mother would never have survived so long. I'm confident you'll figure something out."

The tears came now and I didn't care what Lloyd thought. She'd nursed him back to health, not me. She could have ended it…a pillow over his face. That simple. Maybe he was right. She loved him to the end.

"Here's what you're going to do. You're not going to the police, and you're not going to say a word to your little friend or your uncle or that hag from the motel. Just get the money and text me where to meet you. Understood?"

"I'm telling you I can't. I won't," I said.

"This can be easy or this can be hard. Your choice." My stepfather put on his sunglasses and exited through the side door of the restaurant.

Only after he left did his words sink in. He warned me not to talk to the "hag from the motel." Did he mean Dora? If he'd seen her, why wouldn't she have told me?

As the waitress delivered the meals to the table, I pushed past her and ran from the restaurant. School would have to wait. I needed information before I could determine my next move.

* * *

When I reached Dora's motel room, she answered the door wearing a tattered robe and large wool socks pulled up over her calves. She looked as if she'd just woken up, but it was already nine. "What's wrong? Why aren't you in school?" she asked.

I pushed past her into the motel room. It smelled of coffee and cigarettes. How long until the scent of things didn't surprise me?

Dora closed the door behind us. "What is it?"

"My stepfather's in Durango. I just saw him."

She groped for the back of the chair and sat down. "Lloyd's back? Did he hurt you?"

"You know him?"

Dora pointed at the other chair, signaling for me to sit down. "I don't know him. I met him only the one time."

"The day Mom died, right?" My knee popped up and down as I braced for her answer.

She nodded. Everything about her looked tired and apologetic, as if coming clean added years to her age.

My heart ached as I put together the pieces. "I asked you point-blank if anyone was with Mom the day she died. You made me believe she left me on purpose when Lloyd murdered her."

"I don't think he killed her," she said.

"But you just—"

"I said he was here the Sunday she died, but she was alive when I saw them. They were shouting at each other. I stopped and asked if she needed help. When I threatened to call the police, she yelled for me to mind my own business."

"Did you see him leave?"

"I did. Then your mom wanted to talk to me."

Dora said Mom had been frantic. "She rambled on about the explosion and stealing money to take care of you. She said he wanted the two of you back in Albuquerque. She lied to him and said you'd run away a long time ago. That you were probably living in Texas with your uncle."

I stood, hands on my head, trying to stop the internal chatter. I felt assaulted by the lies and half-truths that had been told for my own good.

"You knew about Frank too?"

Dora moved to put her arms around me, but I shoved her away.

"She asked me not to tell you unless something happened to her," Dora said. "She was afraid you'd leave her."

Would I have? I'd tried to once and changed my mind, but I didn't know anymore. I couldn't keep track of the things I was learning about my mother's past, but in my gut, they all felt like betrayals. Choices she made to protect herself and Lloyd instead of me.

"Why didn't you say anything?" I asked. "Why did you let me get sucked into foster care when Frank could have been contacted sooner?"

"At that point, would you have welcomed the life you have now?" she shot back. Angry tears flowed.

I didn't know the answer, but she'd never given me the chance to find out.

"I would have told you, Arlie. I swear," she said. "But then you showed up that night to tell me about the funeral. When you mentioned your uncle, I figured it was best not to say anything. It would have only upset you."

"You were selfish," I said. "Just like my mom."

Then I remembered Mom's notebook. *Dora will know what to do.* She'd counted on her friend to tell me about my uncle, to help me start a new life away from Durango.

Dora wept freely now. Her stooped shoulders shook while her arms hung at her sides. She no longer tried to hug me.

"I got to get out of here," I said.

"Wait. *Please.* What does your stepfather want?" she asked. "Are you all right?"

"Don't worry about it," I said. "I'll handle Lloyd."

"Please go to the police," she begged.

My phone beeped several times, alerting me to texts. *Frank.*

He was at the school, wondering where I was and why I wasn't answering any calls.

"I have to go. Frank found out I skipped school this morning," I said. "Don't you dare call the cops, Dora."

I grabbed my backpack and ran from her room, not knowing whether she'd listen to me or not.

* * *

The school secretary had called Frank when I didn't show up for first and second periods. He'd run into Mo in the hallway and was standing with her near the front steps of the school when I got there.

"You promised Frank you wouldn't go off by yourself. You said you'd stay safe." Mo was beyond pissed. I could tell she'd been crying. Fine strands of hair still clung to the cheeks she'd failed to wipe.

"Why wouldn't I be safe?" I couldn't look them in the eye so I held up my hand as if squinting against the sun.

"You go AWOL and we're not supposed to wig out?" Frank worked hard to keep his anger in check, but he was clearly as upset as Mo.

"I had an early therapy appointment," I lied. "Jane couldn't see me at our regular time this week."

"Why didn't you tell somebody?" Frank asked. "The school obviously didn't know. And neither did Mo. Then you didn't answer your phone."

A headache banged like a drum section behind my eyes. Lying was hard to stomach, but I wasn't about to disobey Lloyd's instructions to keep quiet. "My phone was off during my appointment. I thought I'd left the note from Jane at the school office, but I'd accidentally stuck it in between the pages of one of my textbooks," I said.

"From now on, the phone stays on twenty-four seven. And you let me know where you are and where you'll be," Frank demanded.

"I said I was sorry. I promise it won't happen again. Can we just talk about this after school? I've missed two classes and don't want to miss calculus."

Mo wrapped her hair into a tight ponytail and wiped her face with her sleeve. "She's right. We should get back to class."

Frank nodded and said he'd pick me up from school after choral. I'd scared him enough this morning that he wouldn't let Mo drive me anywhere. She and I waved as he got in his Suburban and left the school parking lot.

I removed my hoodie and let it drop to the ground. My sweaty T-shirt clung to my chest and back, so I pulled the bottom edge away to let in the cool air. I shivered like someone with the flu— hot, then cold, unable to control the shakes.

"You look like you've been crying. What'd you and Jane talk about?" Mo picked up my hoodie and handed it to me.

"Just the usual. Mostly Lloyd. And how worried Frank has been." I wrapped the hoodie around my waist and bent to retie the laces on my sneakers to avoid looking at Mo.

"Yeah, Frank must be really worried. So much so that he can't tell when you're lying."

I stood up slowly. "Lying?"

"Oh, please. Are we really going to do this?"

Sometimes I resented that Mo could see all of me. I had nowhere to hide.

"You can't tell anyone what I'm going to tell you," I said.

"That's where you're wrong."

* * *

The bell rang, giving me an hour in calculus to decide how much to share with Mo and how to deal with Lloyd. Brittany sat a few desks behind me, but I still heard her remark that I'd either run a marathon or forgotten to wear antiperspirant today. I stole a quick glance at the perspiration stains on my tee while two of her friends laughed.

I couldn't be bothered by their petty comments. Mo was the only thing on my mind. She'd made it clear she didn't mind risking my friendship if it meant I'd be safe. She guessed I'd seen Lloyd earlier, but I hadn't had time to say any more. I didn't tell her he had stolen her phone or that he wanted me to steal money from Frank. Throughout class, I imagined she'd already gone to the police and that they'd be waiting for me in the hall. Thankfully, they weren't.

At lunch, I dodged Cody. I'd proven myself a terrible liar once today, but he seemed to believe that Mo had a boy problem needing my undivided attention. His playfulness and tender kiss did nothing to calm my nerves. I'd make it up to him when this was all over, but for now, lying was the only way to keep him safe.

Mo rolled her eyes but played along. When Cody was finally out of earshot, she grabbed my elbow and dragged me toward the school parking lot.

"I'll drive you to the police department," she said. "We can call Frank on the way."

"Whoa, whoa. You don't even know what happened this morning."

"I have an idea and I'm mad as hell you didn't take my advice when I said not to get involved."

"But I am involved. And now I've put you and Frank and Cody in danger as well. I want to handle things on my own."

Mo kept interrupting my attempts to explain the meeting with Lloyd. "Why didn't you just run up to the policemen and scream for help? They could have had him right then and there."

"I thought he had a gun. I couldn't risk people in the restaurant getting hurt."

"Then why didn't you tell Frank once you were away from Lloyd?"

How could I explain things to Mo when I couldn't think straight? I needed water and food and aspirin. And I needed to get my emotions in check or I'd start screaming and never stop.

"Please get off my back. Just for a minute. I've had a friggin' terrible morning and I need some quiet so I can think."

Mo's expression was granite hard. "I'm sorry, but a dangerous man is out there and you're running out of time. He's demanding money you don't even have. You have to go to the police."

I tried to think of another option. Mo and Cody were safe as long as they stayed on campus. An officer was probably watching the trailer so Frank wasn't in danger. The smart thing to do would be to call the police and wait for them in the principal's office. Lloyd couldn't touch me there.

"Please call Frank." Mo shook my shoulders, momentarily stopping the vertigo in my head.

"I can't."

"Then let's tell my parents. They'll know what to do."

"No! Your dad would say he was right all along, that all I am is trouble."

"This isn't your fault. He won't blame you."

I blamed myself. Mr. Mooney would have every right to do so too. Especially if he knew that Lloyd was close enough to his daughter to swipe her phone.

"Then what's your plan?" Mo grew impatient and I felt more pressured.

When Mom and I first left Albuquerque, she couldn't eat or sleep. Terrified that Lloyd would follow us, she let her fear creep into all our conversations and guide every move we made. I couldn't be sucked into that kind of life again.

Maybe I could trap Lloyd. Make him think I have his money. Illogical, TV-inspired scenarios filled my thoughts, but nothing grounded in reality would stick. I couldn't tell Mo that all I really wanted was for him to admit he killed my mother. I don't know how he did it, but I knew she hadn't committed suicide, no matter what Dora said. He wasn't the type to forgive and forget—especially when Mom betrayed him and stole almost everything he had left.

"I don't think he'll hurt me, Mo. Let me handle it."

"Looks like a decision's been made for you." Mo pointed to the police car that slammed to a stop near the school's entrance.

Officer Daugherty and Detective Monroe emerged from the car and made their way up the front steps, obviously in a hurry. They hadn't seen me.

"Hey!" Mo called out. She yanked me in their direction, eager to finally get them involved.

"Miss Betts, you need to come with us immediately." The officers wasted no time with pleasantries. Detective Monroe's face was pinched.

"Why? What's wrong?"

"We'll explain in the car. Please come with us."

Monroe reached for my arm, but I jerked away. "No. Tell me what's wrong. What's happened?"

"Your uncle's in the hospital," Officer Daugherty said. "It's urgent that you come now."

"I'm going too," Mo said. "I'll call Mom when we get there."

"I need to know what happened." *Frank. Hospital. Urgent.* My body seemed to float above the unfolding scene.

"He suffered a severe head injury in an assault," Monroe said. "He's in the ER."

"Did he say who did it?" I didn't have to ask though. Lloyd had gotten to him regardless of the steps the police took to protect us, but why? He said he'd give me a day to try to get money from Frank or the Mooneys.

"Your uncle's not conscious." Officer Daugherty's delivery couldn't have been more emotionless.

I made my way to the cruiser, not wanting to hear any excuses they could offer.

"You said you'd keep us safe."

CHAPTER 27
NINE YEARS AGO—NIGHT RUN

Lloyd looked less scary when he was asleep. I sometimes put my face very close to his to see if he could feel me standing over him. He hardly ever woke up, which made me feel like a ghost. If I started to giggle, I'd run and hide so he wouldn't find out I was messing with him again.

Tonight, I poked his stomach.

"Mom's sick." I spoke directly into his ear and he batted at me like I was a fly.

"Tired…leave me alone." He groaned and turned to face the back of the couch. His bare back was covered with skulls and snakes and other scary tattoos.

I poked him again. "Mom's not waking up."

"Go away, girl. Don't make me tell you again." He mumbled into the cushion.

I stood and watched him, afraid to poke him one more time. But I couldn't go back to Mom. She scared me more than Lloyd right now. After a while, he turned over again and opened his eyes.

"How long have you been standing there?"

"Not long," I said.

"What time is it? Go back to bed."

"It's nighttime," I said. "Mom's sick. Please go see."

He stretched his arms above his head and yawned, then swung his legs around and sat up. I grabbed his hand and pulled with all my might.

"Come on. I'll show you."

He stumbled after me, still holding my hand. I pointed to Mom on the bed. "She won't wake up. I shook her real hard."

Lloyd seemed suddenly very awake. He ran to the side of the bed and kept saying, "Sarah, Sarah," over and over. He stuck two fingers in her mouth and scooped something out onto the bed where she had already thrown up.

He put his ear very close to her nose, then lifted her off the bed. Mom's arms flopped backward, and I was afraid he'd bump her head going through the doorway.

"Get your shoes, *mija*. Now!"

I put on my fuzzy slippers. When I went back into the living room, Lloyd had already gone outside, but he'd left the front door open.

"Wait for me!" I ran as fast as I could to catch up to them.

He was at the car, trying to fit Mom in the backseat, but her arms and legs seemed to be in the way. I pushed around him to try to get in after her.

"No, get in the front," he said.

"I can't. Mom says I'm too small for the seat belt."

"Now, Arlie!"

Lloyd grabbed my arm and hurried me to the other side of the car. One of my slippers fell off, but he wouldn't let me pick it up.

Once I was in the car, he slammed my door and went to his side.

"What's wrong with Mom?" I began to cry because I'd never seen Lloyd scared. "Where are we going?"

"Your mama needs a doctor. Just shut up while I drive."

I tried to look around my seat to see if Mom was awake yet, but Lloyd pushed me back.

"Don't look," he said.

He wouldn't let me hold his hand so I made myself into as small a ball as I could. My face was wedged near the door so that I could almost see Mom in the backseat. I smelled throw-up.

I turned around and looked out my window. There were so many lights and so many sounds for the middle of the night. I watched the freeway lights whiz by until my tummy felt sick.

When Lloyd turned the car too fast, Mom rolled partway into the floorboard. I tried to look again, but he pushed me back.

The car came to a stop.

"Stay here," Lloyd said.

He opened the backseat door and pulled Mom's legs until she was almost all the way out. He then lifted her over his shoulder and carried her to the hospital entrance that had sliding glass doors. Carefully, he lowered her to the ground, his hand behind her head.

Then he got back in the car.

"What are you doing? You can't leave her on the sidewalk!" I pounded my hands against the glass. "Mom! Mom, wake up!"

A man and a woman rushed out of the hospital. They wore light blue pants and shirts, and white shoes. The woman pointed at our car as Lloyd drove away. The man was touching Mom.

"Stop crying. We couldn't stay." Lloyd gripped the steering wheel and leaned into it like a race-car driver.

After we'd gotten back onto the freeway he said, "How about we stop for doughnuts, huh? Krispy Kreme opens at three a.m."

"I'm not hungry!" I yelled. "We have to go back for Mom."

I cried until my throat hurt. Then Lloyd finally held my hand.

"If we stayed at the hospital, they would have said your mom was not a good mom and then the police would come and take you away from us. You want that to happen?"

"She is a good mom," I said.

"Not tonight," he whispered.

"I want to see her." I kicked my feet against the dashboard.

"She'll probably be home tomorrow or the next day," he said. "They just need to make her well."

I wanted to cry again.

"Can I please stay at Rosa's?"

Lloyd didn't look at me. "Your mom and I are getting married soon. I'll take care of you."

"I want Rosa."

"Well, you're staying with me."

"I don't want you," I said.

Lloyd never answered. He pulled the car into the apartment parking lot and into our regular space, which was still empty. I jumped out and began looking for my lost slipper while Lloyd went back inside.

"Lock the door when you're done," he said.

CHAPTER 28

Frank seemed an inanimate extension of the machines and wires anchoring him to the hospital bed. It'd been an hour since they moved him from the ER to the intensive care unit. His bandaged head immobile, my uncle lay completely still except for the subtle rise and fall of his barrel chest beneath the hospital gown.

"There's swelling in his brain." A nurse adjusted the IV protruding from Frank's forearm. Her name tag said Amy. "He's stable but needs rest."

She touched my shoulder briefly before leaving me and Mo alone.

"Lloyd did this. I know he did." I held Frank's calloused hand, its strength apparent even in this frozen state.

Lloyd had gotten close enough to Mo to steal her phone. And he'd knocked Frank out with a two-by-four piece of lumber at the construction site. No one else had a reason to hurt Frank. Not one goddamn neighbor saw a thing. The city's permit officer had found Frank and the bloody piece of wood on a visit to check the progress of the house. Thank God for that.

"Cody…he's in danger too. I have to tell someone." I jumped from the chair and headed for the door where a police officer stood guard.

Mo stopped me and led me back to the chair. "You don't even know if your stepfather's seen you with Cody, but I called James. Cody's with him. He's safe."

I turned to the window. The glare of the hospital-room lights made it impossible to see into the dark night. I only saw my reflection and that of Frank in the bed. Until another reflection appeared behind me: Detective Monroe.

Heartbreak had a physical pain to it. "What did you do, Mo?"

"What I should have done earlier," she said.

"Miss Betts, would you join me?" The detective motioned to the hallway. "I have some questions for you."

Mo moved closer to Frank but didn't look me in the eye. I followed Monroe down the hall to a small waiting room. We were alone.

"Your friend said your stepfather confronted you this morning. You should have said something at the high school." He took out a small notepad.

"I had other things on my mind. Like my uncle almost being killed."

"She thinks you're cooking up a scheme to deal with your stepfather yourself. Is that correct?"

My best friend had crossed a line. It was one thing to be worried about me. It was another completely to blindside me like this. By telling the police about Lloyd, she'd stolen any chance I had to think things through.

"I've had a pretty rough day," I said. "I haven't been thinking straight."

"That's understandable," Monroe said. "So let's start from the beginning. Tell me everything you remember. Don't leave out a thing."

I didn't admit Lloyd had stolen Mo's phone. I lied and said he had been waiting for me at the trolley stop. The phone was my only means of contacting Lloyd, and I didn't want to risk the police tracing it. Thank God I hadn't trusted Mo with that bit of information.

"Some druggie my mom knew ran into Lloyd in Albuquerque. He told my stepfather we lived in Durango," I said. "He knew she'd died."

"And did he tell you what he wants? Do you have idea why he'd attack your uncle?"

I told him Lloyd wanted me to steal money from Frank, but that I didn't know why he went after Frank so quickly. I was anxious to find that out myself.

"He was high. He wasn't making a lot of sense," I said. "I told him I would figure something out."

"That wasn't very bright," Monroe said.

"I was stalling. To keep him away from Frank and Mo."

Detective Monroe closed his notepad and cracked his knuckles as if dealing with me made him beyond exhausted. His reproachful stare made me even more uncomfortable.

"What do you want from me? I'm telling you everything now."

"I want you to take this seriously," he said.

He had no idea how seriously I was taking it. I'd make Lloyd pay for hurting Frank, for coming back into my life.

"Well, at least we know why he's in Durango," he said. "We'll get a description out to the police and the sheriff's department. After you say good-bye to your uncle, an officer will take you to the Mooneys' residence."

I rushed back into the hospital room. I had no intention of leaving Frank's side. And I definitely wasn't going anywhere with Mo.

* * *

I leaned over the side of the bed and laid my cheek against Frank's chest. The rhythmic pounding could almost drown out the beeping machines. By closing my eyes, I shut out the sterile, gray hospital room and the slackness in his features. I imagined him standing in the trailer's kitchen with his stupid apron on, cooking dinner and teasing me about Cody.

"The doctors are doing all they can," Mo said.

"Why don't you just leave?" My friend had betrayed me and I didn't need her to comfort me.

"We're both leaving. The police are taking us back to my house. You can be as mad as you want. I told you I'd do anything to protect you."

I stepped away from Frank and leaned against the cabinets near the bed. I needed water and food, but I couldn't focus enough to make any decision. Even breathing felt like a chore.

"I don't need you to protect me." I rubbed my temples to stop the throbbing.

"Then I'm protecting myself," she said. "I want you around. I want Frank around. In the last few weeks you've been differ-ent…*happy*. I want that back, for both of us."

My brain had no room for Mo's excuses. Instead it niggled at all that had transpired since Lloyd had made his demands. Why hadn't he texted?

"He didn't even give me a chance," I said more to myself than to Mo.

"Who?"

"Lloyd. He went after Frank almost immediately."

"You're questioning the logic of a drug dealer? Did you think he'd keep his word?"

"I could have fixed this if you hadn't messed things up," I said.

"Me? You think I messed things up?" Mo's chest heaved as if she would explode. "I'm so tired of your bullshit. Face it, Arlie. You're the reason Frank's here."

"Get the fuck out!" I yelled at her.

"You keep forgetting you're sixteen years old," she shot back. "You've handled things on your own for so long that you've lost a grip on reality. You can't fix this."

Her shrill voice carried through the glass wall and to the nurses' station. It wasn't two seconds before the officer on duty and nurse Amy burst into the room.

"Be quiet this instant or you're both out of here, do you understand?" Amy's harsh command hung between us.

The officer surveyed the scene, tugged at his collar, and exited as fast as he could. The door clicked behind him.

Like a mother hen, the nurse pulled us toward her and into a huddle of exhausted emotion. "Girls, you've got to respect that this is a hospital and this is the ICU. People are seriously ill. You can't raise your voices."

Amy released us and softened her tone. "You've got five minutes and then you'll have to go. Understand?"

I broke away from her and went to Frank's side. He lay so still that I couldn't help but think of him as lifeless. The image of another funeral drove spikes of panic into my heart.

"Arlie…if anything happens…you know, to Frank…"

"No. Don't say it. You can't say it."

Frank couldn't leave me too. It just wasn't possible. He had to wake up. He had to finish our house.

"Your stepdad is unstable. What makes you think he won't kill you when he finds out you can't get him the money? Arlie? Are you listening to me?" Pale and exhausted, Mo no longer raised her voice. She'd sensed I'd shut myself off.

I hugged my uncle and stood up. "I need to use the restroom and splash some water on my face. Then we can leave."

Mo nodded and went out into the hallway, giving me the chance to contact Lloyd.

* * *

I lowered the lid of the toilet and sat down. *Don't make him mad, Arlie. Remain calm.* My shaking hands almost made it impossible to tap out a message.

I thought I had more time. Why'd you hurt Frank? I typed.

When my cell phone rang, I fumbled for it and lost my grip, sending it bouncing onto the tile, screen side up. Mo's name and number appeared.

"You could've killed Frank, you bastard." So much for remaining calm and not pissing him off.

"I followed you after breakfast. You went straight to the motel, then to your uncle. I saw you outside the school."

"But I didn't tell them anything." I whispered in case Mo came back into the room. "They were worried that I hadn't shown up to school. Everyone is being extra careful now that—"

"That I'm in town."

"We could still meet." Detective Monroe's warnings tapped at my consciousness, but all I could think about was the chance to see Lloyd.

"You said you couldn't get the money."

"I lied before. I can get some. Maybe not fifty thousand, but—Frank keeps a little in the trailer. And I can get more from Mo's parents."

"You're a lying bitch, just like your mother," he said.

I bit back my anger. I couldn't risk scaring him off. "Just meet me at the trailer. Two a.m. I promise to be alone."

The line went dead. I could only pray he'd show up.

* * *

Warm lights illuminated Mo's house, the glow of family and safety and normalcy pouring from the multipaned windows. Two police cars on the street in front shattered the idyllic scene and reminded me I was essentially under house arrest.

Mo walked up the sidewalk to her front porch and I followed close behind. "Mom's cooked supper. Cody and James are here too."

"Why are they here?" I pulled on Mo's arm to stop her.

"I told them what happened. They wanted to see you."

"And your parents?"

"I told them everything too."

My legs grew weak and I grabbed for the porch railing. Mo didn't wait for me to object or complain. Instead, she walked into her house, assuming I'd follow. So I did.

* * *

As soon as we entered the kitchen, Mo's mom pulled me into a hug and kissed the top of my head. Without thinking, I wrapped my arms even tighter around her waist. During the whole day, no one else had offered any comfort or understanding, and my frayed nerves welcomed the soothing she provided.

Mo's dad stood in the doorway to the dining room, a beer bottle in his hand. When I caught his eye, he turned and left.

I expected a hug from Cody, but he sat down with the others. I took the chair next to him.

"Cody?" My voice shook. I didn't know the extent of the harm I'd done to us. I squeezed his hand, but he barely squeezed back.

"I'm glad you're okay, but let's just eat."

"Cody's right. I'm sure Mo and Arlie are starved," Mrs. Mooney said. "They've been at the hospital most of the day." Mrs. Mooney reached for plates in the cabinet and filled them for us.

After not eating or drinking all day, I was grateful for the warm meal and gave it my entire attention. Everyone else picked at their food and said little except to ask for more bread or tea.

"So we're going to pretend this is some normal get-together?" James let his fork drop to his plate, which caused both me and Cody to jump.

"Cool it, James," Cody said. "We can talk later."

"Actually, no, we can't." James stood and laid his napkin across his plate. "We're leaving now."

Mrs. Mooney jumped from her seat. "Please, let's stay calm. Arlie's been through enough for one day."

"Oh, she has, has she?"

James's anger shouldn't have surprised me, but I found myself shaking, barely able to keep it together. I felt cornered and utterly alone.

"Hey, man, lay off," Cody said. "We're all tired. We're all worried. Blaming Arlie right now won't solve anything."

Even though Cody came to my defense, his tone suggested a distance that would be difficult to bridge, at least tonight.

"I'm sorry—" I began.

"You should be," James said, sitting down.

"Let her finish," Mo interrupted.

More than anything, I wanted to apologize for thinking I could be part of their normal lives. I was the square peg that'd never fit, no matter how hard I tried.

"Why didn't you let us help you?" Cody's tone had softened, but hurt punctuated every word. When he finally leaned in to hug me, I'd never been so grateful.

"He told me not to say anything. I needed time to think of a plan. I was trying to protect you. All of you." I buried my face in the nap of his flannel shirt.

"And yet your uncle is in the ICU." Mr. Mooney had come back to the kitchen without me noticing.

"Rob, that's uncalled for," Mrs. Mooney said. "She's just a girl."

"He's right. This is all my fault." I pushed away from the table and ran up the stairs, two at a time, until I reached the hall bathroom. I slammed the door and locked it. Slumping down, I wedged my back against the vanity. The chill in the tile floor seeped into my jeans.

Thankfully, no one followed. I sucked in air, but my lungs refused it. Everyone downstairs expected me to do the "right" thing—let the police find Lloyd, arrest Lloyd, punish Lloyd. Emotions ran high. They were all angry that I hadn't gone straight to the detective as soon as I left the restaurant this morning.

How could I explain my fear that Lloyd would slip through the cracks once again, only to resurface later? I couldn't imagine how we'd live day to day. No one could protect us twenty-four seven. Frank was proof of that. And Mr. Mooney was right. I was to blame.

I heard Mo leading Cody up the stairs before I heard a faint knock on the bathroom door.

"Let me in. Please."

From my sitting position, I leaned over and unlocked the door. Cody motioned for Mo to leave us alone and then closed the door behind him.

"I'm on the floor. Here, take my hand," I said.

Cody dropped to his knees, his hands outstretched to determine which direction I faced. He sat down, legs crossed and facing me.

"I didn't mean to upset you. Any of you," I said. "My decisions had nothing to do with you."

"Do you know how awful it'd be to lose you?" he asked. "And your actions do affect me. Because we're together now."

With his head bowed slightly, his hair fell in a blond curtain, shielding his eyes. I brushed it out of the way, only to have it fall again. So I grabbed his chin and lifted it up so that I could see his whole face. I ran a finger over his bottom lip and he drew it in.

"Don't," he whispered. "We should go downstairs."

I placed my hands on his cheeks. "You're beautiful, Cody. Inside and out. I don't deserve you."

"Arlie—"

"Shhh." I kissed him softly. He kissed me back, gently at first, then more forcefully. His tongue darted around mine. I didn't think I could kiss him hard enough to show how much I wanted him.

My fingers fumbled at the buttons on his flannel shirt. He brushed them away with a quiet "no" but kissed me hungrily. I kept at the buttons until I could push the shirt off his shoulders. He struggled to free his arms so I pulled on the sleeves until the shirt came free. He grabbed my T-shirt and lifted it over my head. Goose bumps dotted my skin as Cody pushed me against the cold tile floor, the clasp of my bra digging into my back. His chest was blistering hot against my skin. He leaned on one elbow, keeping his full weight off me.

"We can't do this now, here." His breath tickled my ear. "With everyone downstairs."

"I don't care." I groped at the zipper on his jeans. I felt he wanted me as much as I wanted him.

"Not like this." He pushed off me and sat with his back against the bathroom door. The distance between us felt enormous. He ran both hands through his hair and closed his eyes.

Embarrassed at what I'd started, I pulled on my T-shirt, but felt chilled through and through.

"I'm sorry," he said.

"Don't be. I don't know what I was thinking." But I had known. Lloyd represented death and I wanted to feel alive, supercharged in every cell of my body. To drink every last drop of what Cody represented: love and hope and normalcy.

"I wanted to," he said. "I did."

"You don't have to say that."

He pulled on his shirt, but didn't button it. He helped me to my knees and held on to me as if there was a chance I'd disappear forever. Cody spoke directly in my ear.

"I haven't done this with anyone. I want it to be right."

He kissed my neck and hair. I closed my eyes and wanted nothing more than to sink into his words like into a warm bath.

"I want you to be my first too," I said.

Mo's sharp rap on the door wrenched us back to reality. "James wants to leave now."

CHAPTER 29

Mrs. Mooney had made coffee by the time Cody and I joined everyone back downstairs. Mo's dad was in the living room, speaking to one of the officers tasked with watching the house. I overheard that they'd stationed one car in the front and one in the alley behind the backyard.

"Here." Mo handed me a steaming mug.

I closed my eyes and breathed in. All those years, I couldn't smell this aroma. Now freshly brewed coffee was one of my favorite scents. Even with everything that had been said at this table earlier, a sense of family filled the room.

"This is just plain old Folgers," Mo said. "With enough sugar, it's not bad."

"I remember Rosa used to drink instant," I said. "She'd have coffee every afternoon with little rolls that had pink sugar designs on top."

"Conchas," Mo's mom said. "Rob and Mo love them. The Mexican bakery near the Laundromat on Eighth sells them every Saturday. You'll have to try them sometime and tell us if they're as good as Rosa's."

I couldn't see Mr. Mooney and me bonding over our love of Mexican pastries, but it was sweet of Mrs. Mooney to try to keep things upbeat and normal on a day that was anything but. And she managed to stay positive, straddling the conflicting emotions of her daughter and husband.

She stood behind Mo, rubbing her shoulders. She had to know what a rough day it'd been for her daughter. And she sensed that my friendship with Mo was on shaky ground.

James cradled his mug but didn't seem eager to talk. Yet I couldn't let him leave without trying to make him see what Cody meant to me.

"I'm sorry, James. Please tell me what I can do to make this better."

Cody turned in his brother's direction. Their bond was evident in the way that James reached over and took his hand.

"Sometimes we do stupid things in the name of love," he said flatly. There was no sign of happy, joking bookseller James. His clenched jaw said he was holding back what he really felt.

Mo's eyes were red and glassy. I reached across the table and offered my hand, palm up. I held my breath waiting to see if she'd take it. When she finally did, I let my own tears spill.

"Well, at least we can all agree that I've been stupid." I wiped my face and snotty nose with the arm of my hoodie.

Cody and Mo's mom smiled, but James and Mo remained distant. I turned to Cody and he leaned in for a kiss, connecting with my lips on the first try.

"Nice aim, kid." James's joke eased some of the tension at the table. I found my shoulders loosening a bit too.

"I'm not completely helpless," Cody said and kissed me again.

I'd underestimated what I meant to these people and what they meant to me. My heart ached to think how they'd react if they knew I still intended to meet Lloyd. It could mean an end to these relationships, but there was no way I'd risk Lloyd slipping away now. I was sure he'd return when we least suspected it to carry through with his threats.

"Can we call the hospital and check on Frank one last time tonight?" I asked.

Mrs. Mooney grabbed our unfinished mugs of coffee and placed them in the sink. "Sure, honey. I'll call right now, but I think it's time for you and Mo to get some sleep. Cody is welcome to come back first thing in the morning."

* * *

James waited on the porch while Cody and I said good night in the foyer. I leaned my forehead against his.

"Promise me…no more secrets," he said.

I couldn't make that promise without lying. "So, you'll be back in the morning?" I asked.

"I'll go with you to the hospital."

"Thanks. It'd mean a lot to me. And to Frank."

He kissed me softly.

"Should I call later?" He nuzzled my neck and then stepped back.

"No, I'm going to turn in."

"I could stay," he said. "On the couch, that is."

James held the door open for Cody so I touched his hand one last time. "Go before I change my mind," I said.

* * *

Mo and I lay on her bed in the dark. Her parents had already gone to sleep, but the caffeine had me wired. That and trying to figure out how I could sneak out of the house without Mo or the police knowing. My plan would destroy the trust I'd built with Mo over the years. But if I thought about the pain my deception would cause her, I'd lose my nerve.

"The nurse told Mom he opened his eyes. That's a good sign," Mo assured me.

"He's still not talking," I said. "What if there's permanent damage?"

"They can't know until the swelling goes down. It's been less than twenty-four hours. Give it time."

Minutes and hours didn't make sense. My world had stopped the moment the police said Frank was in the hospital.

I turned my phone to vibrate in case Lloyd decided to call or text. I couldn't risk Mo finding out that I was still planning to meet him. I kept the phone at my side, praying nothing had changed since I gave him instructions to meet me at the trailer.

"Mo, about today..."

"Let's just go to sleep," she said. "We'll talk tomorrow."

"But I want you to know—"

"I do know," she said. "But you've got a lot to learn about friendship."

I thought back to our first meeting outside the motel where Mom and I had been staying. Mo had been so bold, so sure of herself. She'd entered my life and stayed no matter how many times I tested our friendship.

"But it doesn't matter how mad everyone is. You're not alone in this." She turned her back to me and pulled the quilt up over her shoulder.

She was wrong. Tonight, I'd be completely alone.

CHAPTER 30
FOUR YEARS AGO—FRIENDSHIP

Watching cartoons with a growling stomach wasn't working. Mom had been gone two days, and all we had in the motel room were tortilla chips and bean dip—and I'd finished those the first night she was gone.

The last two days, I'd crossed the highway and sneaked into the Holiday Inn breakfast room to steal a bagel and a small box of cereal. I needed something I could grab fast. Part of me wished I could smell the freshly made waffles the tourists were having before they went hiking or rafting.

The young guy at the front desk caught me the second day. His eyes were sleepy and sad. When he shook his head no, I knew I couldn't go back a third day.

Mom had warned me not to leave the room when she was away, that it'd look suspicious for a twelve-year-old girl to be out alone. But if she didn't care enough to make sure I wasn't hungry, then I didn't care enough to obey her.

Anyway, it was Saturday, not a school day. No one would think it was weird for me to be out walking around. I pulled on a ratty, long-sleeved T-shirt that one of Mom's friends had left behind in our room. I'd learned never to wear anything nice where I was going.

I jogged down the alley for three blocks, then ducked behind a delivery truck that was parked in the back of Mama's Boy Italian restaurant. I only had to wait fifteen minutes before two kitchen workers brought out the trash.

When the guys had gone back inside and I was sure no one was looking, I hoisted myself to the edge of the dumpster and jumped inside. I wore heavy hiking boots so I wouldn't accidentally cut myself on broken glass or the sharp edge of a tin can.

Because I couldn't smell or taste, I wasn't choosy. Still, I didn't want to get food poisoning. I usually looked for pieces of bread left over from the baskets they put on everybody's tables. I also looked for discarded pizza slices because the meat and cheese made me feel full longer.

I'd been in the dumpster a couple of minutes before I noticed the police car. A female officer approached and she didn't look happy.

"Hey, there. Want to tell me what you're doing?"

I loved how authority figures asked the obvious and didn't expect a kid to reply with a snarky comment. I didn't say a word though. I thought through my options. Getting out of the dumpster and then outrunning a cop car didn't seem like a good one.

Before the officer could speak again, Mo pushed herself through the hedge lining the alley. She brushed off leaves and twigs that clung to her hair.

"Sorry, Officer. That's my sister, CeeCee. I dared her to go dumpster diving, but I never thought she'd take me seriously." Mo rolled her eyes for effect.

"And who are you?" the officer asked.

"I'm Maureen Mooney. We live a block over."

While the officer listened to Mo's explanation, I pulled myself out of the dumpster and walked toward them.

"You smell awful," Mo said. "Mom and Dad are going to be mad."

"Only if you tell them," I played along.

The officer let us off with a warning, but not before scolding us for trespassing on private property and endangering our health and safety by going through other people's trash.

I saluted her as she drove off.

Mo yanked my arm down. "You want to get in even more trouble?"

Ever since I'd met Mo the year before, she'd been showing up at the motel with schoolwork and books even though I wanted nothing to do with school. More than once, I told her to leave me alone, but she kept at it. I don't know how she showed up at exactly the right time in the alley, but I'm glad she did.

"You stalking me now?" I asked.

"Whatever." Mo took off walking down the alley and I followed.

"Why are you mad?" I asked.

Mo turned and faced me. "Because you needed something to eat and you didn't ask me for help."

My cheeks grew hot. I thought about lying, but that'd be stupid considering she'd caught me going through garbage to find food. She thought of us as friends, but I didn't have friends.

"You don't have to be embarrassed," she said.

"I'm not."

"You're red."

I brought my palm to my face. "What do you know anyway?"

"I know that friends count on each other," she said.

When I didn't answer, she walked away. I let her get to the end of the block before calling out. "Hey, Mo! Wait up."

We didn't say much as we walked. I let her take the lead.

"Where are we going?" I finally asked.

"My house," she said. "You stink."

I didn't want to know where she lived. I didn't want her parents to see me like this. And I didn't think it was safe that someone knew so much about me and Mom.

"They're not home," she said.

"Who?"

"My parents."

She had an almost creepy way of reading my thoughts, but I was grateful she offered the information before I decided to run back to the motel.

Mo's house was everything I didn't want it to be: a life-size dollhouse painted light blue with curly white trim around the edges of the porch. Inside, the furniture seemed brand new, as if no one ever sat on the chairs or sofa. The kitchen was almost all white, except for the stainless-steel refrigerator and stove. Every surface was shiny. In this too-perfect world, I felt dirty and checked the soles of my boots to be sure I wouldn't mess up the floor.

"So, was that a fake name you gave the cop, or do you really have a sister named CeeCee?" I sat on a bar stool, careful not to put the arms of my stained shirt on the counter.

"I had a sister. Celine's dead now." Mo offered no further explanation as she grabbed bread and peanut butter and honey, and set about making sandwiches for us. "Would you get the milk from the fridge?"

I didn't ask about CeeCee, although I was curious. I figured

Mo would tell me more some other day. And one day I'd tell her that I couldn't smell or taste, and that sticky peanut-butter sandwiches were one of my least favorite foods in the world.

CHAPTER 31

With Mo's back to me, I couldn't tell if she'd fallen asleep or not. If I waited much longer, Lloyd would reach the trailer before me. I needed to get there first so I could grab Frank's gun.

I sat up as slowly as I could manage. No movement from Mo. When I swung my legs over the side of the bed, she sighed but made no other sound. The moon cast enough light in the room for me to find my jeans and T-shirt. I couldn't find my jacket so I borrowed Mo's fleece and a ball cap.

When we were younger and I didn't want to risk running into her dad, I'd climb the oak in her backyard to reach the roof of the sunroom, which was just below her bedroom window. The tree would be my means of escape tonight.

The window opened without a sound, although the rushing in my ears made it hard for me to determine how loud I was actually being. Light rain had left everything with a glossy sheen. Much to my relief, the rubber soles on my sneakers gripped the shingles on the roof.

I quickly closed the window and scrambled down the tree,

careful not to lose my grip on the wet limbs or drop my back-pack. The moonlight that had helped me get dressed now made me feel like a burglar caught in the lights of a police helicopter.

Brittany and her parents still lived next door to Mo's family, but thankfully the house was dark. I shivered to think how much more complicated things could get if she spotted my escape.

I crouched low and made my way to the fence gate. The space between the boards gave me a good view of the police car posted in the alley. It faced away from me, opposite the direction I needed to go. Still, all it would take was one quick glance in the cop's rearview mirror and I'd be busted. I needed a diversion.

I scanned the ground for a rock or brick, something heavy enough to throw over the fence and squad car that would get the officer's attention. Mo's dad kept the backyard immaculate—definitely nothing in the immediate vicinity for me to pick up. I crept back over to the patio and grabbed a small flowerpot filled with soil, praying it'd do the trick.

I heaved the pot over the car and down the alley. It soared for a good way before hitting the pavement and shattering.

As soon as the officer leaped from the car with his flashlight, I opened the gate and took off running. I didn't dare look behind me until I'd reached the side street. From there, I cut across the parking lot of a gas station and disappeared into the darkness.

* * *

It took me longer than I thought to jog back to our trailer. I had told Lloyd to meet me at two a.m. and it was already ten minutes past that. The city still hadn't fixed the street lamp and Frank had never gotten the chance to install motion-detecting lights, but the full moon illuminated the entire yard.

As I rounded the back of the trailer, I spotted Lloyd on the top step near the front door of the Airstream, working at the lock. He had a handgun stuck in the back of his jeans. If I had shown up just a few minutes later—a few *seconds* later—I wouldn't have seen him arrive. I would have unknowingly opened the door.

A weapon. I needed a weapon. The gun in Frank's fake Bible was now useless. One of Frank's tools might suffice, but he locked them in the small shed every night. Even if it wasn't locked, I couldn't get to it without crossing the yard and risking that Lloyd would see me.

He had a gun. Fear washed over me, draining every bit of strength I had. Of course he had a gun. I felt foolish. A little girl thinking she could fight back against the monster in her nightmares. I wanted nothing more than to be back in Mo's bed, warm and dry under the quilt.

Crashes and thumps erupted from within the trailer. He was probably trashing the place, looking for the cash I said Frank had stashed there. Crouching beneath the trailer's bedroom window, I pressed my back to the metal exterior and inhaled, struggling to fill my lungs and squelch the doubts paralyzing me. The rain had soaked my jeans and fleece hoodie. I'd lost the ball cap on my run from Mo's. Water dripped from my hair and I swiped it from my eyes.

An image of Frank in the ICU, tenuously connected to life via tubes and wires, failed to steel my nerves. I was going to totally lose it right here and now, when I was so close to finding the truth.

Mom, tell me what to do. I'm scared.

Then I remembered the wheel chocks. The red triangles of heavy-duty rubber kept the wheels of the trailer from rolling. A loop of synthetic cord made it easy to remove the one closest to me. It was heavier than I expected and definitely not easy to hold with one hand, but like a medieval spiked ball and chain, the wheel chock would do some serious damage if I could catch Lloyd unaware. Otherwise, the chock was useless against a gun.

I crab-walked along the side of the trailer until I stood on the far side of the front door, shaking violently from adrenaline overload. I bent down beside the steps. I needed him to exit the trailer so I hammered my fist against it.

The screech of the metal screen sent an additional jolt into my limbs. He walked out on the first step, his cowboy boots at eye level. He held the gun in one hand and a flashlight in the other. I stood and swung the chock upward, connecting with Lloyd's groin. Doubled over and cursing, he tumbled down the steps and onto the muddy ground. He reached for me with one outstretched arm. I wound up one more time and brought the chock down on his head.

* * *

The street remained quiet, empty. No one had witnessed what I'd done. Lloyd didn't move, but he was still breathing. His ball cap and wig had come off in the fall. The gash on his head bled profusely. I looped my arms under his armpits. With short bursts, I heaved backward, dragging his body only inches with each pull. I'd never get him up the steps to the trailer.

The rain came down harder now. Ignoring the searing pain in my arms and back, I dragged Lloyd toward the construction site. The slick mud made it easier to pull him except that my feet also slipped as I struggled with that much deadweight. One last heave and we were inside the shell of the house. I felt a bizarre sense of elation, as if I'd accomplished something heroic instead of hiding a person I'd injured badly.

I backed away, letting Lloyd slump to the floor, then shucked off my backpack. The house was dark except for moonlight that shone through the window openings cut in the plywood sheathing. A black stain widened on the floor near Lloyd's head, but I couldn't see how bad his wound was. I took off the fleece and balled it around my hand. The fabric, soaked from the rain, made a squishing sound when I pressed it to his skull to stop the bleeding. *All that blood.*

I needed light. Even though the house didn't have wiring yet, Frank had used heavy-duty extension cords to run electricity from the trailer to his thousand-watt halogen work lights. The powerful bulbs could illuminate the entire first floor while he was putting up drywall. I saw the outline of one at the far side of the room. I carefully made my way to it and felt along the floor for the extension cord. My shaking hands managed to fit the plug into the lamp's socket.

The instant shock of light and heat stunned me, and I stumbled backward. I turned to Lloyd. He moaned in pain but lay still.

I gasped when I saw his face. The wheel chock to the head wasn't his only injury. One eye was swollen shut, and his chin and cheek had cuts. Frank must have put up a fight before Lloyd knocked him out.

I spotted another extension cord on the floor. Maneuvering behind Lloyd's back, I wrapped the cord around his wrists and then around a wall stud. He groaned into consciousness and I backed away quickly. He looked like the subject of an interrogation gone very wrong.

"Didn't think you'd come." He spat blood onto the floor, but most remained in the spit that clung to his chin.

I hadn't smelled gasoline before, but now the stench filled my nostrils and burned my throat.

"What were you planning to do?" I screamed at him.

Lloyd smiled at the panic in my face. "What's it smell like? I was going to teach you and your uncle a lesson by burning down your little dream house."

The gun. Lloyd had been holding a gun before I hit him. I ran out into the rain and searched the ground near the trailer's steps. Moonlight glinted off the metal of the gun, making it easy to spot. I grabbed it and ran back to Lloyd.

"You won't shoot me," he said weakly.

"Shut up!" I pointed the gun at his face. My shaking hands struggled to maintain a tight hold.

"What are you afraid of, little girl? Pull the trigger."

Lloyd twisted his body until he had worked himself into a sitting position.

"No one would blame me for killing you," I stammered. "I'd tell the police I was protecting myself."

"Self-defense, huh? Hitting me in the nuts, cracking open my head, tying my hands, then shooting me. Yeah, that would qualify as self-defense."

"Shut up!"

I shivered in my wet clothes. *Don't let him get to you. Stay in control. You're in control.*

My phone vibrated in my back pocket, which sent another surge of adrenaline through my already shaken body. I put the gun under one arm and retrieved the phone. Its screen cast blue light around me.

Where are you? Call us NOW!

Don't be stupid. Call me or the police.

The messages were sent from Mrs. Mooney's phone, but Mo was texting. The phone buzzed again. This time, she tried calling. I returned the phone to my back pocket.

I strained to stay focused. My original plan was to trap Lloyd, to have the police close by to arrest him. Yet I'd asked Lloyd to meet me here alone. Had I really only wanted a confession, or had I planned something else all along? I sucked in air, hoping it'd ease the burning in my lungs. The fumes in the house sickened me and fueled a surreal new panic.

"Why'd you have to track me down?" The futility of the conversation began to sink in. With one hand, I reached for the phone. Mo had been right all along. I needed to call the police now.

"I needed money," he said. "You can still get me some and I'll walk away."

Images of my mother's body, lifeless and small, flashed before me. Every emotion I felt that day returned with the same intensity. I'd never see her again. Ever.

"You didn't have to kill her. You didn't have to." I lowered the gun but kept my finger on the trigger.

"I didn't kill your fucking mother." Lloyd appeared to be regaining his strength. He now sat more upright, even though the blood still seeped down his neck and shirt.

"Dora said you were at the motel that day. She said you were angry at Mom." I cried freely now, not caring what my stepfather thought.

"She was alive when I left her," he said. "I can't be responsible if she OD'd on the crank I gave her as a parting gift. Too bad the bitch never had no self-control."

The roar in my ears unhinged me and I dropped to the floor.

Had I pulled the trigger? I tried to focus, but the floor seemed to heave from side to side like a ship at sea. The gun slipped from my hand. Lloyd's animal-like screams were unlike anything I'd ever heard.

"You shot me, you bitch!" Lloyd slumped to his side but writhed with newfound energy. He'd worked his hands free from the cord and was groping for my legs. I kicked at him wildly and lost my balance, falling into the floodlight.

The casing around the bulbs shattered. The heat was enough to ignite the gasoline-soaked wood. A whoosh of hot air flew up around me. The flames whispered for me to run, so I did.

* * *

The rain was so cold…too cold. My fingers dug into the wet ground. The sticky mud clung to my skin. I rubbed the cool mud over my face, making it feel smooth. Was it my face? Lloyd's screams pierced through the fogginess in my brain. Why was he screaming like that? I pawed at my bloodstained shirt. Lloyd's blood.

A siren. Flashing lights. Car doors slamming. Mo screaming.

"Oh my God, Arlie. What have you done?" Mo's distant voice pulled me back to reality.

The rain pelted me harder now. An orange glow spilled from the windows of the house.

Not this way, Arlie. Not with fire.

As Mo and the police officers ran toward me, I covered my face with my forearm and ran back into the house.

* * *

The flames were confined to the sides of the room where Lloyd had poured the gas. He was pulling himself along the floor, his screams no more than hoarse pleas now because of the smoke.

When he saw me, he reached out with both arms.

"Don't let me burn. Just don't let me burn." His frantic pleas made it harder for me to concentrate.

I lifted him to his feet and dragged him by the elbow. He shuffled as best he could, holding the leg I'd shot. The heat engulfed us, threatened to melt us. There was no way in hell I'd let us be permanently joined in this inferno. I pulled with the remaining strength I had. Together, we fell through the doorway and onto the wet ground. He landed on top of me. I pushed against him, but he was too heavy. On his own, he rolled to his side.

I coughed, straining to find air. Strong arms lifted me. I was weightless, flying. The rain and night sky blurred. My mouth and nose burned with a familiar taste and smell. I was on the wet ground again. Hands patting me, rolling me. More sirens. More shouting.

"Is she breathing?" Mo's screams were too loud.

Hadn't I asked her to be quiet? *Just for a minute, Mo. Just let me rest a moment.*

CHAPTER 32

My head ached. For that matter, every muscle in my body ached. I pulled at the tubes in my nose, but Mo touched my hand to make me stop.

"You need the oxygen," she said. "Do what you're told for once, okay?"

"Water." The excruciating pain in my throat made me regret uttering a word.

Mo held a straw to my mouth. The cold water eased the burning. I closed my eyes in gratitude. Then the images assaulted me. *Lloyd. Blood. Fire.*

Tears flowed freely. "Mirror," I croaked.

"No. Not now," Mo said. "Just rest."

"Mirror!" I didn't care about my throat. I didn't care that my body begged me to lie still. I needed to know.

"Shhhh. You weren't burned, Arlie. You weren't burned."

My body shook uncontrollably. Mo climbed into the hospital bed beside me. She held me tentatively, conscious of my bruises. She burrowed her face into my neck. I couldn't tell who cried harder. Then sleep claimed me again.

* * *

The scent was unfamiliar. Very sweet. Almost overpowering.

"They're lilies," Mo said. "Mom wanted you to have something fragrant."

Mrs. Mooney never ceased to amaze me. She'd chosen a bouquet based solely on my newfound sense of smell. "Tell her thank you."

"You can tell her yourself. Mom and Dad will be here a little later to see you. They came by earlier, but you were sleeping."

"How long?"

"About seven hours. You needed it."

I brought my fingers to my nose. No more oxygen tube. I rubbed my cheeks—one smooth, one pocked with my old scar.

"The firefighters said you didn't get burned because you were soaked in rain and mud. They said you were very lucky."

"And Lloyd?"

"Airlifted to Denver. Smoke did a number on his lungs. Plus, you cracked his head open and shot him in the leg. He lost a lot of blood."

"But he lived?"

Mo nodded.

The sky outside had turned a purplish gray. Dusk. At this time yesterday, I was in Mo's bathroom with Cody. The last moment everything seemed right.

"How's Frank?" I asked. "I want to see him." I kicked feebly at the sheet and blanket, but then collapsed back against the bed.

"That can wait. Frank's stable. The swelling has gone down considerably, but he's pretty out of it. Sleeping mostly."

"I have to explain everything," I said.

"It can wait." Mo smoothed the hospital blanket and tucked it around my body.

"I was wrong. All of it was wrong," I said. "You've given me every reason to trust you and I still didn't let you in. I don't expect you to forgive me."

"We're broken, Arlie. I'm so hurt that I can hardly stand it, but it's selfish to think about that now."

Mo was the least selfish person I knew. She should be able to ask for anything she needed now or anytime. I'd foolishly thought I was protecting others by not asking for help. That was the height of selfishness and stupidity.

"Did Cody come by?" He and I were likely broken too.

"Cody was here almost the whole time you were sleeping. He'll be back. I'm sure of it."

Mo frowned before catching herself.

"What? What is it?" I asked.

"I don't want to scare you, but the police are waiting to question you. Mom said you don't have to answer anything until Frank can be present."

Police. I'd risked everything to confront my stepfather. It wasn't worth the price I was sure to pay. Thank God, Lloyd had lived.

* * *

James peeked his head around the door after a quick knock. Cody gripped James's elbow and followed him to the side of my bed.

"Thanks for coming." My voice, though hoarse, was getting stronger. And with the analgesic spray for my throat, I no longer felt like I'd swallowed razor blades.

"I see you got a new hairdo," James said.

"What new hairdo?" Cody asked.

"The fire singed a good bit of my hair on one side. I have a lopsided punk look going on," I said.

Cody leaned down to kiss me so I guided him toward my lips.

"You'd be beautiful bald," he whispered.

I couldn't believe he was actually here, that he was speaking to me. "That may be an option. If the stylist can't work with this mess."

James coughed, so Cody pulled away. Although I wished he hadn't.

"I appreciate you bringing Cody to the hospital," I said. "Mo said you've both spent a good deal of time here."

"Just promise me you're done being so stupid," James said. "Things could have ended badly. Much worse than a sore throat and crap hairstyle."

"I was stupid. So stupid," I said. "And I know you were worried about Cody...and what he'd gotten mixed up in."

"Cody's told me he doesn't want me worrying about him and that he can make his own decisions."

"Well, I can," Cody added.

"So...I'll leave you two alone," James said. He headed to the hospital cafeteria to get ice cream for the three of us. My throat could almost feel the soothing coolness.

"Lie beside me." I patted the bed and then grabbed Cody's hand.

"Is that allowed?"

"Who cares."

Cody set his cane against the chair, kicked off his sneakers, and climbed onto the bed. He smelled like mint and something earthy, like grass or bark or pine needles. I nuzzled against him and breathed in. Such a nice change from the antiseptic smell of a hospital room mixed with lilies.

"I want to be angry with you, but I can't," he said.

"Everyone else is, and I don't blame any of you. And when Frank wakes up… I don't even want to think about how disappointed and angry he'll be. He may want to rethink being my guardian."

"He'll be grateful and relieved. Just like the rest of us," Cody said. "Even Brittany stopped by to see how you were."

"She probably came to dig up dirt," I said.

"Not at all," he said. "Claire was here in the waiting room. She warned Brit not to start any shit. Brittany said she was sorry to hear what happened and to tell you to get better soon. She left some magazines."

Her change of heart made me suspicious, but I was too tired to figure it out. "That's so freaking hard to believe."

"Well, believe it," he said. "And it gave me the chance to tell her she needed to accept that you and I are together. That we're for real."

His heartbeat was so steady. I closed my eyes and listened to its strength. I pulled myself around him even tighter.

"Hey. It's okay, Arlie. It's all going to work out."

I hoped he was right. Upon my release from the hospital, the police were going to arrest me. After that, I didn't know how things would play out.

"I won't be able to sing in the community concert," I said. "My throat won't heal fully by then."

"Small price to pay for not dying," he said.

Dying. I'd never allowed myself to believe that. Otherwise, I wouldn't have been able to confront Lloyd. But what if I hadn't seen him enter the trailer? Or if it hadn't been pouring rain? I shuddered now at how easily things could have gone horribly wrong. Lloyd and I were both very lucky to be alive.

I touched Cody's lips and then ran my hand along his jawline, pulling him toward me. I kissed him and kissed him until he responded. The world disappeared just as I had intended. I pushed his collar with my chin and kissed his neck and shoulder. His skin was warm against my face.

"Hey," he whispered. "You sure pick inappropriate places to try to undress me."

"I'm not trying to undress you," I said. "Well...maybe a little."

"At least Mo's bathroom door had a lock."

"Please don't remind me of how stupid I can be. I love you and I want you, but I agree we should wait."

I'd said it. Out loud. I buried my face in his shirt and groaned.

"What is it?"

"Nothing," I said.

"Oh, I thought I heard you say you loved me." He beamed with the joy of a kid on Christmas morning.

"So you heard that, huh?" I longed for a bucket of ice water to douse my flaming cheeks.

"Hell yes, I heard it." He kissed the top of my head and hugged me tighter.

I waited for him to say more. The silence was excruciating. "Well?"

"Well, what?" he asked, still grinning like a goof.

"Nothing." I gave him a halfhearted punch to the ribs.

"I'm messing with you. I love you too. And have for a long time."

* * *

A nurse knocked and then entered without waiting for me to

respond. Cody scrambled to get out of bed and almost fell. She winked.

"I thought you'd like to know your uncle is awake and talking. A lot, in fact," she said. "Can I help you to his room?"

"Go," Cody said. "I'll wait for James."

My heart hammered with both excitement and dread as the nurse helped me into a robe and slippers.

* * *

Frank's hospital bed was in the upright position so he could sit up.

"Nice turban," I said.

"Nice hair," he said.

When I walked closer, he held out his arms. I fell into his embrace and didn't want to be anywhere else. His body shook and the emotion reverberated through us both.

"Thank God, you're all right," he said.

I didn't know how much he'd been told. Enough to know I was also in the hospital. Enough to know I'd been in a fire but survived intact. Still, Cody had been right. Frank wasn't angry.

"Enough of this." He loosened his grip so I backed away. He pulled the sheet up to wipe his tear-stained face. "What a crybaby."

"I think it's nice, Frank."

I sat down in the chair next to the bed and held his hand, careful not to touch his bruised knuckles. He looked like the same old Frank except for the gauze dressing on his head wound. Even his color had returned.

"I was so worried about you," I said.

"Now you know how I feel."

"Point taken."

"I've gotten bits and pieces of the story from the nurses,

and a little from the police. Now I'd like you to tell me what happened," he said.

I took a deep breath and told him everything. That I'd been contacted by Lloyd. That I'd purposefully kept it from him and the police. That I'd sneaked out of Mo's to meet Lloyd, not knowing what I was even going to do. I told Frank I'd lied to Lloyd about being able to get him the money he wanted. As I spoke, it became apparent how insane my thinking and actions had been. At the time, though, I'd been operating on autopilot. Each step led to another and another until I found myself doing horrific things. Things I didn't know I was capable of doing.

"When will you get it through your thick skull that people love you? You're not alone anymore. Jesus, Arlie, I don't know how to make it any plainer."

I nodded. I did believe him now. I believed all of them.

"What I did was wrong. I'm sorry. For everything."

"We'll get through this," he said.

"I don't know. Mo…she's so hurt. And the police…I'll go to jail." A hitch in my voice betrayed how frightened I really was.

"No one will blame you for what you've done. He threatened you. He assaulted me. He's responsible for three deaths."

Lloyd's words came rushing back to me. Claiming self-defense didn't seem like a viable option considering all I'd done to hurt him.

* * *

Since Frank wouldn't be released for a few days, the police agreed to interview me in his hospital room. After the questioning I'd be taken into custody. Juvenile detention, they'd said. I tried deep breathing, but I couldn't shake the feeling that my life had veered so off course I'd never find my way back again.

"Miss Betts, do you understand your rights as they were read to you?" The officer was young, maybe in his thirties. He had kind eyes, but that didn't put me at ease.

"Yes, sir."

"And you are answering our questions today of your own volition?"

"Yes, sir."

"And your guardian, Frank Betts, is here with you?"

"That's correct. He's my uncle."

Frank rubbed my back, but I found it more irritating than comforting. I watched the other officer, a female, who worked the tape recorder. She was all business but smiled nonetheless.

"Tell me about your relationship with Lloyd Hanson," the male officer began.

Relationship? I shuddered to think we were connected in any way. "He was my... He *is* my stepfather."

The investigating officer was thorough. He asked me about my childhood, how Lloyd treated Mom and me, what happened the day of the explosion. He listened as I described how terrified Mom was that he'd find us in Durango.

"She considered him dangerous?"

I nodded. Tears pricked at my eyes. The female officer handed me a tissue. "You're doing great," she said.

"And he contacted you on the morning of April 26?" The male officer took notes even though the recorder was running.

"No, sir. He had stolen my best friend's phone. He texted late on April 25. I met him the next morning at Denny's. He told me not to tell anyone."

"And did he threaten you?"

He'd threatened me. He'd threatened to hurt Frank and Mo

if I didn't do as he said. And he followed through on his threats, almost killing Frank. I tried to explain why I thought I could handle Lloyd on my own and why I hadn't called the police.

"Why did you agree to meet him at your residence at two a.m. on April 27?"

The way he phrased the question suggested that Lloyd asked to meet me, not the other way around. I should've admitted I orchestrated the confrontation. A voice inside said not to offer any more information than necessary.

"I was going to ask him to leave me alone. To leave all of us alone."

"You thought he'd listen to you?"

"I don't know. I wasn't thinking. I thought about calling the police to trap him there, but things got out of control fast." My voice rose. Frank whispered for me to calm down. "Don't tell me to calm down. I just felt I had no choice."

The officer asked if I wanted to take a break, but I said no. I wanted the interview to be over. He asked me to describe everything that happened once I arrived at the trailer. My body shook. I was afraid I'd say something wrong. Something that would convince them I'd planned to kill Lloyd all along. And a little part of me wondered if I had.

"When I got to the trailer, he was already there. He had a gun. That's why I grabbed the wheel chock. To protect myself."

"Once he broke into your trailer, why didn't you just leave or call the police?"

"I don't know! I never had a home before. Never had a family. I couldn't let him take that too. If I didn't confront him then, I might not ever get the chance." I got up and went to the window. I covered my mouth to stop the sobs.

"Are you okay?" Frank stood behind me, his hands on my shoulders.

"I'm trying. Really I am."

"Just answer as best you can," he said.

"But they're going to put me away. I almost killed someone." I buried my head in his chest.

"Miss Betts, we're not here to put you away." The female officer turned off the recorder and stood. "You've been through a horrendous ordeal. We know this is difficult. We just want to get your side of the story."

I took a few deep breaths and sat down. After the female officer turned on the recorder again, she motioned for me to speak.

"I suspected he killed my mom. I wanted him to admit it. I needed some closure."

I explained that I lured Lloyd out of the trailer and that I hit him with the wheel chock. I told them I tied him up with an extension cord so he couldn't hurt me while we talked.

"Tell me about the gun."

"It was his. He dropped it after I hit him. I was just trying to scare him. I wanted him to feel powerless. Like I felt after he'd hurt Frank."

"But you shot Mr. Hanson?"

"He admitted he helped Mom overdose." I bit my lip to keep from crying, but it did no good. "I swear I don't remember pulling the trigger. I heard a loud pop, and he was screaming and screaming. He wouldn't stop screaming."

"And you said Mr. Hanson brought the gasoline to the scene."

"Yes. He was going to burn down the house that Frank is building. He said he didn't think I'd show up."

"And what about the fire?"

"It was an accident. When he lunged at me, I knocked over the floodlight, but I don't remember much else. Not until I was outside again."

My ribs ached from sobbing. Frank put his arm around me and I leaned against his shoulder.

"And that's when you went back in?"

I nodded. "I couldn't let him burn. I'm not that kind of person."

"You risked your own life for a man who almost killed your uncle and threatened to kill you," the officer said.

"Yes, sir."

"That took a lot of courage."

His words only made me cry harder. I hugged Frank. "Don't let them take me."

Tears filled Frank's eyes too. He tried so hard to remain calm, but his voice cracked. "It's only for a while. Don't be scared. We'll both be home in no time."

The female police officer patted me on the shoulder. "We should go."

I nodded and followed her into the hall. Mo and Cody waited just outside the door. Their faces were splotchy and tear-stained. They folded me into their arms and I collapsed against them.

CHAPTER 33

I only stayed in juvenile detention for a couple of days before they released me back into Frank's custody. I underwent two psych evaluations, but no one told me I'd been crazy to do the things I did at the trailer that night. The district attorney offered a plea agreement that included probation and counseling. I'd been lucky.

Two weeks after my release, Frank and I sat at the picnic table outside the charred remains of the house, sipping coffee and eating doughnuts. Frank wasn't strong enough to clean up the debris left from the fire. He needed at least a couple of guys to help. Last week, he'd placed an ad in the *Herald* for short-term construction help, but he hadn't received a response yet.

"At least the foundation didn't burn," I said.

"What an optimist."

"I'd live in the trailer forever and be happy."

"It was too small all along," he said. "I should've rented us a house. When I got the call about becoming your guardian, all I could think about was how fast I could get here."

I rubbed Frank's back. I hated seeing him so down. He wasn't used to being sidelined, but he wasn't one hundred percent yet. At least he had the good sense not to push it.

"It still smells like a campfire," he said. "But without the happy feelings." The morning dew seemed to intensify the smell, which dissipated as the day heated up.

In a way, I was glad the cleanup hadn't progressed. The charred shell served as a reminder of just how close I'd come to dying. It reminded me how lucky I was not to be in jail. It reminded me that Lloyd was out of my life for good.

I ran my hand through my short hair—another reminder of that night. The day I was released from the juvenile detention facility, Mo's stylist had cut off all the singed parts of my hair. After that, it was already pretty short, so I asked her to keep going. She cut it into a pixie and used a razor to soften the edges. My scar showed more, but as the hair fell to the floor, it felt like pieces of my past had been cut away. I added a shock of bright blue dye to the front, something Cody's friend Claire heartily approved of.

Frank's hair was just growing back. They'd shaved his head in the hospital to stitch up the four-inch gash from Lloyd's assault. His beard, however, was as unruly as it'd always been.

"So, everything's on track for Mom's memorial?" I asked.

A while back, Frank asked what kind of headstone I wanted for Mom's grave. I said I'd rather do something more positive, that I wouldn't be visiting a cemetery to remember her. That's when he suggested something huge. Something that still made me cry when I thought about it.

Frank had approached the board of directors of the women's shelter in town. He explained that we wanted to donate money for a special wing just for women who were recovering addicts and who needed a fresh start. We'd call it the Angel Wing.

The shelter agreed and was already using the money to renovate several previously unused rooms. There'd be a dedication ceremony at the end of the summer. Even though it was money from Frank's inheritance, he gave me free rein with the details. I said I wanted the plaque to read *In Memory of Sarah and with Love for Mo.*

"Why haven't you told Mo yet?" he asked.

"I want it to be a surprise," I said. "I'll tell her soon though." In truth, Mo and I were still working through the damage I'd done to our friendship. I wanted to wait until we were on firmer footing before sharing something so huge with her.

"Speaking of Mo…"

He saw the Toyota pickup pull into the yard before I did and nudged me to look. It was James. Mo's dad was also in the front seat. Mo and Cody crouched in the jumper seats.

"What's this about?" Frank walked toward the truck and I followed, wondering the same thing. I stayed behind him as if he were a protective shield.

Mr. Mooney reached out and shook Frank's hand. "Glad to see you're doing well."

"Finally on the mend," Frank said. "If I'd known we were expecting company, I'd have bought more doughnuts."

"No worries. James and I thought we'd give you a hand with the cleanup. Looks like a lot of wood and ash to clear before you can start building again."

I looked at Mo for some explanation of her dad's change in attitude, but she just shrugged as she helped Cody from the truck.

"Great timing. The dumpster arrived yesterday," Frank said.

"I can use the muscle."

"Those I have," Mr. Mooney said. "And I'm happy for the chance to get to know you better... since our girls are best friends."

"I'd like that," Frank said. "Let's get started."

Our girls. He saw Frank as my dad. I guess I'd started to view him that way too.

James followed Frank, but Mr. Mooney stayed behind. I tensed from my neck to my toes. Without realizing it, I took a defensive step backward.

"My wife said you like Mexican pastry," he said. "They're a favorite of mine too. We stopped by the bakery this morning. They're fresh." He took a deep breath and held out a white paper sack. He clearly felt as uncomfortable as I did.

The gift and his kind words caught me off guard. I accepted the bag but couldn't think of a thing to say.

"I'm sorry for how I've treated you," he continued. "You mean a lot to Mo, and I've hurt you both by not taking the time to get to know you. I hope you can accept my apology."

Mo sidled up beside her father and hugged him around the waist. "You're embarrassing Arlie. Go help her uncle. That's why you're here."

He kissed the top of Mo's head and jogged over to where Frank was already showing James something on the foundation.

I felt choked up and confused. "I might just faint."

"Not before you try these conchas," Mo said. "I ate one on the drive over. Amazing."

I grasped Cody's hand and we walked over to the picnic table. We sat on one bench seat while Mo sat cross-legged on the tabletop.

"Good thing Frank's picnic table didn't catch fire," she said.

"He treats it like some family heirloom."

"He made it himself," I said. "And it suits us more than a formal dining room."

I watched James and Mr. Mooney scoop shovelful after shovelful of ash into the dumpster. Frank moved slowly, being careful with each movement.

"I can't believe all his hard work is gone," I said.

Cody squeezed my hand. "You didn't start the fire. I seem to remember it was Lloyd who brought the gas can."

He was so good at knowing what was going through my head. His freakishly acute senses never missed a thing. He and Mo were alike in that respect.

"You'd grown attached to the idea of having a house," Mo said. "Admit it."

"I had. I just didn't realize how much until it was taken from me," I said.

"I already have an idea of how you should decorate your room," she said. "We totally need a road trip to Albuquerque to shop."

It'd been Thanksgiving when I'd last thought about returning to the city of my childhood, the day Mom had found me at the bus station. Mo was the perfect person to help me make new memories and chase away any lingering ghosts.

"I'm up for a road trip," I said. "But only if Cody drives. You're a mess behind the wheel."

We laughed and dug into the conchas. They weren't as good as the pastries Rosa used to bake, but they signaled a new start for me and Mo's dad—and possibly for me and Mo. Nothing could taste better.

***

After everyone had left for the day, Frank ordered pizza. We'd eaten takeout almost exclusively since he was released from the hospital because he didn't feel up to cooking and was tired of my scrambled eggs.

"Don't you get sick of this?" he asked.

"You've got to be kidding. I'm making up for seven years without taste buds. I could eat pizza every day for a year and not be tired of it."

We finished a large pepperoni and then divided the cinnamon breadsticks evenly. My appetite hadn't waned since I'd regained my sense of taste. Cinnamon was my second favorite scent next to coffee.

"We'll be in the house by late July," Frank said, stealing an extra breadstick for himself. "But we have a lot to do before then. I'm counting on you to help with the painting and trim work. We can do some of that after we move in."

"No problem," I said. "I'm thinking purple walls and yellow trim."

"I'm thinking I trust Mo more than you when it comes to decorating."

Since he was in such a good mood, I decided to broach a sticky subject again. "Any chance you've changed your mind about a television and cable?"

"Funny, you should mention that. I have a TV as well as a bunch of furniture in storage in Corpus Christi."

"Road trip?" I'd never been anywhere but Colorado and New Mexico, so the thought of going to Texas with Frank was appealing. We could even go to Padre Island and the beach.

"Yeah, about that. I've been meaning to tell you something," he said.

My gut clenched. "I thought we said no more secrets."

"I wasn't keeping a secret. I was just waiting for the right time to tell you."

I raised my eyebrows, indicating he'd better fess up. I couldn't take the suspense.

"Lily found me on Facebook," he said. "We've been texting and emailing for about three weeks. We've spoken a few times on the phone as well."

Lily? His old girlfriend? And Frank on Facebook?

"Okay. Mind completely blown," I said. "Start from the beginning."

Frank explained that his stay in the hospital—and my almost fatal confrontation with Lloyd—had made him see how tenuous life was and that we needed to do everything in our power to be happy, to live each day to the fullest. When Lily contacted him on Facebook, he took it as a sign that they might have a second chance.

"But you were together twenty years ago. Didn't she ever get married?" Lots of people reconnected with old sweethearts through Facebook, but my Frank? It was surreal.

"She's divorced now," he said with a slight smile. "Isn't that just the saddest thing you ever heard?"

I was having a hard time synthesizing the news and Frank's playful mood. "What does any of this have to do with your television?"

"Well… I asked her to get some stuff from my storage unit… and, uh, bring it when she visits next month."

"Holy cow."

I don't know what my face looked like, but worry clouded Frank's in response.

"I'm sorry, Arlie. I should've said something sooner. Don't be angry with me."

"No…no, it's okay. I'm just stunned. This is good news. I mean, it's great news." No longer hungry, I put down the half-eaten breadstick I'd been holding.

"Really? Because I'm pretty psyched and I'd hoped you'd be too." The furrow eased from his brow. He was now animated, explaining all the things I'd love about her and all the things we could do when she visited.

Jealousy pricked at my heart, but I hoped his happiness would help dispel it. After all, I had Cody. Why shouldn't Frank have someone special? I just needed to take it one step at a time instead of reacting to all the what-ifs—especially the "what if Frank and Lily marry and then I'll have a pseudo mom" scenario.

"You sure you're okay with this?" he said. "I still sense storm clouds brewing."

How could I tell Frank I wanted it to be just us for a while? Our first few months together had been anything but normal.

"It's just a visit, Arlie. It's not like we're getting married."

"Oh, I know," I said. "I'm happy for you. Really. And I'm happy for us. To start over."

Part of me was glad I was still seeing Jane and going to therapy. I had more to sort out than I'd thought.

***

In the chaos of the last few weeks, I'd forgotten to donate Mom's clothing and her old suitcase to the thrift store. When Lloyd trashed our trailer, he'd dumped the contents onto the floor. I'd stuffed them back in until I was ready to deal with it again.

After Frank went to sleep, I opened the suitcase. I knew each piece by heart—which shirts used to be her favorites and which she rarely wore. I brought one of her tees up to my nose, hoping some last bit of her scent lingered. It didn't.

It was time for me to move on. Frank was obviously excited about building a new life with Lily. I'd been given so many second chances that I'd lost count. Tomorrow, I'd wash the clothes and bring them to the thrift store.

I opened the drawer to the nightstand and retrieved Mom's notebook. That, I'd keep. The writings might just be gibberish, but they obviously meant something to her. Mo suggested I use the words or phrases in the notebook to write a "found" poem. I'd never heard of using words found in everyday objects like magazines or books or menus or even a cereal box as inspiration for poems, but I liked the idea of creating something new out of the old.

Also in the nightstand was something else I planned to keep. Recently, Dora had left an envelope in our mailbox. A sticky note on top read, "I should have given this to you sooner. I love you and want to see you again when you're ready."

The envelope contained a letter from Mom, written the day she died.

> Baby girl,
>
> I hope you know I'd never let anyone hurt you, but today your stepdad was here. He found us. And it's my fault. I stole some money from him before we left Albuquerque. I was stupid to think he wouldn't track us down. I told him you'd run away to Texas. I have a brother there, in Corpus Christi. Frank. I know he'll take you in.
>
> I asked Dora to give you this letter if something

happens to me. Just ask her or Mo for bus fare and get out of Durango.

Please be safe. Please go to college. Please find someone who'll love you to the moon and back. You deserve it.

Love, Mom

I *was* safe now. And I'd found someone to love me to the moon and back. I hoped Mom knew these things now.

CHAPTER 34

Cody and Mo sat on either side of me. We'd been watching kayakers do rolls in the river. The Animas had hit its peak the first week in June so it was teeming with kayaks and commercial rafts holding a dozen people each. Every time a raft overturned, Mo and I described the frantic, bobbing tourists to Cody. Most of them just laughed after being plunged into the ice-cold water.

"I don't understand why we couldn't have gone rafting." Mo handed me sunscreen, but I waved her away.

"Because the water is forty degrees," Cody said. "And there are too many tourists. We'll go soon."

I was glad to just be on the shore with Mo and Cody, enjoying the warmth of the sun and the sense of normalcy they brought to my life. Since the beginning of summer, both had stuck to me like glue holding together a fragile, once-broken vase. I couldn't blame them. The incident with Lloyd had made us all very aware of the importance of friendship and trust.

I hadn't been able to rebuild trust with Dora as easily and

hadn't seen her since the day Lloyd confronted me. Still, I vowed to call her and ask if we could meet for coffee in the next few days. How could I still punish her for lying about Lloyd and Frank if everyone had forgiven me for my lies? Neither of us felt we had choices, and both of us were protecting people we loved.

Dora believed Mom's overdose was an accident, but there was no way to know for sure. For a while, I tortured myself with speculating about whether she'd left me on purpose, what she could have done differently, and what I could have done differently. From time to time, I still wondered if Lloyd had played a larger role in her death.

Cody leaned in closer. "I don't have to see your face to know you've gone somewhere dark."

"What's Cody talking about? You okay?" Mo was super-sensitive to my moods, and his remark drew her back to the conversation.

"Not too dark," I assured them. "I have some complicated feelings to work through."

"Well, you have me and Mo and Frank to talk to. And, of course, Jane," Cody said.

"Especially Jane." Mo rubbed my arm and then quickly turned her attention back to the river.

Since my arrest and subsequent release, I'd been seeing my therapist twice a week again. Although the plea bargain mandated it, I'd have gone on my own. Yes, it was difficult to look at how close I'd come to killing another human being, but I had to understand that piece of myself—the anger and fear and desperation that drove my actions. And I had to find a way to forgive myself and move on.

Mo and I had also worked hard to mend our friendship over

the past month. She even suggested we see Jane together a couple of times, and it had made all the difference in how quickly
we could trust each other again.

"I'm telling you, we're missing out!" Mo pointed to another
capsized raft. "Can we please go tomorrow?"

"Whatever you want, Mo," Cody answered for us. We were a
couple now, one unit.

When she ran down to the river's edge to heckle some of her
friends thrashing around in the water, I moved to Cody's lap and
wrapped my arms around his neck. I loved that when he kissed
me, he was never the first one to pull away. I liked to think we'd
go on kissing forever if I didn't stop.

He reached up and ran his fingers through my hair. "I like it
short. Will you keep it like this?"

His touch sent an electric current down my spine. "Definitely,
if you promise to keep doing that." I kissed him again.

I glanced up to see Mo had jumped in the river, fully clothed,
and was now holding out a lost paddle to her friend.

"It's so freaking cold!" she shouted to us.

"That maniac changed my life," I said. "I'm a better person
for knowing her."

"I think you both changed each other's lives for the better,"
Cody said. "I know you've changed mine."

"And you, mine." Our lips met again and I shut out the summer
sounds around us until Mo's shouting broke through our PDA.

"Hey, look! It's Frank and Lily!" She motioned for us to join
her.

I took Cody by the elbow and guided him over the boulders
until we reached the sandy strip near the water's edge.

We whistled and hooted to get their attention. Lily waved

first. When Frank spotted us, he raised his paddle above his head. A silly grin stayed plastered to his face as the raft went by. He looked like a love-struck teenager. I hoped that was the way he felt. It'd just be one more thing we had in common.

ACKNOWLEDGMENTS

Although writing can be a solitary endeavor, I've never felt alone on this journey. My husband, Andy, has been the consummate cheerleader/therapist/coffeemaker who reminded me countless times that it was a question of "when," not "if."

First, many thanks to my agent, J. L. Stermer of N. S. Bienstock, and her assistant, Sammy Bina, who embraced Arlie's story and found it a home at Albert Whitman and Company. I'm grateful that my editor there, Wendy McClure, championed the project and made it even stronger.

The book, though, had many readers long before it went to press. I'm indebted to my critique partner, Micki Browning. Thanks also to the family members and friends who enthusiastically read first (or second, or third) drafts: Camm, Hunter, Haley, Erin, Tessa, Char, Kathy, Tracy B., Mari, Jenni, Wendi, and countless others.

I'm especially grateful to two dear friends who've made this author business seem more real: Jenni Baker for designing my website and McCarson Jones for taking my professional photos.

It didn't take me long to realize what a supportive community of writers exists online as well. These friends are so real to me that I sometimes forget they live all over the world and not just down the street. One special author and mentor, Summer Heacock (FizzyGrrl), championed the book in an online contest that resulted in substantive feedback and a much stronger story—the version that caught my agent's attention. Fizzy taught me that laughing every day is the only way to stay sane.

And lastly, this book will forever be entwined with memories of my sweet nineteen-year-old cat, Lily, who stuck beside me (literally) for every word I wrote on this book. She deserves coauthor status.

DISCUSSION QUESTIONS

1. After her mother dies, Arlie makes the decision to not hide any longer. How would her life be different if she had decided to run away?

2. Arlie lost her sense of smell and taste in the explosion that scarred her face. In what ways did that distance her from others even more?

3. What role does Mo play in Arlie's life? Is she more like a friend or sister or mother figure? Do you have someone like Mo in your own life?

4. How does the relationship Arlie shared with her mother and stepfather influence her decisions about drugs?

5. In what ways were Arlie's and her mother's roles reversed because of her mother's addiction?

6. Why do you think Arlie has a hard time adjusting to living with her uncle Frank?

7. In what ways does Frank make it easier for Arlie to accept him as a guardian?

8. Frank decides to build a house for himself and Arlie. How do Arlie's feelings about the house change over time?

9. One of the first things Mo recognizes about Arlie is her love of reading. What role do books play in Arlie's life?

10. How does music allow Arlie to express herself?

11. In what ways is Arlie like other teenage girls? How is she different?

12. Why do you think some students make fun of Arlie's scars and call her names while others do not?

13. Both Arlie and Cody have disabilities. In what ways does that bring them together? In what ways does it pull them apart?

14. Arlie makes some decisions that may appear dangerous or foolish. How does her childhood explain her decision-making process as a teen? Would you have made different choices?

ABOUT THE AUTHOR

Red Scarf Shots

Mandy Mikulencak has been a writer her entire working life, first as a journalist, then as an editor and PR specialist for two national nonprofits and a United Nations agency. Today, she lives in the mountains of Southwest Colorado with her husband, Andy. She writes both YA and adult fiction. *Burn Girl* is her first novel. Visit her online at mandymikulencak.com.